MW00343279

BEYOND THE GRATE

ROB NETO

Published by Chipola Publishing, LLC,
Greenwood, Florida 32443, U.S.A.
www.chipolapublishing.com

Cover photography and design by Rob Neto

Author photography by Jen Neto

Printed in the United States of America

PUBLISHER'S NOTE

This is a work of fiction. Names, characters, places, and incidents either are the product of the author's imagination or are used fictitiously, and any resemblance to actual persons, living or dead, business establishments, events, or locales is entirely coincidental. While the names of certain locales, such as Morrison Spring, are used to add depth and reality to the story, they are in no way meant to disparage such locales or past or present ownership of such establishments.

ISBN: 9781961612006

DEDICATION

This book is dedicated to all the trained cave divers in the world following the established training guidelines and doing safe cave dives every day.

ACKNOWLEDGMENTS

I'd like to thank my wife for supporting me in this endeavor even though there was so much more I could have been doing other than sitting on my butt writing a book of fiction. Not only did she support me but she read through the early editions and provided me with invaluable feedback. The final version of this story is much improved than the early editions because of her advice and recommendations.

FOREWORD

The idea for this book came about after Ben McDaniel's disappearance in August 2010. McDaniel was last seen on August 18, 2010 about to do a dive in Vortex Spring. He was a certified scuba diver but did not have any formal training as a cave diver. Two days later, on August 20, his vehicle was still parked next to the spring basin but McDaniel was nowhere to be found. It is typically assumed when a vehicle is found at a cave diving site that the owner never made it out from the cave dive. Because of this, McDaniel's vehicle was reported abandoned to local authorities and it was assumed he had perished in the Vortex Spring cave.

The afternoon after the vehicle was noticed the first set of recovery divers entered the cave to look for his body. Their objective was to locate the body and make sure a continuous guideline leading from the body to the opening of the cave was left in place so the second team of divers could recover it. They were unsuccessful in locating the body. The second team's objective changed from recovery to searching and they went into the cave to continue the search. This team, which included the author, searched the entire length of the cave. The author and one other team member even penetrated the fourth restriction at the end of the line. McDaniel's body was not in the cave. Many rumors spread around the internet about what happened to McDaniel. No one knows, or at least is willing to tell, what really happened. To this day, McDaniel's body, dead or alive, has never been found.

* * *

This book is a work of fiction. The characters, incidents, and dialogue are drawn from the author's imagination and are not to be construed as real. Any resemblance to actual events or persons, living or dead, is entirely coincidental. While the idea for the story did come from the disappearance referenced above, that is the only similarity. This story is simply one in which the author creates a story based on his imagination of what could have happened. There are some snippets of fact embedded in the story, such as some of the information about Ponce de Leon, Morrison Spring, and St. Andrews State Park. These things are included simply to give the story more depth and reality. They are by no means implicated in any wrong doing in the disappearance of McDaniel.

There is no Joey Simmons. There is no Earl Hewitt. There is no Lindsey Carter. There was no body found beyond the grate, even after multiple attempts searching for it over the months following McDaniel's disappearance. These characters, as well as the other characters in the book, and the body, are all imaginative creations. This work of fiction simply takes one of the rumors that was going around and expands upon it.

No one knows what became of Ben McDaniel, or at least

no one is willing to say. All that is known is his truck was left parked close to the spring basin and he hadn't been seen in two days. No body was found. No one was implicated in any type of foul play. He was simply never heard from again. He could be anywhere…or nowhere. I hope you enjoy this one possible version of the course of events. I certainly enjoyed writing it.

PART 1

1

August 4, 2011 2pm

Joey Simmons sucked in his last breath as he swam the final length of the small water filled cave passage. He pushed past the hole that was just barely big enough for him to fit through into the large cavern at the bottom of the chimney-like opening located at one end of the spring basin. As he popped out into the wide gaping room, he let go of the pipe resting on the floor below him and let the water current carry him toward the rope that lead up to a large white buoy floating at the water's surface 50 feet above him. He tried to take another breath from his regulator but there was nothing left in his scuba tank. He could hear an incessant beeping coming from somewhere nearby. The thought that this was it for him, these were his last moments alive, and that the beeping was the countdown timer for his final seconds on this earth, rushed through his mind. He was still too far from the surface and he was certain he wasn't going to make it back up to it with all of the air drained out of his tank. Yet, he wasn't quite ready to give up.

Swimming as fast as he could Joey shot up toward the rope. Once he got to it he could use the rope to help pull himself to the surface even faster. He might just make it out alive. It was only 50 feet. But with no air in the tank on his back 50 feet might as well have been a mile. As he got close to the rope he reached out to grasp it with his left hand and finally realized where the beeping he had been hearing was coming from. It wasn't a death timer counting down his last moments on earth. It was the dive computer he had rented from the dive shop for the day. Not only was it beeping but its display was wildly flashing numbers, indicating something was drastically wrong. *Well, he didn't need a stupid computer to tell him that!* And the beeping certainly didn't help him one bit in his current situation. If anything, it only made his panic level worse.

He grabbed the rope and yanked himself up hand over hand. As he reached over with his right hand to continue pulling himself up, Joey risked another glance at the dive computer display screen. It was still flashing numbers at him but he had no idea what they meant. The dive computer was supposed to tell him his depth, how long he had been underwater, and how long he was allowed to stay underwater. He had learned in his open water scuba class three months earlier that dives had "no decompression limits" meaning if a diver stayed down longer than a specified amount of time he could get the bends. The bends wasn't a good thing. In fact, it could cause paralysis or even death. The realization came to Joey that not only had he breathed through all of the air in his tank, but he had also stayed underwater far too long and if he did make it to the surface he might be paralyzed.

Well, no time to worry about that. Without air it wouldn't matter if he got the bends or not. He couldn't breathe water. Joey could feel his chest getting tighter and his lungs starting to ache from the lack of air. He continued to pull himself up the rope one hand over the other. As his depth got shallower he could feel the pressure on his lungs relax, or rather, he could feel the small amount of air that was still left in them start to expand. He was still starving for oxygen. He couldn't hold his breath any longer and tried to inhale. He was able to get about a quarter of a breath from his regulator. There must have been a little air in his hoses that also expanded as he ascended up the chimney. It was just enough to ease off some of the burning in his lungs.

Glancing at the flashing display screen of his dive computer he saw he was 23 feet deep. Still deeper than what he had done during his controlled emergency swimming ascent skill in his open water scuba class, but no longer greater than 50 feet. He had a tiny glimmer of hope that he might just make it. Of course, he still had to deal with the flashing, beeping dive computer telling him he had stayed at depth longer than he was supposed to. And he was ascending a lot faster than he was taught was safe.

But he desperately needed to breathe.

Continuing to pull himself up the rope Joey felt the tightness in his lungs ease off as the air in them expanded little by little with every foot of depth he eliminated. He could just start to make out the white buoy on the surface directly above him. He stole another glance at his dive computer display and saw he only had another 14 feet to go before breaking through the surface. Fourteen feet more before he could fill his lungs with pure wonderful oxygenated air.

He might just make it.

12 feet.

The annoying beeping seemed to be getting louder.

10 feet.

He could almost taste the air above him.

7
5
3

Joey broke through the surface of the crystal clear 68 degree water into the warm sunshine of the hot summer day. It was a beautiful day. And Joey had made it back to air. He could feel the warmth of the sun on the top of his head. He immediately tried to pull a breath of air into his lungs. But there was still no air!

What was going on?!? He was on the surface. He should be able to breathe! Yet, nothing was happening. No air was getting into his lungs. The realization suddenly came to Joey that he still had the scuba regulator in his mouth. He was trying to breathe from it, but without any air in the scuba tank, he couldn't get a breath from the regulator. The regulator was designed to not let water in. On the surface it wouldn't let ambient air in either.

He pushed the regulator out of his mouth with his tongue and gulped in that much needed lungful of life sustaining air. He could feel his chest expand as the air swooshed in through his mouth, past his vocal cords, and into his airways.

It felt so good to breathe again.

He coughed out that breath and sucked in another one. And a third. Joey felt himself start to sink underwater toward the chimney and back to the dark cave as if it was pulling him back into its dark recesses. He pressed the power inflator button on his buoyancy compensator but nothing happened. Pressing that button should have shot air into his buoyancy compensator so he could float. He didn't have any air in his scuba tank though, and the power inflator was connected to a hose connected to the tank.

He was coughing too hard and was too busy trying to breathe. He knew he couldn't fill the buoyancy compensator by mouth. He grabbed the white buoy floating in front of him that marked the cave entrance below and held on for his life. Exhausted from the efforts of the last several minutes, he continued to cough and breathe as he clung to the buoy wishing he could just lie back and pass out.

It seemed like it would never happen but Joey finally caught his breath and was able to relax a little. He grabbed his power inflator, closed his lips around the opening on it and depressed the exhaust button so he could blow air into it like he had been taught. He could feel the buoyancy compensator, or BC as it was called, tighten around him as air filled its bladder. In response, the BC pushed his body up out of the water slightly. He also became aware of that annoying beeping again.

Looking at his dive computer Joey saw it was still flashing at him and beeping much more loudly on the surface than it had in the water. He quickly dropped his wrist underwater to muffle the sound. He studied the display screen carefully but still didn't know what the flashing numbers meant. He could see a large 0 for depth. He also saw the number 45 for dive time. Under those numbers was the number 10 flashing at him. He thought that meant he should have stayed at his safety stop for 10 minutes but he wasn't sure. All he knew was the dive computer only beeped when something was wrong so this wasn't good.

Joey looked around the shoreline of the small spring basin and up the green grassy hill surrounding it. No one was in sight, not even Earl, the manager of the scuba park. So no one had seen the exhibition Joey had put on at the buoy. He wasn't sure if that was a good thing or a bad thing. If he did have the bends and was paralyzed he would need someone to get him out of the water.

He was holding onto the buoy so his arms weren't paralyzed. He moved his legs back and forth. They seemed to work as well. But, from what he could vaguely remember, paralysis could start anytime during the 24 hours following a dive.

He would have to worry about that later.

Joey let go of the buoy and slowly swam toward the steps where he had entered the water, careful to not overexert himself in case he did have the bends. He kept the dive computer underwater so the beeping remained muffled. He wasn't sure how long it would keep doing that but he hoped it would stop after the 10 minutes had passed. It was bad enough he was going to be turning in an empty scuba tank, especially after being warned by Earl to watch his gauge, but he didn't want to turn in a beeping computer.

And what about the dead diver?!?

Joey just remembered he had bigger issues to deal with than an empty tank and an alarming dive computer. He had found a dead diver inside the cave. Joey shouldn't have even been back there himself. He had to tell someone about it though. He couldn't just leave and pretend he didn't see anything. The nightmares he was going to have about what just happened would haunt him for a long time. He couldn't add guilt to that by leaving without reporting it.

Once Joey got to the steps, he looked at the dive computer display again. It was still flashing 10 on it. Joey wasn't in the best of shape and it had taken him at least 5 minutes to swim the hundred feet or so from the buoy to the steps. Was it going to keep doing this until he did what it wanted and went back underwater to 15 feet for 10 minutes? He couldn't just stay on the surface of the water until it stopped beeping. Especially if it kept this up the rest of day.

Looking around the basin and up the hill again he still didn't see anyone. He looked over at his car parked at the top of the hill and thought he might be able to rush up there and toss the computer in the trunk wrapped in a towel. That should muffle the sound enough. Joey pulled his fins off his feet and tucked them under his arm. Another look around and he grabbed the railing and pulled himself up the steps out of the water. He glanced around one last time before he rushed out of the water toward his car.

As he was half jogging, half walking up the hill as fast as he could with the scuba gear and tank still on, he saw Earl step out of the dive shop. In spite of the 60 pounds or so of gear, Joey quickened his pace up the hill and started to release the clasp of the dive computer wrist band so he could pull it off his wrist. As the computer fell away from his wrist the constant beeping got louder. The small speaker was on the back side and pulling it off his arm had exposed it. Joey took the dive computer and pushed it against his pudgy belly to muffle the sound. That worked.

When Joey got to his car he quickly flipped open the gas tank door and reached in to retrieve the keys he had hidden there. His fingers fumbled the key chain and the keys fell to the ground. He started to bend over to grab them until he remembered the heavy scuba tank on his back. Joey grabbed the side of the car with one hand to steady himself and knelt down slowly until the keys were within reach. As he reached down with his other hand, the one holding the dive computer, the beeping increased in volume. He snatched up the keys and shoved the computer back into the fat of his belly. Straightening back up, he grasped the keys with the hand he had been using to steady himself on the car and unlocked the trunk. He grabbed his towel from inside and shoved the dive computer in the middle of it, rolling it up into a ball. He set it back inside the trunk and slammed the lid closed, sealing the dive computer and the beeping inside. The beeping was just a faint sound that disappeared as he stepped away from the car.

With that done, Joey walked over to one of the picnic tables situated at the top of the hill in front of the Grande Vista Chalet and started to remove his scuba gear. That was when Earl approached him.

"How's yur dive?" Earl asked with what looked to Joey like a suspicious expression on his unshaven sunburnt face.

Joey paused for a moment as he thought about how he

wanted to handle this. He should tell Earl. Earl managed the property after all. If Joey didn't tell him, the next diver to go back to the grate would see the body just beyond it and Earl would find out then. The basin was pretty small and Earl would know he had gone in the cave when he saw the bubbles from his regulator disappear from the surface. He had to tell him. Besides, Earl could hardly blame him for coming out with an empty tank after finding a dead diver.

"N-not so good," stammered Joey.

"Oh? Furget yur weights agin?" Earl asked with a wink.

Joey finished pulling his BC off and placing it on the picnic table and then pulled off the weight belt.

"N-no, nothing like that." Joey paused for a moment. "I-I'm not sure how to t-tell you this."

Chuckling, Earl said through his crooked yellow stained teeth, "Wut happen'd? Ya come back wit 200 psi dis time?"

Grabbing his pressure gauge Joey thrust it toward Earl and said, "A-actually, m-my tank is empty. I-I had a little issue on this dive."

Earl placed his hands on his hips, looked down at the ground in between them, and started shaking his head. The hair on the top of his head fell forward and Joey watched as it swung back and forth in front of him. Earl tilted his head slightly and looked up at Joey through the strands of hair.

"Boy, ya gotta watch dat gauge more kerful. Not only isit bad fer da tank but is dang'rous. How'd ya let it git so empty?"

"W-well..." Joey started off slowly, "I-I-I heard some other divers talking about the c-cave and the g-grate back there and I wanted to see it. I thought it w-would be okay since there are lights along the tunnel."

As he went on Joey was talking faster and faster and started running his words together.

"WhenIgotbacktothegrateIsawadiverontheothersideofit. Iswamoverandtriedtogethisattentionbuthewouldntlookupatme."

Earl brought his rough calloused nicotine stained hands up signaling Joey to stop. "Whoa, boy! Hold on thar! Wut'r ya talkin' bout? Wut diver? Thar ain't no'ne else heah t'day."

Joey continued on talking just as fast as he had been before he was interrupted, no longer stuttering but barely understandable.

"That's what I thought too until I saw him there. When he wouldn't look up at me I reached through the grate and tapped him. He still didn't look at me so I grabbed him and shook him and his regulator fell out of his mouth. I don't know anything else. I was so freaked out I just pushed back away from the grate and tried to get out of there. Then I couldn't see anything because all the mud from the bottom got stirred up. I don't know how I got out of there but I did."

"A'ight. Les jus stop a minute an' think 'bout dis." Earl walked around the picnic table, sat on the edge and placed his right foot on the bench. He signaled to Joey to sit on the bench next to him.

"A'ight, so y'all was swimmin' in da cave an' foun' a dead body trapt on da'ther side of da grate?"

"Yes, sir"

"He wa'n't breathin'? "

"No, sir." Joey thought a moment, "Now that I think about it I never saw any bubbles coming from his regulator."

"Dis ain't good. Dis ain't good t'all." Earl looked down at the table shaking his head, the long hair from the top swinging back and forth like a pendulum again.

"We gotta git dat body outta thar without nobuddy know'n 'bout it."

Earl got up from the table and paced back and forth a few times. He stopped and looked over at Joey. "Son, I'm gonna need y'all's help."

2

August 4, 2011 8am

That's how it all started. Well, actually, it started earlier that morning when Joey decided to play hooky from work and go scuba diving instead. His mother had always told him nothing good comes from shirking your responsibilities. Here she was being right again.

It was a typical searing hot and humid summer day in the Florida panhandle. Joey had decided to call in sick and take an extra-long weekend off from work and go scuba diving. He already had a three day weekend. Why not make it four? With the extra money he was saving in rental fees from owning his own scuba equipment he could afford a few more days underwater.

The cool refreshing 68 degree water temperature of the Florida springs would feel good in the blistering August heat. The combination of the heat and high humidity made it so it wasn't possible to walk out the door from his air conditioned house without breaking into an immediate sweat and soaking his shirt all the way through! And the gnats were especially bad this year. They formed a bubble around his head every time he stepped outside and followed him. Some even dive bombed his ears! The strongest bug spray didn't do a thing to keep them off.

Joey left his house early in the morning. Well, it was actually his parents' house since he was 19 and still lived at home with them. If they knew he was ditching work to go scuba diving they wouldn't be pleased with him one bit. He was supposed to be saving up during his summer break from school. They were already upset with him for spending money on a scuba class.

He knew he should be saving money but he couldn't pass up the great deal the local dive shop had offered back in May. Only $99 to get open water scuba certified! What they didn't bother mentioning in their advertisement was that the $99 was only for the class. He still had to buy his own mask, snorkel, and fins and pay for rental gear and air fills for the checkout dives. He also had to pay to get into the scuba park where the dives were done. After all the extra expenses were added up he had ended up spending an additional $700 for everything. That had put a real dent in his savings and he had to borrow some money from his parents, which he was still paying back. If anything, he should be working extra, not skipping out from work to go play.

3

3 months earlier
May 11, 2011 6pm

The $99 was a great deal. Even when the shop told him it didn't include a student manual, which cost $60, it still seemed like a great deal. He bought the book and read every chapter, twice! He showed up for class the first night ready to go. They spent a few hours reviewing all the material and taking the written exam, which Joey aced! Then they went to the pool next door to do their swim and float tests.

The float test was effortless. Joey wasn't exactly thin so he could float all day. The swim test was another thing though. The extra 20 pounds or so around his midsection didn't make physical activity easy. By the end of the 200 yard swim Joey was so out of breath he could barely talk. He was also a little embarrassed because he was the last one to finish the swim. The last one by about 10 minutes. The good thing was it wasn't a timed test so it didn't matter that he was last. All he had to do was finish. And he did get 100% on the written test so that had to count for something.

After the tests in the pool they dried themselves off and went into the dive shop to look at scuba gear. That's when the instructor told the class, "Y'all are all gonna need to buy your own mask, snorkel, and a pair of fins before we meet Saturday for the next pool session."

Joey was in shock. No one had said anything about buying scuba equipment when he signed up and paid the $99. As they walked through the dive shop the instructor showed them the different types of masks, snorkels, and fins. The instructor explained that not every mask will work for every diver.

"Cause we all have differently shaped faces one mask might work better for one person but leak like a sieve for another," he told them.

They all tried on several masks, putting them on their faces and sucking in through their noses to see if they could form a seal. The mask that fit Joey the best thankfully wasn't the most expensive one. That one was almost $150! He ended up finding one that cost about $80 that fit pretty well.

Next they looked at snorkels. The least expensive snorkels were $20 and the most expensive were more than the mask he had chosen. Almost $100 for a piece of tube to breathe through! *Wow!* It was sure looking like this was going to cost significantly more than Joey had initially thought. He grabbed one of the $20 snorkels and followed the instructor to the fins.

The instructor explained the difference between fins that looked like paddles and fins that had a slit up the middle of them. He called those split fins. He explained that split fins were better because they made swimming through the water much easier. The least expensive pair of split fins was going to cost Joey $180. His head was spinning. Where was he going to get another $280 for this stuff? He was going to have to ask his parents for a loan and pay them back over the next couple of months. Maybe he could pick up a few extra days at work.

So much for that idea.

A cute young blond girl about Joey's age who worked in the shop brought out several different sizes of fins and in a sweet southern accent asked everyone for their shoe size. She wrote all of these down and disappeared through a door in the back of the dive shop. A few minutes later she returned with neoprene booties. *Oh no!* Something else to buy. The girl, with a big smile on her face, handed Joey a set of booties.

"Here ya go, sweetie."

Joey blushed as he took the booties and almost dropped them because he was having a hard time taking his eyes off her. She had long beautiful blond hair that draped over her shoulders and bright blue eyes that popped out at him from the deep dark tan of her face.

Joey managed to hold onto the booties as he glanced at the price tag - $50! He almost dropped them again! This just kept getting worse. He was up to over $300 for the equipment and they weren't even done going through the dive shop. If he hadn't already spent almost $170 on the class and book he would just quit.

As it was, that was the last of the expensive scuba gear that had to be purchased before the pool sessions began. The instructor showed everyone the different types of BCs, scuba regulators, and dive computers and told them all about the differences in the brands and models the shop carried. Thankfully they didn't have to buy any of those because they were all several hundred dollars each! This was all so much information, and an obvious sales pitch to try to get them to spend more money. At least the class fee included BC and regulator use during the pool sessions.

Finally, the instructor brought them over to a small display with little plastic bottles and mesh bags full of more plastic bottles.

"These bottles here are real useful for y'all's everyday divin'. We've got defog to keep y'all's masks from foggin' up underwater, some stuff to clean off y'all's underwater writing slates after y'all write on 'em, and this stuff right here." The instructor held up a medium sized bottle with a dive flag symbol on it. "This right here is the most important thing y'all 'll need. It'll help keep the stink out of y'all's wetsuits...because there are only two kinds of divers – the ones who pee in their wetsuits and the ones who lie about peeing in their wetsuits. This'll help y'all with your lies."

The class burst out in laughter. But as Joey was laughing he was recalculating the amount of money he would need to borrow from his parents. He was up to $330, and that didn't even include tax.

After the tour the instructor and the pretty blond set everyone up with gear and got ready to take their money. Some of the other students in the class looked as surprised about the additional expenses as Joey but everyone pulled out a checkbook or credit card and bought their mask, snorkel, fins, booties, and other odds and ends.

When it was Joey's turn he stepped up to the counter and stood across from the attractive dive shop employee at the cash register. He thought she had said her name was Lindsey. Joey glanced into her deep blue eyes and quickly looked away, embarrassed at having to tell her he couldn't pay for the gear that evening. Not that he thought he had much of a chance with her. She was way out of his league.

Joey wasn't a bad looking guy. His light colored green eyes were a stark contrast to his dark brown hair and often attracted attention to him, unwanted as it was. He also had other pleasant features. But his gut. Thanks to his mother always pushing food on him and his lack of self-control, he could stand to lose about 20 pounds. Then, he might be only a notch or two…or three…below Lindsey's league.

He sheepishly said, "I didn't know we had to buy anything else tonight and didn't bring any extra money."

The girl gave Joey a bright toothy smile, tilted her head to the side, and said, "Oh, that's fine sweetie. That happens all the time. The instructors forget to tell everyone about the extra gear. We take credit cards," she offered as she tilted her head slightly to the side again.

Joey felt another flash of heat creep up his cheeks. He was blushing because she called him sweetie. And the way she tilted her head each time almost made Joey melt right there in front of her. He was even more embarrassed at having to tell her he didn't have a credit card.

"I, uh, I don't have a credit card. C-can you just put this aside and I-I'll show up early on Saturday and pay for it then?"

The smile on her face transformed into a frown but somehow made her look even more beautiful.

"The shop won't be open until a couple hours after you start your class Saturday morning but you can come in tomorrow or the next day if you want. I'll put the gear aside for you. I'll be here both days so when you come back just look for me."

Joey got excited at the thought of seeing her again and told her he'd see her the next couple days and walked off wondering if he was going to be able to borrow the money from his parents or if he was going to embarrass himself even more and have to drop out of the class.

The instructor told them that was it for the night and reminded everyone to be at the shop bright and early Saturday morning ready to scuba dive.

"Oh, and despite what I said about peeing in your wetsuits, there's no peeing in the pool so don't drink too much coffee that morning!"

Joey walked out to his car and drove home dreading the conversation with his parents.

* * *

When he got home, Joey's mother asked him how his scuba class had gone.

"U-um, it was okay. I got a hundred on the written exam! The swim test was pretty hard but I-I passed it," Joey said with a quick grin. After a short pause, "Mom, c-can I ask you a favor?"

Joey's mother looked at him with an all too common look of suspicion, and what he swore was disappointment, on her face. "Sure, Joseph, what's going on?"

Joey wasn't sure how to bring it up so he just went right into it.

"W-well, tonight I found out we have to buy some more scuba equipment. Just a mask, snorkel, fins, and some boots. I-I need the equipment to do the class this weekend but I don't have all the money for it. I-I didn't know about this before tonight. If I don't get it I'll have to d-drop out of the class and I'll lose the money I already paid."

Joey watched the wrinkles on the corners of his mother's mouth drop into a deep frown as she began to scold him.

"Are you serious, Joseph? Your father and I knew this scuba thing wasn't a good idea from the beginning. We told you it was too good to be true. Businesses can't make any money by selling classes that take 3 or 4 days long for only $99."

After a short pause she asked, "How much do you need?"

"Well, um," Joey paused, "$300 should do it."

"$300 dollars?!?"

4

August 4, 2011

Joey's parents had obviously lent him the money. He had every intention of paying them back as soon as he could. But then after that next weekend of scuba class he found out he would need to rent a BC, regulator, and tanks for the checkout dives plus the entry fee to Eddy Spring. That would cost him another couple hundred dollars. So he had to ask his parents for another loan and hold off starting to pay them back for another couple weeks.

Since Joey had gotten his scuba certification two months prior, he paid his parents back a little each week. He didn't make very much money. But he picked up extra shifts when he could. He was also holding some of the money he earned aside so he could go diving on his days off. He hadn't had his own gear and each day of diving meant spending over $100 for rental gear, tanks, and gas for his car to get to the dive site and back home.

Joey lived about an hour's drive from Eddy Spring and his car was older and didn't get great gas mileage. He still owed his parents $340. That's why they would be so upset about him ditching work. But he needed a break. It was only a summer job anyway and school was starting back up in a couple weeks. Once school started, with that and having to work weekends so he could continue to pay his parents back, he would hardly have anytime to dive. And he really loved scuba diving.

Whenever Joey was in the water he felt completely free. Being a little overweight, he got tired and out of breath fairly easily whenever he exerted himself. In the water he was weightless and, while he couldn't move very fast, he didn't have to. He could just swim around slowly and look at the fish while enjoying not having to lug around the extra weight he had put on over the past few years.

Another advantage to scuba diving and being overweight was Joey could save a little money by not having to buy a wet suit. He had what his scuba instructor had called *bio*prene to keep him warm. And it did work. While the thin divers were all shivering after only 20 minutes in the cool water, even with 7mm thick wetsuits on, Joey was pretty comfortable. The extra fat on him was insulating and helped keep him warm in the 68 degree water.

After a couple of weekends of renting equipment and tanks Joey decided it might be better to buy some used scuba gear. The dive shop had already gotten about $75 for the rental gear each time and that money would be better spent on gear that Joey would have all his own. He reasoned that he would save a lot of money in the long run by not having to pay that $75 every time he went diving.

Joey found some great deals on used scuba equipment on the internet and decided on a set someone local was selling that looked lightly used and was reasonably priced. He picked up a few shifts without telling his parents, skipped a couple of days of diving, and used the extra money to buy the gear. This was the first time he was going to have a chance to dive with it. He couldn't wait. The few weekends of scuba diving he had to give up to be able to afford the gear meant he could go scuba diving a lot more often because it would only cost him a rental tank and a couple of air fills. He no longer had to shell out so much money on rental equipment!

5

August 4, 2011 9am

Joey arrived at Eddy Spring, located just outside of Ponce de Leon, Florida, around 9:00 that morning. Eddy is located in the Florida panhandle about 20 minutes south of the Alabama state line. The Florida panhandle is littered with springs. Eddy is the only one privately owned but still open to the public. Driving by on the highway you wouldn't even know this place existed if it wasn't for the faded blue billboard sign looming over the entrance to the dirt road proclaiming "*Crystal clear water!*"

Driving north from I-10 on FL-81 past the small town of Ponce de Leon, named after the Spanish explorer who allegedly searched for the fountain of youth in the area, Joey wondered if there was a cave in Ponce de Leon State Park similar to the one at Eddy Spring. He had been to the state park and swimming in the spring located there a few times with his parents over the years. That was long before he had even thought about becoming a scuba diver, though. He didn't remember seeing anything during his dips in the cool, clear water that Juan Ponce de Leon may have thought was the fountain of youth, but Joey hadn't been looking for that either.

He turned off the asphalt highway onto the tree lined dirt road next to the billboard. The road looked freshly graded. Rain ruts always formed on the road after it rained giving it a washboard feeling when driving over it. The Eddy Spring staff kept it maintained since their patrons used it the most. There were lines of dirt along the sides of the road formed by the blade that had scraped the road smooth earlier that morning. Preparations for the busy weekend ahead were already in motion.

About a half mile down the road Joey saw the perimeter fence for Eddy Spring to his left. He could just make out the campsites and one of the bathhouses through the trees. He followed the road around the bend to the left and continued down the road toward the entrance The fence ended and Joey turned left toward the entrance shack that was situated about halfway between the road and the dive shop building. Since it was a Thursday no one was at the shack. They only staffed that on weekends. So Joey drove past it and pulled up to the dive shop, parking in front of it.

Joey was always overwhelmed with all the scuba gear lining the walls and stacked on shelves throughout the store. He walked around the store for what was probably the hundredth time to take it all in, stopping a little longer at the locked display cases to examine the smaller, more expensive items like dive computers, regulators, and cave diving reels. After his requisite walk about the shop he signed in at the counter and paid the entrance fee and scuba tank rental. It was nice to not have to pay for rental gear.

"No rental gear today, sugar?" the employee checking Joey in asked.

"I-I finally bought my own set. I-It's used but it l-looks in good shape," Joey replied.

"Well, you be kerful then. We don't need no one gettin' hurt while divin'."

"I will!" Joey called back as he turned around to walk out the door.

With his color-coded wristband indicating he had paid to scuba dive, Joey left the cool air conditioning of the shop and got back into his car to move it closer to the water. He looked around the parking areas on both sides of the Grande Vista Chalet, a log cabin style building that sat high on stilts and contained five rooms that could be rented overnight by guests of the scuba park. Underneath the building was what appeared to be an open fireplace in the center, like those often found in ski lodges. Closer inspection of it revealed that it was a scuba tank filling station that was masterfully disguised. Surrounding the fireplace/fill station were several tables where divers could set up gear protected from the hot Florida sun. There was also a rack of full scuba tanks in one corner under the stairs leading up to the balcony where Joey would be able to find a tank to use for the day. The building was located at the top of the hill overlooking the crystal clear spring basin just south of it.

Joey scanned the area and noticed there were no other cars around. He was the only one there that morning. In addition to the tables under the Chalet there were also several picnic tables scattered around it on the grass to make it easier for divers to set up their gear. On weekends it was almost impossible to find an unclaimed table. Today, Joey had them all to choose from.

He continued his scan down the slope of the hill to the spring basin. The basin, the size of a small pond just under 200 feet wide and about 250 feet long, narrows down and empties into a creek that disappears into the woods to the west. On the other side of the basin from Grande Vista Chalet sits the house that the original owner of the property lived in and still visited from time to time. *How cool would it be to have a spring basin right in front of your house?* Joey thought.

The water coming from Eddy Spring flows to the west into Otter Creek and then bends south into Silty Creek a few miles away. It eventually passes through Ponce de Leon State Park where its waters mix with the waters coming from the Ponce de Leon Spring. The land around Eddy Spring was purchased back in the late 1960s and developed into a popular scuba diving destination. Divers from all over the southeast drove several hours to dive and train at this spring. Joey felt very fortunate to live in Santa Rosa Beach less than an hour south from it. The only thing better would be living in the house overlooking it!

The weekend Joey completed his certification dives it was so busy he had to park pretty far from the water. Fortunately, his instructor had brought all the scuba tanks so all Joey had to carry from his car to the picnic table his instructor had arrived early enough to claim was the gear he had rented at the dive shop the day before. All the divers there that weekend didn't help maintain the crystal clear visibility claimed on the billboard back on the road turnoff. Visibility in the spring basin was terrible by Saturday afternoon when they did their second dive. But that was typical, not only for Eddy Spring, but for most scuba training facilities.

The bottom of the spring basin was covered with dirt that divers called silt. It was really easy to disturb and when it was disturbed that crystal clear water wasn't so clear anymore. All the divers in the water had stirred up the silt on the bottom so badly he could hardly see his instructor a few feet away from him. Joey had been diving at Eddy Spring since he completed his class but it was always on weekends and conditions were no different. This was the first time he would be diving Eddy Spring during the week and he could hardly wait to get in the water and *see* what it looked like. It was also the first time he would be diving alone.

His scuba instructor had emphasized buddy diving and told everyone solo diving was dangerous. But he had seen other divers alone at Eddy Spring, even during his certification dives. The basin was small and shallow, less than 25 feet deep throughout most of it and less than 200 feet across. It was impossible to get lost. And if there was a problem all Joey had to do was ascend to the surface. How dangerous could it be? They had done CESAs in class, controlled emergency swimming ascents, which meant he had to swim from the concrete platform, located 20 feet deep, to the surface without taking a breath. He was able to make it almost all the way to the surface the first time with no problem. He did take a small breath but his instructor either didn't catch that or didn't care. Some of the other students had to try it a couple times before they were passed on that skill.

As Joey got out of his car he noticed a pickup truck he hadn't seen when he first arrived. The truck was parked in a grassy area on the other side of a fence, off the scuba park property on the adjacent property where they could enter the basin without having to pay the entrance fee. When Eddy Spring had been sold a couple years back

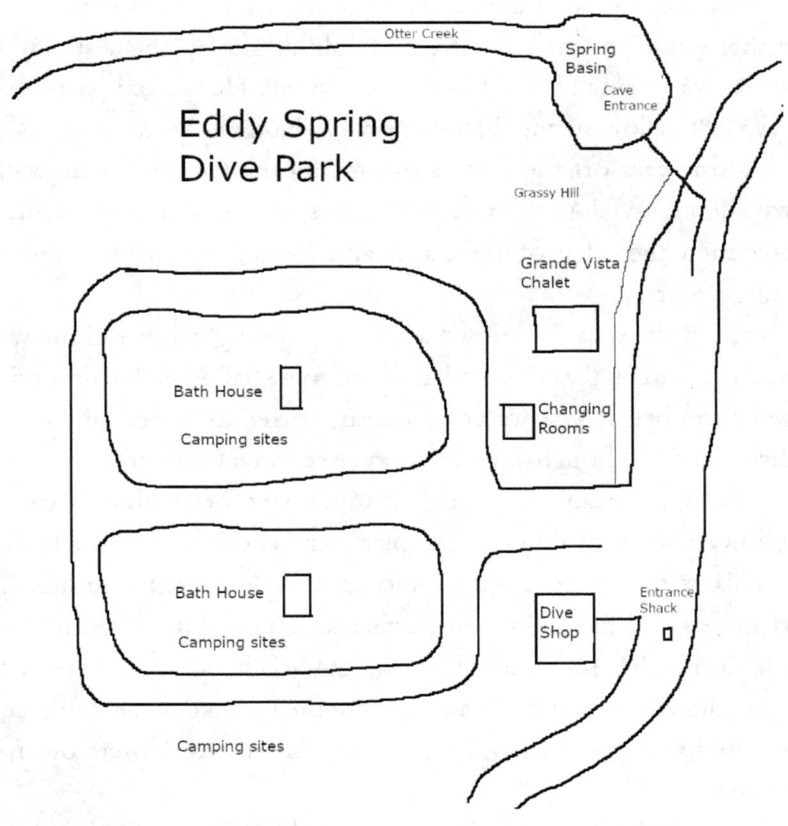

the property was divided so the original owners retained the east side while the scuba park got the west side. The owners didn't live on the property. They kept it as a vacation home.

Some divers chose to park on that side and forgo paying the scuba park entrance fee. Joey had thought about doing it too so he could save some money, but he needed to rent a tank so he still needed to go into the shop. He didn't feel right about renting a tank and then parking on the free side. Besides, anyone who paid the entrance fee got a break on rentals and air fills and got to use the restrooms and changing rooms. And the scuba park did do a lot of work to keep the place nice.

Joey was a little disappointed once he realized he wasn't the first one there, but one or two divers shouldn't stir up the visibility too badly. It was a small basin but not that small. He walked past the big heavy dark yellow metal chains that were hanging between posts and keeping the cars off the grass surrounding the Chalet. As he walked down the grassy slope he noticed he was already dripping sweat. He approached the edge of the basin and looked down into the clear inviting water.

Joey decided to cool down a little by dipping his feet in the water at the metal steps that descended down to a shallow ledge around the edge of the basin. The water was clear, correction - crystal clear like the sign said. Although Joey had never seen real crystal so he wasn't sure what that meant other than it must have been pretty clear. He could even see the old concrete platform where he had knelt to do his skills with his scuba instructor a couple months earlier. The platform was 20 feet below the surface and he had never been able to see it during his previous visits on the weekends, not even while floating directly above it. Standing there on a weekday, he could see it from where he stood and it must have been at least 20 feet out from the steps.

He looked around the basin and could make out the shapes of

the large, fake metal caverns that had been placed in it many years prior. He hadn't been in the caverns yet but maybe today he would just take a peek inside. He had been to the basin a couple times since getting his certification card and even though he still loved scuba diving, the basin was getting a little boring. How much could you do in a 200 by 250 foot spring basin? He thought it would be really cool to swim through those metal caverns. They had plenty of openings cut out from the top and sides to make them safe.

Joey stepped down a couple of metal steps so the water was up to his knees. The cool water felt really good! It was a welcome relief from the intense heat of the day. He could barely wait to get his gear on and explore the manmade caverns. After a few minutes of standing with his legs in the water and daydreaming Joey turned around and looked back up the hill toward the Grande Vista Chalet. From that vantage point the Chalet definitely looked grand. He

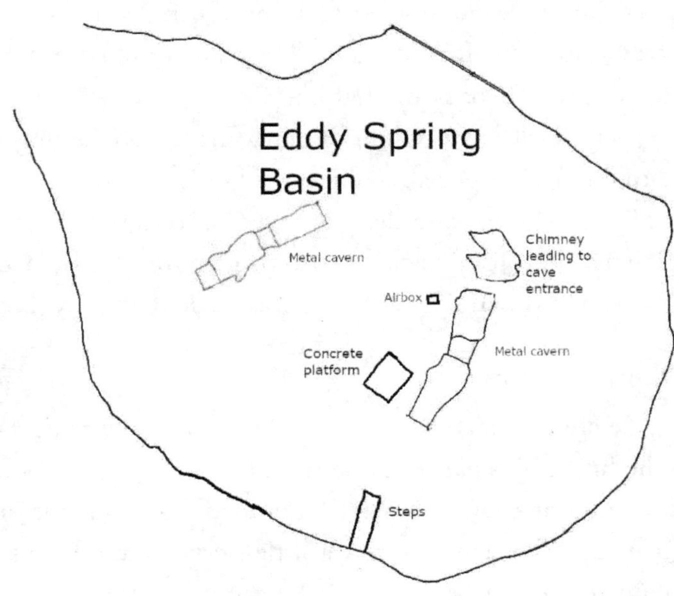

would have to sneak up the steps to the balcony during his surface interval to take in the view from there.

He turned his attention back to the hill. That steep hill wasn't any fun to climb, especially in this heat. That was part of the price one had to pay for diving in such a beautiful location. He begrudgingly climbed to the platform at the top of the steps and headed back up the hill toward his car so he could get his gear and go scuba diving.

Even after dipping his legs in the refreshingly cool water the sweat was still pouring out of Joey. With as much sweating as he was doing one would think he had just come out from a full dip in the water. His clothing was completely soaked through! He got to his car and started unloading his gear onto a nearby picnic table. Placing his rental tank on the ground, he slid the cam straps of the buoyancy compensator down over the tank. Suddenly he remembered his scuba instructor had told everyone to wet the cam bands first to make them loosen up so when you tighten them on the tank they stay snug. He wished he had remembered to bring the BC with him when he first arrived and went to the water. He really didn't want to walk down and, even worse, back up that hill.

Joey did it anyway. He didn't want to risk having his tank slide out of his BC, especially while diving alone. He headed back down the hill to the steps and dipped his BC into the water to get the straps wet. This time Joey decided to dip his entire body in the water and cool himself down. His clothing was soaked anyway. He strapped his BC to the rail and dove in head first.

What a relief!

He should have done this earlier when he was at the steps. Back up the hill at his gear Joey slid the BC back on the tank and tightened the cam straps snug. Next he grabbed his regulator set and slid it onto the tank valve. He was a little nervous about this. He had just bought the regulator and when he got it he called his local dive shop to ask about having service done on it to make sure it was in good working condition. They wanted to charge him over $150! He hadn't even paid that much for the regulator set. He would have to save some more money to get that done.

But first he had to pay his parents back. He couldn't spend any more money on scuba equipment before he paid them. They didn't even know he had bought this equipment. And he couldn't have the gear he just bought sitting around without taking it on a dive. He would start off nice and slow and stay shallow while he made sure everything was working properly. His scuba class was all about learning how to deal with problems underwater. If something happened he would do what he had been taught to do.

Once the regulator was on the tank valve Joey turned the pressure gauge so it was facing down like he was taught. If it blew up when he opened the valve and sent 3000 pounds per square inch of pressure into it the plastic facing would explode toward the ground. He slowly opened the tank valve. Phfffffft. He could hear the air filling the regulator and hoses. He opened the valve all the way then turned it back a quarter turn like he was taught. He rotated the gauge so it was facing him. 2800 psi. Not quite full but he didn't expect much better. He hadn't seen a single tank filled to 3000 psi since he started scuba diving a couple months ago. No one seemed to fill scuba tanks to their rated pressures.

Joey stopped and listened for a moment but didn't hear any air leaking from the regulator. That was a good sign. He leaned in and placed his right ear close to the first stage regulator and valve and still didn't hear any leaking air. Maybe it didn't need to get serviced by the dive shop after all. He took a couple of breaths off the second stage regulator and it breathed about the same as the rental regulators he had used. So far, so good.

Joey lifted the heavy tank and BC onto the picnic table so it would be at a better height for him to put it on. He placed his fins, mask, and snorkel on the bench and then put his right arm through the opening in the BC. He pulled the shoulder strap up and dropped his left arm through the other opening and pulled the BC up so it was resting on his shoulders.

It felt a lot lighter than the gear he had used before. This wouldn't be as hard to walk up and down the hill, he thought with a smile. Joey pulled the cummerbund ends snugly together over his belly and snapped the smaller waist strap over it. He pulled down on the shoulder straps to tighten them and grabbed his fins, mask, and snorkel before heading down the grassy hill to the water.

Joey got to the top of the platform and slowly stepped onto it, careful to keep from slipping on the slick surface. He walked the length of the platform to the steps at the other end. At the top of the steps he slowly stepped down holding onto the rail so as to not slip and fall. That would be bad with a 40 pound tank on his back. He continued holding onto the rail with one hand while he reached down with a fin in the other hand, slipped his right foot into the foot pocket, and pulled the fin strap over his heel. He swapped sides and did the same with the other fin. He then gathered some spit in his mouth and directed it into his mask to keep the glass from fogging up.

He hadn't bothered to buy the bag of bottles that contained mask defogger. He saw plenty of divers using defogger on their masks but he had also learned spit worked just as well. And it was free! Just don't eat anything with onions before diving.

Joey rinsed the mask and slipped it over his head onto his face. Lifting his feet off the steps, he pushed himself away from them, lifted the inflator hose to let all the air escape from his BC and waited to descend into the heavenly crystal clear water of Eddy Spring. Only unlike during his previous dives, this time he didn't descend. He just bobbed on the surface. He lifted the hose higher in the air while pushing the exhaust button harder. He shook it around but no more air came out and nothing happened. Had he bought a defective BC?

Suddenly Joey realized he forgot to rent a weight belt. The BCs he had previously rented were weight integrated, meaning they had weight pockets built into them. The used BC he bought wasn't. There were no weight pockets to hold weights. He had to use a weight belt to secure the weights necessary to get him negatively buoyant enough to sink below the surface. No wonder it felt so light when he put it on! He would have to take his fins and mask off, get out of the water, walk back up that hill to the picnic table, take his gear off and walk over to the dive shop to rent a weight belt and some weights. He was exhausted just thinking about it.

Joey made his way to the steps and pulled off his fins and mask. As he was climbing out of the water an older man he had seen working around the dive shop and the spring basin on previous days Joey was there was walking toward the steps.

"Y'a'ight?" he asked in a heavy southern accent making what he said sound like one drawn out syllable.

Quite a bit embarrassed at forgetting a weight belt and looking bad in the water, Joey looked away from the man and down at the water and said, "I-I'm fine. I-I just forgot a weight belt. This is my first time d-diving my own scuba equipment and stupid me forgot to rent a weight belt when I rented the tank."

"New t' divin'?" The accent made it so Joey almost couldn't understand what the man was saying. Thinking he knew the question he responded.

"Yep. I-I just got my certification card about six weeks ago. M-my name is Joey."

"M'name's Earl. Ah manage dis place."

Apparently Earl wasn't one much for enunciating complete words but Joey was really impressed that he was talking to the manager of the Eddy Spring Scuba Park. He looked up at him wide-eyed, "Wow! That's really neat! I'd love to work at a scuba park!"

"It's fun, but's lotta work too. Hard work. Well, ifya need thin', lemme know."

"Thanks."

Earl just stood there looking out over the basin, sweat stains under his arms and around the neck of his shirt, as Joey walked back up to the picnic table and undid the straps and pulled his BC and tank off. Joey couldn't believe he had just met and talked to the manager of Eddy Spring. How cool was that? Wait till he told his dive buddies. They would be pretty envious. Maybe he could become friends with Earl and get a discount on the entry fee or maybe even get in for free. He might even get a discount on gear in the shop.

Joey stopped his daydreaming and walked to the dive shop. He added the weights and weight belt to his rental ticket. He had only brought enough money to get in, rent a tank and get air fills for two dives, and lunch. He had forgotten about the weights. He'd have to cut back on lunch today. He'll never make that mistake again!

He slid the bare metal weights into the pockets of the weight belt and zipped them securely in place. He had used 24 pounds in class and that worked fine the other times he'd been diving so that's what he got today. The other times he had gotten the weights with his tank and rental gear and put them in his car to drive over to the parking area. This time he had walked. So he had to carry the heavy 24 pound weight belt back to the picnic table. His muscles were already starting to hurt just thinking about it.

Once back at the table Joey put the weight belt around his waist and then slipped his arms into his BC so it was situated over the weights. This time it didn't feel so light. What an idiot he was! He slowly headed back down the hill toward the water, walked across the platform, and descended the steps even more slowly so he wouldn't slip with all the additional weight he was carrying. He slid his feet into his fins, placed his mask over his face, and backed off the steps once again.

As soon as he moved away from the steps Joey immediately started sinking, his head quickly dropping under the surface. *Uh oh!* He forgot to fill his BC with air and he didn't have his regulator in his mouth so in a second he wasn't going to be able to breathe. This was not turning out to be a good day.

He quickly found his inflator hose and pushed the inflator button. He felt the BC start to squeeze him as it filled with air and he slowly started to ascend to the surface. His head popped up above the surface and he took in a big gulp of air. He looked up the hill and saw Earl looking down at him and shaking his head. Well, that wasn't good. He certainly wasn't making a very good impression on his new acquaintance. Earl was probably some sort of world class diver and here Joey was almost drowning himself right in front of him.

* * *

Joey had a fantastic dive! He had the entire spring basin to himself and the visibility was the best he had ever seen. He could practically see from one end of the basin to the other! He swam around chasing after the koi that he didn't even know lived in there. He peeked inside every hole in the fake metal caverns. He could see light coming from all the other openings and thought he might just do a quick swim through one of them on his next dive. Finally he headed over to the air box someone had bolted to the bottom of the basin around 20 feet deep. The air box was just large enough for two divers to swim under and stick their heads up into so they could talk to each other.

He noticed a couple of scuba tanks with no regulators attached to the valves hanging off the side of the air box, which he thought was strange. He had never seen those there before. Joey had heard that a diver goes in the basin every morning and fills the box with fresh air. He did this so divers who pop their heads up into the box can breathe it without worrying about passing out from not having enough oxygen.

He had learned in his scuba class that in every exhalation there's only 16% oxygen left so breathing from air bells and boxes and air pockets in caverns and wrecks wasn't too smart. But because this was a scuba park divers went into the air box a lot just to talk, so the staff refreshed the air in there every day to make it a little safer for those who forgot.

The guy who had that job must have forgotten to bring his tanks back out, Joey thought. Joey had heard there was another air box back in the cave right before a metal grate that had been installed in the passage to keep divers from going beyond it deeper into the cave. He recalled some divers talking about this room where the second air box was located. They called it the Opera Room. They were climbing up the steps out of the water talking excitedly about their dive as Joey was getting ready to go in the water for the first time with his scuba class.

"Can you believe how cool that was!?! That room back there is huge!" As the diver said this he held his hands out at arms' length to illustrate just how big it was.

His buddy had a big smile on his face and responded, "That was definitely one of the best dives I've ever done. I wonder what it's like beyond the grate we saw."

His buddy got a worried look on his face, "I don't know. It looked kind of small. I saw a padlock on the grate but I don't think anyone is allowed back there. If divers were allowed back there they'd probably have the lights go back in there too."

Joey had also heard about the string lights that ran from the cavern opening back to the room right before the grate. This had intrigued him but at the time he was pretty certain he wouldn't venture into the dark cave. It seemed too scary to him.

But that was then. Now, a couple months later, Joey found

himself thinking about the Opera Room and what it would be like to be in it. Maybe the air box diver was back there putting fresh air in that box and had left the two tanks in the basin so he wouldn't have to carry so many tanks with him. If that was the case then it couldn't be too dangerous. If it was so dangerous wouldn't they have installed the grate at the opening instead of beyond the Opera Room?

Joey swam around for about 45 minutes before he noticed the air pressure in his scuba tank was getting a little low. His scuba instructor had taught him to always be out of the water with no less than 500 psi left in his tank. He was down to 700 psi and started wondering once again how he would know when he would be at 500 psi. He would just have to watch his pressure gauge a little closer to make sure he was near the steps where he could exit the water when the needle reached 500 psi.

He stayed in that area for the next couple of minutes watching his pressure gauge closely. He knew that the deeper he was the more air he used. Which meant if he was shallow he was using less air. But that was the extent of his knowledge. What he didn't know was how to calculate when he would have 500 psi left in his tank.

The deepest Joey had been so far was 50 feet and that was during his scuba class when the instructor took everyone down the chimney-like opening to the cavern. They all went through their air quickly at that depth. The instructor and the entire class had descended along the rope to the bottom of this hole that was called a chimney and with the rim at the top about 25 feet below the surface. Once they were there they looked in at the cavern. It was really dark and looked scary back then. It was a big, black opening with some air pockets on the ceiling shimmering in the light. He could also see a rectangular white sign on the back wall but it was too far away and too dark for him to read it. There was also a Florida freshwater eel swimming in and out of the openings in the rocky walls down there.

Joey didn't even know there was such a thing! He had heard

about green moray eels and seen pictures of them on the internet and in books. He didn't know there were any other kinds of eels though. He was a little scared of them when he first saw them but they weren't aggressive and didn't chase after him or try to bite him. The way they swam around it looked like they could see too, unlike what he had heard about the green moray eel. Joey might have to go down and check them out again later during his second dive.

He would have to do that early on during the dive though. Because he had learned that the deeper he was the more air he breathed he knew he should do the deeper part of the dive at the beginning when he had a full tank. This way he wouldn't have to worry so much about his pressure dropping down to 500 psi when he was deeper and breathing more air. It was hard enough to figure out from 20 feet.

Speaking of his pressure, he checked his gauge again and saw that while he was reminiscing about his class and seeing the eels he had breathed past 500 psi and was at 400 psi. *Uh oh!* Joey spun around, caught sight of the steps and started swimming straight for them. Once there he surfaced. He sure hoped whoever was filling tanks today didn't get mad at him for breathing the tank too low.

Joey pulled himself up onto the steps, slid his mask down around his neck, and then reached down to pull his fins off. He turned around and looked back over the spring basin and thought about how much fun the dive he had just done had been. There was no better feeling than floating weightless in cool crystal clear water.

He pulled himself back to reality and slowly climbed up the steps thinking about how heavy the BC, tank, and weights felt. It would be nice to get up the hill and take that gear off. Too bad there weren't any picnic tables at the bottom of the hill right next to the water. He slowly made his way up to his picnic table and backed up against it to remove the BC and tank.

With the BC off, Joey turned around and closed the tank valve, purged the air out of his regulator and unscrewed it from the valve. He then loosened the strap on the BC and pulled it off the tank so he could carry the tank to the air fill station. He went to his car to get a fill ticket that he had bought earlier that morning. He carried the tank and fill ticket to the fill station under the Grande Vista Chalet and left the ticket on the "hearth" in front of the fill whips and quickly walked away before someone came out, attached the fill hose to his tank and saw he had less than 400 psi left in it.

6

Joey opened the glass door to the dive shop and felt the cool blast of air conditioning hit the front of his body. The cold air on his wet skin sent a chill through him and raised goose bumps but it felt great after being in the oppressive heat outside. He turned and walked to the back of the shop to look over what turned out to be a meager selection of food. They usually had a lot more out on the weekends. Joey looked at the price stickers on the food and quickly calculated how much he could afford for lunch. He bought one of the pre-packaged sandwiches, an apple pie snack, and a cola. This would have to do.

He wished he had made himself a lunch before leaving the house but that would have raised suspicion in his parents since he never brought a lunch to work. This summer he had found a job as a busboy at one of the touristy chain restaurants in Destin. The money wasn't great and even though the waitresses were supposed to give the busboys 10% of their tips he knew some of them were stingy and lied about the amount of tips they received. He usually only got about ten extra dollars a day, not even two hours' worth of his hourly pay. And it barely paid for his gas to get to and from work. But that little extra allowed him to set aside money to pay for the scuba diving.

The best thing about working at the restaurant for him was lunchtime. Not the customers' lunches but his own. All employees got their food for a fifty percent discount but sometimes the cooks would screw up and make too many burgers or make the wrong order. Instead of throwing the food away they would put it aside for any of the employees who wanted it. Joey walked by the kitchen every few minutes after bussing the tables to put the dirty dishes by the dishwasher and he made sure to check for the freebies regularly. Usually by the time the lunch rush was over Joey had eaten a couple of burgers and didn't have to buy a lunch. He normally did spring for a dessert since those were made early in the morning and stored in the refrigerator so there was no way to get any of them for free.

Joey walked back to the front of the shop and paid for his small pre-packaged lunch. He ate it while he walked around the dive shop checking out all the neat looking scuba equipment. He had already looked at all the gear that morning when he first got there but he could never get tired of looking at anything related to scuba. So he continued his respite from the hot summer day safe inside the building away from the gnats.

The shop had most of the scuba gear in the front near the counter. The glass display cases holding the expensive items were arranged in a large triangle in the center of the front of the shop with space inside for the employees on duty. The corners of the triangles were formed by shelves that held smaller, inexpensive items like mask defogger. Toward the back of the store, near the food, they had wetsuits hanging against one wall and a bunch of different souvenir type stuff like t-shirts, coffee mugs, and beach towels in the middle. On one of the side walls of the dive shop Joey saw a large map of the Eddy Spring cave system. He stopped in front of it and stared at the map thinking how cool it would be to see what it looked like inside.

It couldn't be too dangerous. Despite what that one diver he heard talking on the steps had said about no one being allowed back there Joey knew scuba divers went into the cave all the time. He had even seen several go in there while he was at the cavern opening with his scuba class. And there were already lights from the opening back to the grate. He wondered where on the map the grate was located but there was no indication of it anywhere.

Joey had also gotten a dive light with the scuba equipment he just bought. He had turned it on during his first dive but the visibility was so good and there was so much light in the basin he couldn't tell how bright it was, even when he pointed it into the darkness of the metal caverns. Maybe he would take a look in the real cavern during his second dive. He wouldn't go all the way to the grate. He would go in just until it was dark enough that he could see how bright his light was.

He walked around to the front of the shop and saw a large table near the door. On the table was a 3D model of the Eddy Spring dive park. It was pretty cool being able to look down on the park as if he was in an airplane flying over it. The spring basin looked even smaller looking down on it from this angle. He noticed the chimney on one side of the basin and saw that the hole went straight down into the model. He stepped back from the model and saw another level underneath the scuba park display. He bent down in front of the table and looked under the ground of the model. It was a reproduction of the cave under the park model.

"Purty cool, huh?"

Joey practically jumped out of his clothes at that. He had been so entranced by this model and his plan for his second dive that he hadn't noticed Earl walk up behind him.

"Y-yes sir."

"Had lil trouble onyer dive dis mornin?" That was the most Joey had heard Earl say in one breath.

"Y-yes sir. I-I'm still getting used to that gear."

"See n'thing good onda' dive?"

"I-I just followed some koi around and peaked inside the metal caverns. It's d-different here during the week. The v-visibility was really great. Not like when I-I've been here on the weekends."

"Yeah, nice ta have sa many scuba 'structors brin thar divers heah 'n weekends but does messup vis in da basin when everun's kneelin n walkin 'long da bottom. We try 'n' keep 's much da silt out thar we can but's hard. Ya doin' 'nuther dive?"

"Y-yes sir." Joey said surprised that Earl had said so much at once.

"Well, y'all b' kerful. 'N make shur ya watch y'alls gauge."

Joey just stared at Earl without saying anything right away. He was mortified. Earl had noticed. He looked down at the floor and said, "I-I-I will sir."

As he watched Earl walk back to an office door on the other side of the shop, Joey realized he hadn't finished his lunch yet. He could usually eat pretty quickly but he was so distracted by the map and model of the cave that he completely forgot about it. He finished the rest of his half eaten sandwich and ate his snack pie as he walked around the shop one more time looking at all the dive gear he wished he could afford and thinking about the cave under his feet deep below the ground.

After finishing his lunch and cola, Joey walked back outside. He felt the thickness of the hot humid air as he opened the door and sweat immediately started to seep out of his skin pores. *Wow! It was really a hot one today!* It had also rained a little the day before so the humidity was up. The air was so thick from the humidity that walking from the shop to the tank filling station was almost like moving through the water. Joey would much rather be in the real water. At least there he wasn't sweating!

His tank was already in the rack marked filled tanks. He grabbed it by the valve and carried it to the picnic table where his gear was waiting for him. The valve felt hot but that was expected after just being filled. The compression of air into the tank generated heat. He could feel that heat on the tank when it bounced against his leg as he carried it to the picnic table.

Earl had said something about watching his pressure gauge. He wondered if the guy who filled his tank told Earl about his tank pressure. He sure hoped not. Maybe Earl just said that to everyone.

Joey slowly set up his gear just like he had earlier that day. This time his pressure gauge read 3100 psi but the tank was still hot. In class he learned that as the tank cools off after being filled, the pressure also goes down. He knew he could expect to see his tank pressure drop a couple hundred psi or so as it cooled off in the 68 degree spring water. Even with the slight drop in pressure he should still be able to get a decent length dive from the tank.

Looping his arms through the shoulder straps of the BC Joey pulled the heavy gear onto his back, clipped the waist strap on, and cinched the shoulder straps. He then turned to grab his fins and mask and saw his weight belt on the table next to them. *Dammit!* The weights had been behind his BC and tank and he hadn't seen them. And again he forgot about it! He loosened the straps and pulled off the BC so he could put his weight belt on.

During the morning dive Joey had felt like he was a little too heavy even at the end of the dive. He was so worried about his pressure gauge being low he hadn't thought about doing a neutral buoyancy check. He recalled doing a buoyancy check in class at the end of one of the pool dives. Everyone got in the water with a scuba tank only filled to about 500 psi, moved over to the deep end, took in a normal breath, and let all the air out of the BC. If you stayed at the surface you didn't have enough weight. If you dropped under the surface too fast you had too much weight. You were supposed to sink to eye level with the surface when you were weighted properly. Joey had dropped under the surface and was ready to pull some weight off but his instructor told him not to remove any. He said he wanted him a little heavy during the class because it would makes things easier.

At the end of the dive earlier that morning Joey remembered having to inflate his BC to get up to the surface. And that was with only 400 psi in his tank. He decided to take off a few pounds. The dive shop had given him two 5-pound weights, two 4-pound weights, and two 3-pound weights to make up the 24 pounds he said he needed. He thought he should only remove 4 pounds but then he would be lopsided so he took the two 3-pound weights out instead. Eighteen pounds would be enough. He put the two 3-pound weights in the trunk of his car for the time being and returned to the picnic table to put his gear back on.

This time Joey put the weight belt on first then looped his arms through the straps of the BC again. He sure wished he could scuba dive with less weight. But while an advantage of having bioprene was that he stayed warm in the water, a disadvantage was he needed more weight to keep him neutrally buoyant. Once he started back at school he wouldn't be working at the restaurant during the week and maybe he could lose some of the extra weight and make it easier. Having two burgers a day certainly hadn't done his physique any good.

By this time Joey had worked up a pretty good sweat. His hair was even soaking wet. He quickly grabbed his fins and mask and headed down the hill to the steps and the cool refreshing water. He walked down the steps feeling the cold water inching up his legs. When the water got to his thighs he stopped for a minute. With as hot as he was the next step had to take some preparation. The one place on his body where he didn't have any bioprene was about to get submerged. It always sent a shiver through him when that region got wet.

He slowly stepped down onto the next step and felt the water moving up his legs. As the shiver went up and down his back Joey took the next couple of steps until the surface of the water was at his chest. He reached down and pulled his fins onto his feet and then pulled his mask over his face. Time for his second dive!

7

August 4, 2011 1:30pm

Joey quickly submerged under the clear crisp water of the Eddy Spring basin and descended to the concrete slab that was located about 20 feet below the surface. He started swimming alongside the large dark steel manmade cavern that was placed next to the slab years ago, passing the air box that was bolted to the basin floor at one end of the cavern. He noticed the scuba tanks were still at the base of one of the legs of the air box. Closer inspection revealed that they were padlocked to the leg. *That was strange*, Joey thought.

He continued on past the airbox and the cavern. As he rounded the air box he made out the large oval shaped chimney located at the other end of the basin from where he had entered. His thoughts went back to his open water scuba class when his instructor had taken all the students down there so they could log a dive at a depth of 50 feet. While the chimney looked big as they approached it from the top it was really crowded with six students plus the instructor once they got within its walls. As they descended down the water column they kept bumping into each other and accidently kicking each other with their fins. They also stirred up a lot more of the silt that seemed to be everywhere.

As Joey approached the rim of the chimney he saw the thick rope that was secured to a large metal pin driven into the stone floor of the chimney. It lead from there up to a two foot long white buoy floating on the surface 50 feet above. He grasped the rope to help him keep from descending too quickly down the shaft. Letting the air out of his BC, he began his descent using the rope to control his speed. The rope slipped through his hands and he felt himself descending rapidly through the water column. He could feel the rope burning his palms, and even worse, his ears were hurting from the added pressure on them. The descent was too fast to equalize the air spaces in his ears. Joey reached up and pinched his nose through his mask like he was taught in class so he could do a Valsalva maneuver and equalize the pressure in his ears and ease the pain off. A few seconds later he crashed into the bottom of the chimney shaft hitting his shin on a large rock on the floor next to the rope.

"Ouch!" He screamed through his regulator as he reached down and rubbed his shin. He felt some broken skin but didn't see any blood. *That was good!* His ears also felt better. He had been able to equalize the pressure before he got too deep.

Pressing the inflator button on his BC to send some air into it, Joey tried to get neutrally buoyant. After a few seconds he started to rise slowly. His ascent increased in speed and his slow ascent turned into a rapid one. He quickly grabbed the rope in front of him while fumbling for his inflator hose to release some of the air. He had put too much air in the BC and not only made himself positively buoyant but he had flipped over and was hanging upside down as both the BC and the water current forced him up toward the surface. He reminded himself that he had taken some weight off his belt and no longer needed as much air in his BC. If only he had remembered that a moment ago.

Air wasn't escaping out of the inflator hose even though he was pressing the exhaust button. Since he was upside down all the air was at the bottom of his BC but the inflator hose was located at the top. But being upside down the bottom had become the top and the top the bottom. He was going to have to somehow flip his feet back under his body so he could get the air to shift to the top of the BC where the inflator hose was located and then exhaust the air from it. He tried to pull his feet down but he didn't have the strength in his arms to do this. He wrapped his legs around the rope and tried to flip his head up over his fins but when he let go of the rope with his hands he started to slide up the rope. This was not a good situation.

Suddenly Joey remembered he had an exhaust valve at the bottom of the BC along his waist. All he had to do was find the short string in the center of it and pull it to open the valve. He reached back with his left hand and felt along the bottom seam of the BC but couldn't feel a string or a valve. He was upside down so maybe the string had dropped down between the BC and his waist. He probed his fingers underneath his BC but still couldn't find the string. *It must be on the other side*, he thought.

Joey grabbed the rope with his left hand and reached back with his right hand. He felt a large plastic protrusion from the canvas-like material of the BC. *There it was!* He grabbed the string and gave it a hard tug. He felt hundreds of air bubbles escaping from the BC and traveling around his hand, tickling the skin, as they shot to the surface. He felt himself descending again, this time head first! Holding on tightly with his left hand so he wouldn't slam his head into the bottom, he was able to flip his body around placing him upright again He continued slipping down the rope. Smack! His shin crashed into the same large rock.

"Ouch!!!" That was going to be really sore later.

Joey tried adding air to his BC again, this time squeezing the button quickly and briefly to give short bursts of air. He slowly rose off the bottom and this time stopped when he was hovering about a foot off the bottom. He was improving.

Looking around the bottom of the chimney shaft he saw the smooth limestone walls with a few holes in them along one side and a very large dark opening leading to the cavern on the other. He also saw some Florida freshwater eels swimming along the bottom and in and out of the holes. *That was cool!* He had only seen one last time he was here but now there were several of them. It was much nicer without so many other divers surrounding him. He looked over toward the cavern opening. It was pretty big. He could see the beginning of what looked like a large white pipe on the floor off to the right and straight in front of him about 25 feet away he could make out a white rectangular sign.

Joey remembered seeing the sign during class but couldn't read it at that time. He swam toward the sign curious to see what it said. As he got closer he made out a drawing and some bold type letters on it. When he was within a few feet of it he could see the drawing was of one of those Halloween ghouls that wear a long robe with a hood on it and he was carrying one of those curved blades on the end of a stick. Suddenly the name came to him – grim reaper. Lying at the reaper's feet were three skeletons wearing scuba gear.

There were words to the right of the reaper which read:

STOP
PREVENT YOUR DEATH!
GO NO FARTHER.

FACT: More than 300 divers, including open water scuba instructors, have died in caves just like this one

FACT: You need training to dive. You need cave training and cave equipment to cave dive

FACT: Without cave training and cave equipment, divers can die here.

FACT: It CAN happen to YOU!

THERE'S NOTHING IN THIS CAVE WORTH DYING FOR!
DO NOT GO BEYOND THIS POINT!

That was pretty dramatic. Joey knew open water divers went in this very cave every weekend and didn't die. He had even heard of instructors bringing their students in here. He remembered the lights that were supposed to lead from the large room where the grate was located back out to the opening. Joey looked to his right and saw a faint glow in the thick darkness of the cave. It looked like the lights might even be turned on.

Joey grabbed his scuba light from his BC pocket and secured the lanyard around his wrist. He flipped the switch on and a faint yellow light from the bulb fought its way through the water. The light wasn't very bright but it looked like the lights in the cave were on so he shouldn't need much light anyway. He swam over to the pipe and saw a string of lights alongside it leading into the darkness of the cave. He squinted his eyes as he peered down the passage but all he could see was the dim string lights being engulfed by the darkness several feet in. They didn't even give off enough light for him to make out how big the passage was.

Kicking his fins a couple of times, Joey advanced into the darkness and started to follow the lights. Suddenly he remembered he hadn't checked his air pressure gauge since he started his dive. The buoyancy issues he had at the rope and seeing the sign had distracted him. Joey reached down feeling for his pressure gauge and found it at the end of the hose it was attached to resting on his back. He pulled it in front of him so he could shine his light on the face of the gauge. He saw the needle was just below the 2000 psi hash. *That should be plenty of air*, he thought. He was only planning on swimming in a short distance and back, just to see what it looked like in there.

Joey continued into the cave alongside the pipe. He watched the string lights in front of him but they never seemed to get any longer. The lights seemed to be moving forward with him. He could feel a slight current coming at him out of the cave making it a little harder to swim forward. He reached down to grab the pipe to use it to pull himself along the tunnel. He grabbed the pipe with his right hand and his left hand dropped into the mud on the floor of the cave next to the pipe. A big cloud of silt billowed up at him from around his left hand enveloping him in darkness. Joey hadn't expected that. He started finning a little faster to escape the silt cloud he had just created and used the pipe to himself pull forward.

Once he broke out of the silt cloud back into clear water he could see the dim string of lights again. They still didn't light up the entire tunnel but they did help him see some of the passage ahead. It was really dark and seemed to be getting darker as he moved farther into the cave.

Joey shined his dim light around. To his left it was pitch black. He couldn't even see the wall, if there was one there. To his right he was able to make out some decent size openings in the wall. He also saw some smaller openings that he knew he wanted nothing to do with. He wondered if the larger openings led to other passages.

The passage was much longer than he had expected it to be. He looked at his dive computer and saw that 19 minutes had passed since he had begun the dive. He estimated it had taken him about 10 minutes to get across the basin and down the chimney. So he had been in the cave passage for about nine minutes. He must be getting near the grate. *No point in turning around just yet*, he thought.

Joey continued finning and pulling himself along hoping he would get to the end of the passage soon. Just as that thought crossed his mind, Joey saw the cave get slightly brighter and he could tell it was bigger than where he had just come from. The string lights looked like they ran along the perimeter of the chamber. He must be in the large room with the grate, the Opera Room.

As the passage widened into the large chamber he noticed a metal air box bolted to the floor of the cave. It looked just like the one in the basin next to the metal cavern. Joey thought that was pretty cool. He left the pipe and swam to the air box to stick his head inside. He popped his head up into the box out of the water, careful to keep his regulator in his mouth though since he didn't know how old the air in there was and if it was safe to breathe. He noticed air escaping out of the bottom edge of the box as he exhaled through his regulator. His breathing was displacing the air in the box probably bringing the oxygen content in the air box even lower.

Joey dropped his head down out of the box and back into the water and saw that it was completely dark in the room. With a slight panic he wondered if someone had turned the lights off while his head was up in the air box. He tried to look around using his light but it was no longer turned on. That's when he realized none of the lights were out. He was looking into another silt cloud.

He must have kicked up the silt under the air box when he stuck his head out of the water. Joey pushed himself out from under the box and started to see a hazy glow of light again. He swam toward it until he could finally see the dimly lit Opera Room in front of him again. He swam toward the light string that was resting on a ledge in front of him. Glancing back at the air box he saw a large cloud of silt enveloping it. He could barely see the top of the box through the growing silt. *He had to be more careful about that!*

Looking back away from the air box Joey saw that the lights illuminated the room much better than they did the passage. There were a lot more of them. He was surrounded by them. He could see from one end of the room to the other and he guessed it had to be at least 30 feet across. He swam along the light string exploring the large room. The wall gave way to a small tunnel leading away in one area and Joey wondered how far it went in. He still hadn't found the grate and wondered if it was back in that passage or in another area of the room hidden from his view.

As he swam around the room next to the lights he noticed the big pipe along the floor disappearing under a ledge about five feet below him. He glanced at his dive computer – 99 feet deep. That was the deepest Joey had ever been. He would take a quick look at where the pipe led and then leave. He released a little air from his BC, careful to not release too much, so he could drop down to the pipe and see what was under the ledge.

Putting his hand out on the pipe Joey stopped his descent but his feet kept falling and crashed into the bottom creating a big mushroom cloud of silt. *That wasn't good!* He hadn't been careful enough! He was really making a mess in here. Hopefully the water current he had felt earlier would carry the visibility obscuring silt out quickly. Joey turned to follow the path of the pipe and he finally saw the old rusted metal grate just under the ledge. He also saw something beyond the grate.

Or rather someone.

Joey saw a diver on the other side of the grate. He was just behind a sign that said "Larry and Matt were here". This must be the diver who owns the truck Joey saw parked on the grass earlier that morning. He wondered if he was Larry or Matt and what made them feel they needed to put up a sign stating they were here. The diver was motionless and looking down.

Joey wished he was good enough to hover motionless like that. He had to keep moving his fins to keep them up off the silty floor. This diver was not moving at all. Joey wondered what was so interesting on the floor. He noticed the diver had two scuba tanks, much larger than his aluminum 80 cubic foot tank, and they were hanging from his sides rather than mounted on his back like every other diver he had seen before. He had heard of a scuba diving configuration called sidemounts but this was the first time he had seen someone diving sidemounts. At least that's what he thought he was seeing.

The water was flowing out much stronger from the other side of the grate. Moving against the heavy flow of water Joey pulled himself along the pipe closer to the grate to try to get the other diver's attention. As he got closer to the grate and the diver he noticed a padlock on the grate. The lock was clasped shut and Joey wondered why anyone would lock himself in the cave. Maybe the diver had dropped the key and was looking for it. Being stuck on the inside of a locked gate underwater would be a really bad situation, Joey thought.

He got close enough to reach out and grab the grate and hold on to keep from being blown away from it by the strong current. The other diver still hadn't noticed Joey. Joey carefully reached through the grate with his other hand and gently tapped the diver on the shoulder to get his attention. The diver still didn't look up. The wetsuit the diver was wearing looked and felt pretty thick so maybe he didn't feel Joey tap him. Joey reached through and tapped him a little harder. The diver still didn't look up.

What was going on with this guy? Why wouldn't he look up? Joey thought about just turning around and leaving but his curiosity was piqued. And if the diver had dropped the key maybe Joey could help him find it or he could help him pry open the grate to let him out. Joey reached through the grate again and firmly grabbed the diver's arm and pulled at him forcefully this time. The diver moved and his body started to swing around with his legs coming toward the grate. Suddenly the diver's regulator fell out of his mouth and Joey realized this guy wasn't ignoring him and he wasn't looking down at anything. He was dead!

8

Upon realizing that the diver he had just tapped on the shoulder wasn't alive, Joey almost spit his regulator out of his own mouth. He thrashed his arms out wildly to push himself away from the old rusted grate. The water current snatched at him and forcefully pushed his upper body up the slope. His fins were snagged by the bottom deep into the silt causing Joey to flip over so his tank was against the floor and he was facing up toward the ceiling. It was quickly getting dark and Joey realized silt was engulfing him and eliminating the clear visibility he had only moments earlier.

Thrashing around even more Joey tried to flip his body over so he could get out of the cave but was having no luck. The scuba tank on his back was too heavy and was keeping him anchored onto the bottom. He kept thrashing and rocking back and forth to try to upright himself. He could feel panic quickly overtaking his emotions but he couldn't control himself. He had just come face to face with a dead diver in a dark underwater cave!

Joey's breathing was getting faster and faster. He could hear the almost constant escape of bubbles rushing from his regulator, interrupted only by the quick brief breaths he took every second or so. He wanted nothing more than to be out of this cave and back on the grassy shore where he could lie back and breathe normally. He remembered he was over 100 feet deep and was breathing away the little air he had in his tank. He vaguely remembered the lesson from his scuba class a few weeks earlier about needing more air the deeper he was. The 2000 psi he thought would be plenty might just not do.

Joey wasn't even certified to be deeper than 60 feet! He knew at 33 feet he needed twice as much air as on the surface. At 100 feet it was 4 or 5 times more. He couldn't remember and was in no state of mind to try to do the math at that moment. It didn't matter anyway. All that mattered was he needed to get out of the cave fast.

In class his instructor had mentioned if there was ever a problem underwater to just stop and breathe. As difficult as it was Joey forced himself to stop moving and focused on slowing his breathing. He tried to relax as much as he could with a dead body beyond the grate just a few feet away from him. He could feel his breathing normalizing and getting a little slower.

He shifted his thoughts to the situation he was in. He was upside down on the floor of the cave, much like a turtle upside down on the top of its shell. Even worse he couldn't see anything around him. All the thrashing had caused so much silt to be disturbed it completely engulfed him and probably the entire room.

The thought of dying in this cave just like the other diver crept into his mind and he felt the panic rushing back in. He quickly pushed it away before it took hold of him again and made him thrash even more. He had let some air out of his BC so he could be negatively buoyant and rest on the pipe and hold himself in place against the water current. All he had to do was put a little air back in his BC, rise off the bottom and flip himself over. He knew his air supply must be running low and every little bit was probably going to be necessary to get him out of the cave alive but he didn't know how else to get out of the position he was in. He would put a small blast of air in his BC. Just enough to get him off the bottom.

Pfffft! He could hear the precious little air he had in his tank quickly escaping. He felt his BC squeezing around him as it inflated slightly. He felt himself become lighter and the floor moving away from him. It was working!

Bonk! Joey felt his body slam against something hard above him and as he let out a little scream his regulator flew out of his mouth. He quickly closed his mouth and held his breath and started reaching around to look for his regulator but there was something large in front of him that was pushing him back. He couldn't move his arms forward.

Joey realized he must have put too much air in his BC again and had become plastered to the ceiling. That would mean the regulator should have fallen off to his right and behind him. He reached back with his right hand and felt the smoothness of the rubber hose from his regulator brush against his forearm. He frantically grabbed at it with his hand and followed it away from his body until he found the regulator. Joey thrust the mouthpiece of the regulator back into his mouth just as he was at the end of his ability to hold his breath, purged it clear of water, and took a giant breath in.

Once he was able to breathe again he reached out in front of himself and pushed away from the ceiling. He flipped his body over so his back was against the ceiling and tried to swim forward. He was still too buoyant and his tank was jammed against the ceiling preventing him from being able to move. Joey reached for his inflator hose and held it up as high as he could before pressing the exhaust button. He heard some bubbles escape from the end of the hose and felt the ceiling let go of his body. He crashed back down into the deep silt on the floor but at least this time he was face down and could crawl out of there if he had to. The silt hanging in the water was still so thick he couldn't see anything.

Joey felt around trying to find the large pipe that was in the room. He knew it lead all the way from the cavern opening back to where he was and if he found it he could follow it out until he could see again. All he felt was a deep soft silty bottom. His hands dug deep into the floor feeling the occasional rock buried in the silt. But no pipe. He started flailing his arms around and pushing forward with his feet frantically trying to find the pipe.

Panic started to force itself back in, this time with a vengeance. His brain was screaming at him that he should be able to see but his eyes got nothing. This must be what it was like to be blind. Joey closed his eyes and the panic started to slowly subside again. It was amazing how such a small action could have such an effect on a person. With his eyes closed his brain no longer expected to be able to see anything. Just closing his eyes had a big calming effect on him.

Keeping his eyes closed, Joey continued to feel around for the pipe. His arms no longer flailing. He tried to do a methodical search but without being able to see he had no idea whether he was going straight or not. He would occasionally feel hard smooth rocks buried in the silt. Some of them felt the same as rocks he had felt before but he knew that didn't mean they were the same rocks.

It was becoming a little harder to pull a breath from his regulator. He remembered the same feeling from his certification class. The instructor had Joey get on his knees and watch his submersible pressure gauge. The instructor then knelt behind him and closed the valve to turn off his air supply. As Joey continued to breathe he watched the needle on the gauge drop down significantly with each breath. During the last breath, when the needle was below 300 psi, he felt it was hard to breathe until the air flow finally cut off leaving him with only a quarter of a breath. His instructor immediately opened the valve and Joey heard the hoses rapidly filling with air and saw the needle shoot back up to 1500 psi where it had been before the exercise. Unfortunately, there was no instructor kneeling behind Joey about to open the valve this time. Once he felt the last breath cut off that would be it.

Joey continued to anxiously feel around the floor for the pipe. He moved his hands forward and sideways quickly hoping he was going in the right direction. Whack! His right hand smacked into something hard and he snatched it back quickly cradling it in his left hand. While he was rubbing his hand it dawned on him that he might have found the pipe. He got excited with the thought of having found his way out and reached back to where he had smacked his hand but there was nothing there but silt. His feelings sank. He was so close but he screwed it up by pulling his hand back.

He continued to feel around. His right hand hit something to his right again. This time he didn't pull it back. Instead he reached toward it and felt the smooth hard curve of the top of the pipe. Instant relief washed over Joey. He was going to make it! He pulled himself toward the pipe and began pulling himself along it occasionally blinking his eyes open hoping to see the silt had cleared. The cave remained pitch black.

Pulling himself along the pipe Joey began to relax. It had taken him 10 minutes to swim to the Opera Room from the opening but he had been moving very slowly taking it all in. It shouldn't take him that long to swim back out, especially if he moved fast. The cave tunnel wasn't that long and it sloped up fairly quickly. His air should last him until he got to the surface.

Joey quickly pulled himself forward hand over hand. His left hand slammed against something small but hard and he pulled it back. He remembered seeing curved rods of rebar holding the pipe in place along the tunnel. That must be what his hand hit. He reached forward, more slowly this time, and felt the bar again. He moved his hand over it and pulled himself forward, this time smacking his head into something hard. Joey's left hand shot up to his head but the movement was quickly arrested by something else. He had violently rapped his knuckles against this obstruction and felt a sharp pain shoot through his hand and up his arm. Reflex made him bring his hand to his mouth so he could suck on his knuckles, a behavior he learned as a child from his mother. But instead of feeling his lips around his knuckles he smacked them against his second stage regulator causing it to purge some of the little precious air he had left.

He bit down on the mouthpiece to keep it from being knocked out again.

Pulling his hand in toward his chest, he cradled it there for a moment. His hand moved back and forth as his chest expanded and contracted quickly due to his labored breathing. After a few seconds the sharp pain began to slowly subside. He opened and closed his hand a couple of times. It felt sore and stiff but it didn't hurt as much as it initially had. Maybe it wasn't broken.

He reached forward slowly to where his head had smacked on something and felt a bar. He slowly traced the bar with his hand and the sinking realization that he was feeling the grate suddenly came upon him. He had gone the wrong way! Even worse was he couldn't see anything and was just on the other side of the grate from a dead body!

Pushing back from the grate Joey moved fast but was careful to also keep a hand on the pipe. He certainly did not want to lose that again. He opened his eyes briefly but still couldn't see anything. He slowly and awkwardly rotated his feet around so he was facing in the opposite direction, toward the cave's exit. He began pulling himself along the pipe confident he was heading out of the cave. During this time a steady beeping started to sound. He had no idea what it was or where it was coming from but it seemed to be right next to him.

Beep Beep Beep Beep

Breathing was getting more difficult. Joey had to really suck in to get air from his regulator. He again recalled this feeling from his brief exposure to his scuba tank being turned off in his scuba class. Hand over hand on the pipe he continued pulling himself out while increasing his speed. He had no idea how deep he was or how far he was from the opening. However, he did remember that once he got to the opening he would still be about 50 feet deep. In class he had done a CESA from 20 feet with his instructor but if he ran out of air this would be more than twice that. And Joey had cheated a little during class. The instructor didn't have them take the regulators out of their mouths.

Beep Beep Beep

The rules for the CESA were they had to continue to exhale the entire time they were ascending and then orally inflate their buoyancy compensators once on the surface. Joey had taken a really deep breath before he started his ascent. As he began his ascent with his instructor he started blowing small bubbles out like he was told. But he had blown too much air out and by the time he was about two-thirds of the way to the surface he couldn't hold his breath any longer. He quickly pulled in a small breath hoping his instructor wouldn't notice. When his head broke the surface he took in a huge breath and then started inflating his buoyancy compensator.

Beep Beep Beep

As it was he could no longer get a very deep breath from his regulator. He had no idea how many breaths he had left. And he was still breathing faster than he normally did. He tried to slow his breathing as he moved along the pipe but he was too worked up trying to get out of the cave as fast as he could. He opened his eyes and saw a faint glow ahead. That must be the opening! He crawled along a little faster and the glow grew bigger and brighter.

Beep Beep Beep Beep

He noticed the pipe seemed to be sinking below him as he was moving along. Then he realized it wasn't the pipe sinking but him rising. He had taken too much weight out of his weight belt before the dive. He should have exchanged the three pound weights he removed for smaller weights. The eighteen pounds he had on his belt wasn't quite enough.

Beep Beep Beep

He grabbed the pipe and held on as tightly as he could so he wouldn't pop up into the ceiling and kept trying to maintain forward motion toward the light. The light kept getting bigger and brighter and he finally came to the small opening where the tunnel transitioned into a big cavern. Joey took his last breath as he swam through that small opening between the water filled cave and the large cavernous room at the bottom of the chimney. He glanced to the right and saw the warning sign with the drawing of the grim reaper and the dead divers at its feet. He suddenly understood why it was there.

Beep Beep Beep Beep Beep

9

Later that night
August 4, 2011 11:30pm

On this dive there was going to be no glow piercing the water from the sun overhead. Joey had returned to Eddy Spring later that same night after the sun had set, the same day he discovered a dead body beyond the grate. He was terrified of what he was supposed to do over the next couple of hours but he didn't have any choice. Earl had tried to convince him he was the only one that could do this. When Joey was still insistent he wasn't going to do it Earl threatened him.

"Lookie 'ere kid. Y'all 'll either come back t'night an' git dat body out or y'all 'll be in dar wid 'im. Y'all's choice. But one ways or 'nuther y'all 'll be in dat cave t'night."

That was all the convincing he needed. From the brief encounters he had with Earl that day he didn't think it was just an empty threat. Joey had been awestruck by Earl at first but that feeling had quickly turned into fear of the man and what he might do if Joey didn't cooperate.

He had tried to talk Earl into calling the sheriff's office and letting them handle things.

"J-J-Just call 911. They will send d-divers to come g-get the body. I-I-I haven't even been certified two months yet."

Nah, kid! Dat'd only bring bad p'blisty. We need ta sneak it out an' git it dis'peared ourselves. An' since y'all found it, it's y'all's 'sponsbility ta git it out."

"B-B-But…"

"Look kid! 'Nuf's 'nuf! Be heah t'night or I'll come an' git y'all heah."

Joey wasn't going to be able to get any sleep anyway after the terrifying incident in the cave earlier that day. He had gotten home at the time he normally would have had he gone to work and went straight to his room. His mother knocked on the door and stuck her head in to ask him if he was coming to dinner. Joey made up an excuse that he had eaten too much at work and his stomach hurt. This happened on occasion anyway so his mom accepted that excuse and let him be.

Shortly after he heard his mother putting the dishes in the dishwasher Joey walked into the kitchen and told his parents he was going to bed. He returned to his room and crawled into bed with his clothes on. He lay there listening for his parents to retire for the night. About a half hour after he heard their bedroom door shut Joey opened the door to his room and looked down the hall toward their room. He couldn't see any light peeking out from under the door. Joey quietly pulled his bedroom door shut and snuck out of the house.

He shifted his car into neutral and pushed it out of the driveway onto the street. He rolled it a few houses down the street. He didn't dare start it anywhere near his house fearing his parents would hear the engine and catch him sneaking out. Florida was a pretty flat state but luckily he lived on a street with a slight slope to it. It didn't take much to get the car rolling and keep it going. Even so, by the time he was far enough to jump in the car and feel safe starting the engine, he was dripping sweat and his clothing was soaked. He was exhausted from the dives earlier in the day and specifically the incident during the second dive, but he still had a long night ahead of him.

* * *

It took him just under an hour to drive to Eddy Spring from Santa Rosa Beach. It was already late and he didn't see any other cars on the road after he had crossed the bay and drove through Freeport. Even on the interstate he only saw a few cars heading westbound in the opposite direction. A few times he thought about turning the car around and heading back home. But then he pictured Earl standing there threatening to "dis'pear" him. He had a feeling Earl wasn't one to make false threats. He would find him if he didn't show up and do something bad to him. Joey continued on toward Eddy Spring.

As he pulled in past the shack at the entrance he cut the lights and drove the last couple hundred feet to park in the same place he had earlier in the day. Fortunately the moon was bright enough to allow him to see. When he cut the engine he could hear the faint beeping of the dive computer wrapped in his towel in the trunk. He couldn't believe it was still doing that. Earl had told him to hold onto it until it stopped beeping. He could return it the next day directly to Earl so no one at the dive shop would find out. He sat in his car for a minute thinking about what he was being forced to do in the next couple hours. He had just wanted to play hooky for one day and go scuba diving. He never thought he'd get himself into this kind of mess.

He was startled by a shadow falling through the windshield of his car. Looking to the left he saw Earl looming over his car waiting for him. Joey slowly opened the car door and stepped out.

It had been pretty disappointing to learn that Earl didn't know how to scuba dive. *Who manages a scuba park and doesn't scuba dive?!?* Even more disappointing, actually, alarming was a better word for it, was what Earl wanted Joey to do. *Scratch that.* What Earl was forcing Joey to do. Joey had to go back into that dark silty cave, open that rusty old grate, and drag a dead scuba diver out. Not only that, but Earl told Joey it had to be done after dark so no one would see.

"It gots ta be afta dark. I can't have ma employ's knowin' nut'n 'bout dis."

Joey begged Earl to get someone else to do it. Anyone.

"D-Don't you know someone else that c-can do this for you?"

"Look heah. If'n y'all aren't back heah t'night y'all 'll wish y'all was da dead scuba diver on da 'ther side of da grate."

So here Joey was, once again back at Eddy Spring…at midnight…setting up his dive gear and preparing to go back into the deceptively clear water. During the day, it looked fresh and inviting. At night, it was completely different. It was like a swamp of black liquid waiting to swallow him in and suffocate him.

Joey hadn't done a night dive in his short month and a half of being a scuba diver. He had planned on checking that off of his list this summer but under the supervision of an instructor. His scuba instructor had told the class about different specialty classes they could take after completing their initial open water class and night diving was one of the classes. Joey hadn't had a chance to take any of the specialty classes yet. He was still busy paying off his parents all the money he had borrowed, and buying used gear. All he knew was that if it was important enough to have its own class then there had to be stuff taught in the class that he certainly didn't know yet. But here he was about to do his first night dive, and even worse, pull out a dead body during the dive.

"Y'all ready ta do dis kid?" Earl whispered quietly to Joey when he stepped out of the car.

Joey looked down to the ground and quietly responded, "I-I guess…but I'm scared."

"It'll be a'ight kid. Alls y'all gotta do is git 'im ta da steps. I'll take care da rest." Joey could smell stale beer on Earl's breath as Earl stepped close to him. Joey recoiled as Earl reached out to put a hand on his shoulder, almost in a fatherly manner, but then Earl grabbed his shoulder and roughly guided him to a table by the scuba tank rack. "I gots ya a fresh tank. Les git dis done 'fore da sun comes up."

Joey started setting up his gear. Even though there was a full moon out, it was dark where they were. They were under the Chalet and the tank rack blocked any moonlight from penetrating the darkness down there. Earl hadn't turned on the lights under the Chalet. Joey was also really scared and nervous and his hands were shaking badly. The shaking was so bad he was having trouble hooking up the regulator to the tank and then connecting the hose to the BC. It didn't help that Earl was impatiently pacing back and forth, chain smoking and mumbling to himself, and coming over to glare over Joey's shoulder every few minutes.

"Wass takin' ya s'long kid?" Earl barked at him in a low whisper, plumes of smoke puffing out with each syllable.

"S-s-s-sorry. It's dark under here. I-I can't see what I'm doing very well."

Earl grabbed the dive light that was clipped to the BC and turned it on. A dim yellow light broke through the darkness and Earl shined it at the BC. Joey turned back to his scuba gear and continued assembling it. His hands continued to shake and he heard Earl from behind him, "Why ya shakin' s'bad kid? Dis dive ain't gonna be no difrent dan da dive dis mornin' 'cept y'all 'll be bringin' out yur buddy."

Earl began chuckling at his little joke but Joey didn't think it was funny one bit. Earl's laugh turned into a violent hacking cough. He sat back on one of the picnic tables and spit out a big wad of snot onto the concrete slab. Disgusted, Joey turned away from him and continued assembling his scuba gear.

Finally finished with the gear assembly Joey slowly walked back to his car to get his mask and fins. He again tried to think of an excuse to get out of this. He looked over at Earl pacing back and forth and quickly gave up on the idea. Earl wasn't about to let him get out of this…not at this point. Joey returned to the table and placed his mask and fins on it. He turned away from the BC and slipped his arms through the openings, checked the inflator, grabbed his mask and fins and started walking down to the water.

"Hold on kid. Ya fergot y'all's weights agin."

Joey turned around and walked back to the table. He backed up against it, removed the BC, secured the weight belt around his waist and slipped the BC back on. *Would he ever remember to put his weights on?*

Back on the platform, Joey began descending the steps. Easing into the water it felt much colder without the hot Florida sun overhead to warm him before the dive. It was also past midnight and the cool night air temperature had dropped about 20 degrees since earlier in the afternoon. He let out a small cry and a shudder went through his body as he felt the water creep up his thighs, past his midsection, and up his back. Earl stood menacingly at the top of the steps above the water holding the dive light and watching Joey.

"Heah ya go kid. I got da lights down thar on but y'all 'll need dis ta get ta da entrance. And heah's da key ta da lock onda grate." Earl tossed the light and key down to Joey and leaned against the rail to the steps. "I'll be waitin' on ya."

* * *

Turning around to face the buoy on the other side of the spring basin at the top of the cave entrance, Joey decided he would swim to it on the surface. He was still spooked about going under the water in the dark. This place looked completely different at night. During the day the water was crisp and clear and looked very inviting, especially on hot humid days like it had been all day. Even with the visibility stirred up by dozens of other divers on the weekends it looked refreshing. At night this was not the case. The water looked black and terrifying and like it was going to swallow him up for good, like it had the diver beyond the grate.

He turned his dive light on and saw the dim yellow light project weakly from the front. It wasn't even bright enough to illuminate the bottom of the spring basin 20 feet below him. He swam toward the buoy slowly while looking around the basin beneath him. He practically jumped out of the water when the dark manmade metal cavern appeared below him. It was just a large black blob that seemed to pop up out nowhere. He decided he would swim around it rather than directly over it even though that was not a direct route to the buoy. He knew no one was down there but he was afraid something would reach out and grab him as he swam by it.

Then he thought of the dead body he had found. There *was* someone down there. Joey hoped the body hadn't somehow made it out from behind the grate. He knew his fears were irrational, just like the fears he had as a small child that a monster was going to reach out from under the bed and grab his ankles. He couldn't help having these thoughts just like he couldn't help jumping onto his bed from the door to his room each night. The difference was as a kid it was just a fear. At the present moment it was a response to finding a dead body earlier in the day. He wasn't sure he could live through it if he came across the body somewhere else in the dark water.

Reaching the buoy, Joey looked around one more time. Despite the full moon all he could see of Earl was his black outline standing at the top of the steps, the occasional glow from a cigarette as he pulled in another lungful of smoke. Joey looked around the basin and could make out the shadow of Grande Vista Chalet at the top of the grassy hill, a few picnic tables, and his car. On the other side of the basin was the old owner's vacation house, not a light on in or around it. Joey and Earl were the only two living beings for miles.

Well, this was it. Earl wasn't going to let him out of the water without getting that body out. Joey put the scuba regulator in his mouth and began his descent down the line below the buoy as his exhalation bubbles quickly rose up around his face tickling his cheeks on their way back to the dark surface above, screaming to be released back into the night air. Joey wished he could be with them. He pulled himself down with one hand and pointed the dim light below him with the other. As he dropped down alongside the rope he thought he saw something moving off to the side. He quickly stopped and held himself in place fearing the worst. What if it was the body? He shined the light around but didn't see anything moving in the dim yellow glow. He slowly pulled himself down a little more and kept shining the light around in circles below him.

As he continued to inch himself down the rope Joey caught more movement off to the side. He quickly moved the beam of the light in the direction of the movement and saw a long gray eel swimming through the holes in the rocks. He had seen an eel on his dive to the bottom of the chimney earlier that day. He wondered if it was the same one. Hastening his pace Joey finished pulling himself along the rope.

Once at the bottom of the chimney Joey shined his dive light around but he couldn't see very far. It looked like the light was getting dimmer. It probably didn't help that Earl had kept it on for about 10 minutes on the surface while he was setting up his scuba gear. Joey had also had it on for part of the first dive and almost all of the second dive even though he was engulfed in the light smothering silt most of that dive. He didn't know how long the batteries lasted but he probably should have replaced them with fresh ones.

He also realized he didn't see the light rope yet. It was even darker at the bottom of the chimney than it was in the basin. At least when he had initially dropped underwater he had some illumination from the moon, but when he dropped below the top edge of the chimney that had disappeared. Down at the bottom with the 25 foot tall walls surrounding him he couldn't see anything except what was barely lit up by the dive light, and that wasn't much.

Joey pushed himself away from the rope toward the cave opening. He started kicking his fins to move a little faster. Remembering how the rope light in the cave was enough to light up the tunnel and room he rushed to get to it. It did a much better job than the dim dive light he had in his hand. Joey saw the big pipe that extended deep into the cave come into the faint beam of his light and turned to follow it into the tunnel. He glanced to his left at the grim reaper sign and a shudder went through his body. He imagined one of the three dead divers laying at the feet of the reaper calling out to him - *Come join us…* He turned away from the sign and continued following the pipe. As he swam through the small opening he was able to make out the lights ahead of him. *This is where I ran out of air this afternoon,* he thought.

He quickly looked down and grabbed his pressure gauge – 2500 psi – still plenty of air. Since he didn't have any issues with his descent this time he hadn't breathed through his air as quickly. He just needed to get down to the grate, open it and pull the body out. Don't look at the body. Don't think about the diver being dead.

Joey pulled himself along the pipe and followed the rope lights. He was moving slowly because he only had one hand available to pull himself so he clipped the dive light to a D-ring located on the chest strap of his BC and used both hands to pull himself along, picking up his pace. He got through the passage much more quickly than he had earlier that day. About five minutes after leaving the buoy anchor at the bottom of the chimney he saw the square shape of the air box in the room at the end of the tunnel. A few seconds later he broke through into the large Opera Room and looked around at the lights running along the outer walls. *This room was really pretty*, Joey thought. He didn't notice how pretty it was the last time he was there. He must have been so excited about it he wasn't able to take in everything at once. He could spend hours in this room enjoying the beauty.

But enough of that. He couldn't waste time daydreaming during this dive. His eyes followed the pipe to the right and he saw the shadow of the grate below the rocky shelf. He was too far and it was too dark to make out the body beyond the grate but he knew it had to still be there. The grate was still closed. What if the body wasn't there though? Or what if he just swam back out and told Earl it wasn't. Earl wasn't a diver. He couldn't dive into the cave and check for himself. But someone else would eventually find the body and Earl would find out Joey lied to him. And then he'd really be in trouble. Earl could find him. He had his address on the release paperwork he filled out when he signed in at the dive shop earlier in the day. Earl would come after him.

Pulling himself along the pipe he slowly approached the old grate. When he was about 10 feet away from it he could make out a dark shape just beyond it. Relief swept over Joey as he realized the body was still there, beyond the grate, and nowhere else. He went the last 10 feet and looked around the grate for the padlock he had seen earlier.

Earl had mentioned there were only two keys to the padlock and both of them had still been in the dive shop earlier in the day. Joey wondered how the diver had gotten beyond the grate without one of the keys. He found the lock, tugged on it with his hand and confirmed it was definitely locked. He looked around the edges of the grate to see if there was a space large enough for someone to shimmy their way through but didn't see any. *That was strange,* he thought.

He grabbed the lock again and inserted the key. He tried to turn it but it only moved a quarter of a turn. He jiggled the key back and forth a little and felt it give a tiny bit. He kept jiggling the key and finally felt the key turn and the tumblers fall into place. He gave the lock a hard yank and it came open. Removing the lock from the grate he hung it on one of the crossbars so it wouldn't get lost in the sandy bottom. He pulled back on the gate and it dragged along the bottom of the cave. He watched as it stirred up clouds of silt. Fortunately, the floor in this area was more like sand and didn't cause great big silt clouds like the stuff out in the middle of the room. The sand poofed up into small plumes and fell immediately back down to the floor.

Joey had to push himself back to allow the gate to swing open. Looking across toward the body he noted it was pushed up across the opening by the current coming out of the cave tunnel. The shoulders were against the grate on one side and the legs pushed up on the other side. He would have to push the body in, straighten it out, then move it to the right to get it to pass through the small opening he had just created by opening the gate.

Joey peered past the body into the darkness beyond. The light from the Opera Room didn't penetrate beyond the grate so all he saw was the pipe disappearing into a black hole. He tried lighting it up with his dive light but it was too dim to even penetrate beyond the body in front of him. Joey snapped himself back to the task at hand.

Slowly reaching through the grate, Joey pushed on the scuba tank mounted on the diver's side closest to him. The body moved slightly but the flow pushed it back against the grate. Joey recoiled afraid of getting touched by the body. After a few seconds he inched forward and pushed on the scuba tank again, a little harder this time, but with the same result. The body was just moving back and forth on the other side of the grate. He had to swing it around somehow.

He grabbed one of the hoses coming off the tank closest to him. If he could do this without having to touch the diver again, that would be good. He pulled on the hose with his left hand and pushed on the scuba tank with his right hand and saw the diver's legs start to swing around. He pulled on the hose harder and the shoulders swung around and into the opening. As soon as the body was free of the grate it started floating out toward Joey bringing with it a cloud of silt caused by the body dragging along the bottom. Joey quickly pulled his hand away and practically jumped out of his BC. His breathing rate increased and he noticed bubbles coming out almost continuously from his regulator.

Joey looked down at his pressure gauge again – 1800 psi. He still had more than half of what he had started with. He tried to slow his breathing and tentatively reached out for the hose again. He carefully closed his fingers around the hose and gently pulled it toward him. The diver started moving toward him again but this time he was a little more prepared for it and didn't get startled.

The diver's legs and fins finally cleared the grate and floated out of the tunnel into the Opera Room. Joey quickly released the hose and watched as the body moved past him. When it was clear of the grate Joey pushed the grate closed while also keeping an eye on the body. Earl had stressed to him several times that he had to close and lock the gate in the grate before he came out so no one would find it open and go in like this diver had. Joey didn't dare turn his back on the body though. More of his unrealistic fears. He couldn't help but think that if he looked away the body would come to life and swim off, or even worse, grab him. Then he wouldn't just jump out of his BC but probably out of his skin.

Joey pushed the gate closed and felt around the haze still hanging in the water from the silt searching for the padlock he had hung on the grate. His hand knocked into it and it fell away onto the floor. *Dammit!* He had to take his eyes off the body to look for the lock and put it in place so he could lock the gate. Quickly looking away, Joey found the lock on the floor just beyond the grate. He reached through one of the larger openings, picked it up and placed it where it had been on the bars of the gate. He turned the lock and tried to close it but it was resisting his efforts. He pushed it against a bar on the grate to try to get some leverage on it and pushed again, still with no success. He tried turning the key in the lock and pushing the lock closed again. This time it relented and clasped shut.

With the padlock locked and the key removed Joey turned to face the body and noticed a huge cloud of silt between him and the body. He could see parts of the diver's gear sticking out around the silt cloud but most of the diver was being swallowed by it. The current from the cave must have pushed the body into the silty floor. Joey's breathing started to get faster and faster as he thought about the last dive he had done earlier that day. He couldn't let that happen again.

Rapidly dumping air from his BC, Joey sank down and grabbed the pipe below him. As he did this he noticed the silt was coming back and engulfing him. *No wait, that wasn't right!* The water flow should be pushing it the other way. Suddenly Joey felt his knees hit the pipe. He had descended too much and his fins and legs were in the silt and he was creating a silt cloud that was engulfing him from behind. The last thought Joey had as the silt completely obliterated the remaining visibility was that this was not a good day of diving for him. Not one bit good…

10

Joey shut his eyes tightly and tried to keep the panic at bay as he held onto the large pipe below him for dear life. He couldn't believe this was happening to him a second time today. He made a promise to himself at that moment that he wouldn't go near any caves ever again if he made it out of there alive. He would stick to scuba diving in water where he could see the surface and just ascend if something went wrong. He obviously wasn't cut out for this.

Taking a quick peek to see if the visibility had returned, all he saw was that the silt had engulfed him again. He thought about just following the pipe out of the tunnel but he had to find the body of the dead diver and pull it out too. If he left the body in the cave Earl was sure to make him do another dive to get it. And he had already decided he wouldn't be going back in the cave under any circumstances, even Earl's threats.

The body had been about fifteen feet in front of him last time he saw it. It looked like the hand might have gotten caught on the metal bars that secured the pipe to the floor. That was good and bad. Good because he would be able to find it easily but bad because he would have to find it by feeling for it. Being in the water with a dead body had freaked him out a little earlier in the day when it was on the other side of the grate, but at the moment there was nothing separating them. And he couldn't see it!

Hand over hand, Joey started to slowly make his way along the smooth pipe. Each time he moved his right hand forward, his muscles tensed just waiting for his arm to bump into the body. He opened his eyes to steal another peek and saw the silt was starting to dissipate. He could barely make out a faint glow in front of him. It wasn't clear enough to distinguish any features though.

Closing his eyes again, Joey continued to move forward with trepidation hoping he'd get into clear water before he found the body again. He opened his eyes every few seconds and saw it was getting clearer but there was still too much silt hanging in the water to allow him to see anything.

Slowly moving his right hand forward past his left hand and tensing again, he found the pipe but no body. He did the same with his left hand and moved another six inches forward. He stole another peek and this time could make out the faint square outline of the top of the air box a few feet away. He could feel the water current pushing him forward toward the box and thought it was possible the body had also been pushed that way and was stuck under it. Moving his right hand forward again he reached around to find the pipe. Still no body.

The visibility was clearing up and Joey remembered his pressure gauge and that he should probably check it. If his pressure was too low, he'd have to abort the dive. *Maybe Earl wouldn't make him come back in here*, he thought. Not likely though. He reached down with his left hand feeling around for the gauge. He felt the stiff hose against his arm and followed it down to the round gauge at the end. Pulling it up in front of his mask, he looked at the face of the gauge. It was too dark to make out the numbers and hash marks on the face. He dropped the gauge and felt around for his dive light. If he could put the light against the gauge face the numbers would glow in the dark for a few seconds, enough for him to see his pressure. He found the light dangling below him from the D-ring where he had clipped it, and probably where it had been dragging along in the silt making the visibility worse. He pulled it up and shook it to get the mud off. It was completely dead. He really wished he had remembered to change the batteries.

All he could do was hope he had enough air left in his scuba tank to make it back to the surface. He placed his left hand on the pipe in front of his right hand. Glancing back toward the air box he noticed he could see more of its straight unnatural outline jutting out from the silt. The silt seemed to be clearing but not quickly enough. Joey decided he would just have to feel around to see if the body was in the silt cloud under the air box. He shut his eyes tightly again and pulled his hand away from the pipe. Tentatively reaching toward the air box, he waved his hand around ready to yank it back if he felt the body. He didn't feel anything so he placed his hand back on the pipe in front of his left hand. He opened his eyes again and saw the silt continuing to clear.

Moving his left hand forward and around his right hand Joey moved another few inches. Once again he closed his eyes tightly and moved his right hand off the pipe and toward the air box. He waved it around and this time his hand brushed across the edge of something smooth and hard. It didn't feel like a rock and he was too far from the air box for it to be that. He moved his hand back and brushed against the hard object again. He stopped, and with increasing apprehension, moved his hand back against the hard object. He slowly closed his fingers over it. It was a scuba fin. Joey almost snatched his hand back but he didn't want to lose the body again. He forced himself to hold his hand where it was.

He grabbed the fin tightly and slowly pulled back on it. He felt some resistance. The body must be stuck on one of the legs of the air box. Grabbing the pipe firmly with his left hand to provide some stabilization for himself Joey pulled the fin a little harder. After some initial resistance the fin finally moved toward Joey. He quickly opened his eyes but still couldn't see anything in the lower third of the room because of the silt. And it looked like the movement of the body as he pulled back on it had stirred up more silt. He felt the fin twisting around in his hand. The water current was rotating the body away from him.

With the fin still in his hand, Joey moved his right hand forward and tried to direct the body toward the exit. He attempted to brace the fin against the pipe so he could move his left hand forward but the current was too strong and was pushing the body out faster than Joey could keep up with. He considered letting go of the fin but he didn't want to lose the body again. He decided to let go of the pipe and hope the current pushed him and the body out toward the chimney and back to the surface where Earl was waiting for him.

The current slowly guided Joey and the dead scuba diver through the dark, silty tunnel. The silt seemed to be decreasing in density as they moved forward. Back in the Opera Room he couldn't see the rope light leading out of the cave. In the narrow tunnel he could make out a faint glow emitting from the floor through the silt. It wasn't enough to light up the tunnel though, just enough to let him know he was above the pipe.

Joey reached back down to the pipe with his left hand to try to guide himself along the pipe and the rope lights as he held on tightly to the stiff fin with his right hand. As they moved along the dark tunnel, he was having difficulty staying in contact with the pipe and he noticed the rope lights were getting dimmer. *That was strange*, thought Joey. The silt should be getting less concentrated as he exited the cave, not worse. The pipe disappeared from under his grasp as the last of the dim light vanished beneath him. Suddenly Joey felt himself bump against something above him. The bump startled him and he briefly opened his right hand and almost lost the fin. He felt the fin sliding along past his fingers and quickly clamped down on it before it got away from his grasp.

The tunnel he was in became more shallow as it stretched out some 200 feet from the Opera Room to the cavern at the bottom of the chimney. Joey had been so focused on holding onto the fin and following the faint glow of the light on the floor that he forgot to let air out of his BC to compensate for the air expansion as he became more shallow. He realized he must have ascended and floated into the hard limestone ceiling above. He felt for his inflator hose, found it, and raised it up. When he felt his hand hit the ceiling he pressed the exhaust button and heard bubbles escaping. A few seconds later he started to drop down and the current caught him again and continued pushing him forward in the tunnel.

Joey had a firm grasp on the fin, which was above him, and felt it pulling his hand up and back. The dead body had also floated up into the ceiling and was still stuck against it. The diver was also wearing a BC that would have expanding air in it. Joey had to figure out how he was going to let that air out of it. He still couldn't see anything because he didn't have a working light and the lights in the tunnel weren't bright enough to light up the ceiling, especially with the silt that was still slowly being carried out from the Opera Room by the water current from deeper in the cave.

Reaching up with his left hand, Joey found the other fin and grasped it tightly. He pulled down on both fins and felt them teeter down. He got them just under his shoulders and began pushing against them. If he could get the body under his own he might be able to find the exhaust valve on the back of the BC and let some air out. As Joey pushed down he felt his scuba tank hit the ceiling again. He had too much air in his own BC and pushing off against the dead diver's legs caused him to rise instead.

Letting go of the fin with his left hand Joey reached for his inflator hose and let more air out. This time as he started to sink in the tunnel he kept his right hand below him and pushed the body down in front of him. He reached out with his left hand and found the other fin so he could use both hands to get the body lower, gain some leverage on it and position himself above it. Finally, something was working. The fins were below Joey and he felt the body move deeper in the water. He moved his hands along the fins until he reached the heels of the boots.

At this point Joey's anxiety started to increase with the thought of having to crawl on top of the body to get to the BC. He remained motionless while trying to summon up the courage to move his hands off the hard surface of the boot soles and onto the soft neoprene covering the legs of the dead body. He started breathing a little faster, almost hyperventilating. Closing his eyes he tried to calm himself. After a few moments his breathing slowed down.

Inching forward ever so slowly Joey walked the fingers of his right hand over the heel and onto the back of the leg while holding firmly onto the heel of the left foot. He felt the soft neoprene squish under his fingers and hoped it was just the neoprene and not the diver's leg. His fingers went as far as the bend in the knee before he couldn't reach any farther. He squeezed his eyes shut even tighter and carefully wrapped his right hand around the leg just below the knee to hold it in place and walked the fingers of his left hand up the back of the left leg.

He continued past the knee up toward the bottom of the BC with his left hand while pushing the legs down more to make room between the body and the ceiling. When he reached the bottom of the BC he felt something flat extending below it. He felt a smooth metal bar on this flat piece that felt similar to a drawer pull and wrapped his fingers around it. He pushed down on it with more force and walked his right hand up the other leg and felt another bar on that side.

Joey was wedged in between the ceiling and the dead body. The BC was pushing up against him. Remembering that the lower exhaust valve on his BC was on the left side, Joey held onto the bar with his right hand and reached up to feel around the lower portion of the dead diver's BC. He could feel the bulge of the air in the BC pushing out against the material. This BC felt different than Joey's. It was smooth with no exhaust valve there and didn't extend all the way around his back like Joey's did. About a quarter of the way across his back the part of the BC that filled with air ended and there was just a hard flat piece that felt similar to the piece Joey was holding onto with his other hand. He brought his left hand back down and grabbed the bar on that side while he reached up to feel the other side of the diver's BC with his right hand. It was also smooth. His BC didn't have an exhaust at the bottom. Joey had spent a lot of time at the dive shop looking at BCs and they all had exhaust valves along the bottom. *This was strange,* he thought.

It occurred to Joey that he was going to have to get the body completely under him and somehow reach over the shoulder, grab the inflator hose, pull it up and dump the air out of the BC. *At least there was a BC full of air between Joey and the dead body*, Joey thought. He continued moving along the length of the body. Holding onto the bar in his left hand he moved his right hand forward and pushed the body farther below him until his right hand was almost all the way to the shoulders.

Once he was almost directly on top of the body Joey could feel it pushing him into the ceiling above even more. Before walking his left hand up the BC Joey found his inflator hose and dumped more air out of his own BC. He felt himself getting heavier in the water and falling from the ceiling, pushing the body down slightly. He walked his left hand up to the shoulder. He needed to reach around the diver's head and find the inflator hose. Fortunately for Joey, the dead diver had a dive hood on. Unfortunately, it only covered his head and ears. The diver's face was still exposed. Well, only the mouth since the scuba mask was also still on his face.

Reaching carefully with his left hand he felt around for the familiar feeling of the corrugated inflator hose that typically routed from an opening on the top rear of the BC and over the shoulder along the shoulder strap. There was no inflator hose there! *What the hell!?!* This BC had no exhaust valves on the bottom and no inflator hose on the top. *What kind of BC was this?*

Joey moved his left hand back on the shoulder of the diver and his hand stumbled upon an exhaust valve. *That was strange.* Why would the exhaust valve be on the shoulder where the inflator should be? Joey felt around for the string and found it coming out of the center and snugged over to the side. It must have been caught on something because Joey couldn't pull the end loose. He squeezed his fingers between the string and the BC and felt it give way slightly. A burst of bubbles shot out from the exhaust valve into Joey's face causing him to pull his head back and bump it on the ceiling. Joey thought to himself, if these little surprises kept up he was going to have a heart attack before his 20th birthday.

With the burst of bubbles releasing from the BC, Joey and the dead scuba diver started dropping away from the ceiling toward the floor. Joey could just make out the faint glow of the lights peeking up at him from below. Just as suddenly as they appeared they disappeared. And immediately after they disappeared Joey felt himself crash onto the body beneath him. He thrashed his arms out trying to push himself off of the dead body. The panic was beginning to set in again.

11

Joey had dumped too much air from both BCs and the body had descended quickly plastering itself to the floor of the cave, partially buried in the silt, and even worse, Joey was plastered to the body. He quickly pushed himself off of the body and could just make out the faint lights, this time in front of him. He grabbed the back of the BC below him with his right hand and found his inflator hose with his left. He shot some air into his BC trying to get himself off the floor…and off the body.

As he ascended he grabbed the other side of the BC with his left hand and pulled the body along with him. He kept an eye on the lights in front of him and the body and watched them disappear below as the body dragged along the bottom and stirred up the silt. Joey tried to go fast enough to keep himself and the body ahead of the silt clouds they were making.

The lights ahead of him suddenly disappeared. Either someone had turned the lights off or they had finally made it to the exit. Joey hoped they were at the exit. He hadn't been able to check his pressure gauge in over 10 minutes and he had no idea how much air he still had left in his scuba tank. It didn't really matter. He just needed to get back to the surface.

He came up to the small opening between the cavern and the cave passage and pulled the body through it. A faint glow appeared, reaching out from his left. It was light from the full moon penetrating through the water column down the chimney. His eyes must have adjusted to the darkness after being in the cave for so long that he could see more light in the dark surroundings. That or the moon had repositioned itself directly over the chimney. Either way, with Joey's dive light being dead, he was happy to be able to see which way to go.

Joey pulled the body along, bouncing it on the bottom toward the light glowing down the chimney. His shoulder hit something rubbery and startled him yet again. He reached out and felt the hard knobby surface of the rope and grabbed onto it. The body felt lighter to him. Moving from the depths of the cave to the more shallow area of the cavern must have expanded whatever air remained in the BC. It wasn't enough to make the body float up but it made it easier to move it.

Wrapping his arm around the rope to remain next to it, Joey kept hold of the body with his right hand and reached for his inflator hose with his left hand. He added air to his BC and felt it begin to squeeze around him. Holding tightly onto the BC he began rising up along the rope. As he became more shallow he felt the rope passing by faster. He pinched the rope in the crook of his elbow to try to slow his ascent. He then let a little air out of his BC. He looked down at his wrist to see how deep he was but he didn't have his dive computer on. It was still in the trunk of the car beeping. He really hoped he hadn't violated any decompression limits on this dive. He was still worried about the dive computer alarming after the second dive earlier that day and he had decided to leave it in the trunk. He was finishing the dive without any idea of how long he had been in the water.

Looking up he could make out the dark shape of the large oblong float at the top of the rope against the light from the moon. He was almost at the surface. All he had to do was get the body to the surface where Earl could pull it out and he could go home and get some sleep. It was all about to finally be over.

* * *

A few minutes later Joey was floating on the black, flat surface holding the lifeless body next to him. He was having difficulty holding it up because he couldn't inflate the BC and get the body positively buoyant. Once they were on the surface he had frantically felt around the front of the body finally finding the power inflator mechanism and pushing the button. He waited to hear the sound of air moving through the hoses and rushing into the BC. Nothing had happened though. It suddenly dawned on Joey that the diver had probably run out of air trapped on the other side of the grate. That's how he must have died. So there was no air in the scuba tanks to fill the BC.

Joey tried to pull the power inflator away from the chest but it was stubbornly trapped on something. He couldn't lift it more than an inch or so away from the diver's chest. Joey wasn't about to put his face in this guy's chest so he could blow into the inflator and get air in the BC. Instead he continued to struggle with keeping the body afloat as he slowly paddled his way over to the steps where Earl stood watching over the water.

Fifteen minutes later breathing heavily from the exertion of pulling the dead body more than 100 feet along the dark surface of the basin Joey felt the metal steps beneath him. Exhausted, he pulled his scuba mask off his eyes up onto his forehead and stared up at Earl standing at the top of the steps, cigarette in his mouth. He shoved the body toward Earl, watched it slowly sink underwater coming to rest on the steps just inches below the surface. He moved out of the way so he could recover from the events he had just endured and catch his breath.

Earl dipped the cigarette in the water to put it out and shoved the used butt into his shirt pocket. He reached down into the water, grabbed a strap on the BC, and pulled at the body. He didn't get it very far before the weight of the scuba tanks and whatever weight belt might be on the body kept Earl from being able to pull it up and out of the water.

"Hep me out heah kid. Pull tho' tanks off 'im."

Joey looked over the strange BC and the sidemounts but didn't know where to even begin. "I-I-I don't know how. Th-those tanks aren't on there in a way I know how to do it." Joey stammered.

Earl barked out at him in a loud whisper, "He shud have a knife somewhar on 'im. Jus' cut'em off."

Joey ran his hands over the straps on the front of the BC searching for a knife, finding one up near his right shoulder. He snatched it out of its sheath. Looking closely at the tanks he saw they were attached to the BC by a couple of clips that were attached to the tanks with string. Joey placed the knife on the string but it didn't seem very sharp. He started sawing at the string with the dull blade until it finally cut through and the tank fell down into the water with a loud bang onto the metal step below.

"Keep it down kid!" Earl hissed, "Ya wanna wake up da whole countraside?"

Joey cringed as he moved over to the other side of the body and began doing the same with the tank there but this time he caught the tank and lowered it down so it wouldn't make such a loud noise.

He looked at the valves and found some bungee material that was holding the valves around the knobs. He started sawing at one of the bungees. However, before the knife was able to cut through it, the bungee snapped off the valve and the tank crashed down. The noise wasn't as loud this time since the bottom was already on a step. But Joey looked up nervously at Earl expecting another reprimand. Earl didn't say anything this time. He just stood there shaking his head.

Moving away from the steps and over to the other side of the body he found the bungee and grasped it in his fingers. He pulled at the bungee until it snapped off the valve and the tank fell away.

"Okay, I-I cut the tanks off sir."

As Earl leaned over to pull the body out Joey detected the smell of beer again, this time not so stale. Earl pulled at the body and it slowly slid up the top step up onto the platform that he was standing on. The tanks started following the body, clanging along the steps.

"Dangit," Earl cussed out, "I thought y'all said ya cut 'em off!"

"I-I-I did sir."

Joey quickly looked over the tanks but didn't see anything else attaching them to the BC. Then he noticed the hoses were still attached to the BC and wrapped around the diver's neck.

"The hoses are still attached," he stammered.

"Well, git 'em off!"

Joey reached up and struggled to unhook the inflator hose from the power inflator mechanism. After some struggle he finally got it disconnected and the tank on the left side slid down a step before it stopped suddenly. Both tanks still had scuba regulator hoses wrapped around the diver's neck. He would have to lift the second stage regulators around the head to get them off the body. He reached for one scuba regulator and tried to push it over the head. Earl snatched it away and swung it around behind the head to the other side and tossed it in the water nearly hitting Joey in the face. Joey grabbed the other second stage regulator and tried to do the same thing but it wouldn't pull away from the neck very far. He pulled at it again and it just snapped back toward the neck. Something was holding the regulator down.

"Sir, th-that one won't come up."

Earl reached down and grabbed the regulator and yanked on it. Something broke off and Earl pulled it around the back of the head and also tossed it in the water. He then pulled the body roughly up out of the water onto the metal platform of the steps.

Joey finally caught his breath and pulled his fins off his feet.

After resting on the surface of the water for a few minutes he started to climb up the steps but Earl barked out, "What ya doin'? Git doze tanks outta thar!"

Joey tossed his fins on the platform making a loud bang and cringed again as he looked over at Earl expecting the worse. Earl just shook his head some more and looked away. Joey grabbed a tank by the valve and carried it up to the platform setting it down next to the body. The tanks were not only a lot heavier out of the water but they were a lot heavier than the tanks he was accustomed to. He walked back down the steps and grabbed the other tank. Once both tanks were on the platform Joey turned to Earl and asked, "C-can I go take off my tank now sir?"

"Yeah, git on up dar. But when yur dun git yur butt back down heah an' hep me widdis stuff."

As Joey slowly walked up the grassy hill the rest of what little energy he had was slowly draining from his body. He thought this night was almost over. All he had to do was get the body out of the water but Earl wanted his help getting the body up the hill. It was after 1 in the morning. He still had almost an hour to drive home. He wasn't going to get much sleep at all. He might not even get home before his parents woke up.

12

Joey removed his scuba gear and dropped it on a picnic table near his car. He debated whether he should take his time and pull the regulator and BC off the scuba tank and pack it away in the trunk or go down and help Earl first. He glanced down the hill and saw the outline of Earl standing over the body looking up toward Joey. That answered that question. Joey reluctantly walked back down to the steps to help him.

Earl moved to one side of the body. "Grab dat arm o'er thar kid."

Joey looked down at the lifeless body. For some reason it didn't seem as terrifying up here out of the water as it had back in the dark cave. He grabbed the arm closest to him as Earl grabbed the other one and they both lifted the upper body of the diver and started dragging him off the platform of the steps toward the grassy hill. The body felt heavy to Joey but it slid fairly easily over the slick wet slippery metal of the platform. And so did his wet scuba boots. As he pulled the body along his feet slipped over the platform causing him to almost fall a couple of times. If it wasn't for the railing along the edge of the platform, Joey would have found himself lying next to the dead diver. Fortunately, the platform was only about fifteen feet long and he was able to get good footing once he stepped off of it onto the grass. However, when the body slid off the platform onto the grass it was no longer as easy to drag. Earl kept pulling his side but Joey didn't have the strength to keep up with him.

"H-h-he's too heavy for me to drag."

"Don' givup on me now kid. We haven' e'en started up'n da hill."

Joey tried to pull the body again, tugging it as hard as he could but his side wasn't budging. Earl abruptly dropped his side and started up the hill leaving Joey alone with the body. With Earl no longer holding up most of the weight of the upper body Joey couldn't hold up his side and the dead diver dropped to the grass. Joey took a few steps back away from the body, keeping it in front of him, and watched Earl angrily stomp up the hill and disappear behind the Chalet wondering where he was going.

Several minutes later Earl reappeared at the top of the hill pushing a large wheelbarrow. He pushed it down the hill and set it next to the body. "A'ight, hep me out heah. Grab tha' side so we can git 'im in da barrel."

Joey grabbed the arm on his side again and heaved it up as high as he could with Earl doing the same on the opposite side. Earl was stronger and able to lift his side up much higher than Joey. They eased the body over to the wheelbarrow and lifted it over the edge. Earl set his side down on the edge and started to grab the legs when the wheelbarrow tipped over. Joey had tried to support his side but couldn't hold it up alone.

Earl snapped at him, "Com'on kid! Look wut ya gone an' did!"

Earl grabbed the body and jerked it into position on its side against the wheelbarrow.

"A'ight, y'all grab da handle an' set dis thin' up while ah pull da body up."

Joey grabbed both handles and braced himself.

"Ona count a 3. 1. 2. 3. Lif' 'er up!"

Joey pulled the wheelbarrow back up on its legs straightening it out on the two legs and the wheel while Earl kept the body inside the barrow.

"Now we jus' need ta git dis up da hill. Why doncha stand on tha' side of it an' push while I pull from da handles."

Joey got in position and leaned into the front of the wheelbarrow. The legs of the dead diver were hanging over the rim and hung limply down on either side of him. Thankfully the mask was still on the face and Joey couldn't see beyond the lenses in the dark of the night, even with the full moon out. If he had been able to see his face and the eyes staring directly at him he wouldn't know how he would handle that. Earl stood on the opposite side behind the body but facing away from it. He grabbed the handles and lifted his end of the wheelbarrow off the ground. Earl took a step forward and Joey grunted and pushed. They started moving slowly. They continued up the hill for a few feet before Earl put the wheelbarrow legs down and leaned back on its edge practically sitting on the head of the dead diver.

"I gotta take a break kid. Dis hill is too much," Earl huffed out of breath. Joey just nodded. He was breathing so hard he couldn't even speak.

Earl pulled a cigarette out of his pocket and lit it. Joey didn't know how he could smoke while he was out of breath. After a few minutes Earl pinched the lit end of the cigarette off onto the ground and stomped it out with his boot. He stood up and grabbed the handles to resume their climb up the hill. They went another several feet before Earl had to take another break. This time he left the cigarettes in his pocket. This went on for about ten minutes before they finally got to the top and were able to push and pull the wheelbarrow the rest of the way to the parking lot on flat ground.

To Joey's amazement Earl headed straight for Joey's car. "Opun da trunk kid."

"Wh-wh-what do you mean?" Joey was in disbelief. Earl wanted to put the body in the trunk of his car. What was he supposed to do with a dead body?!?

"We aint berryin' 'im heah. Opun da trunk so we's can put da body in an' gidit outta heah." Earl snarled at him.

Joey didn't know what to say. "B-but I got the body out of the cave. That was all I was supposed to do. I-I-I can't keep a dead body in my trunk." Joey felt like he was about to start crying any minute. How could all this be happening to him?!? He wasn't one to believe much in karma but everything that was happening to him because he called in sick to go diving was just too much.

Earl stood back and put his hands on his hips. "Com'on kid, ya think ahm gonna jus dump a body in y'all's car an' leave y'all ta deal wit it? We're headin down ta da coast."

"B-but why does it have to be in my car? I-I need to get home before my parents figure out I'm not in bed."

"Don' worry. We're not goin' too far from y'all's house. Den y'all 'll be back in y'all's cumfy bed 'for ya know it."

Joey thought about arguing with Earl. It was one thing to pull a body out of a cave but now he was demanding Joey hide it in his trunk and drive it an hour away. What if they got pulled over? There had to be a law against transporting dead bodies.

He had no idea what to say though. So resigned to the fact that he wasn't going to win this argument, or any argument with Earl, Joey walked around to his gas cap, pulled the door open, and grabbed his car keys out. He walked to the back of the car, unlocked the trunk and popped it open. Earl pulled the wheelbarrow closer so it was lined up sideways next to the trunk.

"Grab 'is legs an' les flip'im o'er."

Joey reluctantly did as he was told and they heaved the body into the trunk. It fell in with a loud thunk. By this time Joey was pouring sweat again. At 2 am and with the air temperature 20 degrees cooler than it had been during the day! He walked around the side of the car and unlocked the doors. He retrieved his scuba gear from the picnic table and placed it on the floor of the back seat so it wouldn't get the seat wet. Earl put the tank and weights Joey had used back in the shop storage. When he came back he said, "Les git dem tanks from da steps an' we're outta heah."

They walked back down the hill to the steps and each one grabbed a scuba tank. Joey again noted how these scuba tanks were a lot heavier than the scuba tank he usually used. One tank had to be at least 20 pounds heavier than one of the ones he rented.

Joey cradled the tank in his arms and slowly started up the hill. About a third of the way up, out of breath again, he had to stop and put the tank down so he could rest a few minutes. Earl continued on up the hill. After a couple of minutes, Joey picked up the tank he had and started back up the hill. He made it almost all the way to the top before having to stop to rest again. After another few minutes of catching his breath he picked up the tank one last time and carried it the rest of the way to his car. Joey knew his muscles were going to be sore tomorrow. This was the most physically demanding thing he had ever done!

With the heavy tanks tightly wedged in between the front and back seat on the passenger side of his car, Joey and Earl began the drive down to the gulf coast. Joey sat nervously behind the wheel as he turned off the dirt road from Eddy Spring and headed south past farm land, a grade school, and a few scattered, dark houses. The smell of beer and cigarettes and sweat mixed heavily in the small quarters of the car so he opened the window a little to let fresh air inside.

Approaching the quiet intersection of the small town of Ponce de Leon, he noticed that the Tom Thumb convenience store and gas station, a place where Joey usually stopped on his way home from Eddy Spring so he could grab some snacks for the hour drive home, was closed at this late hour. Joey glanced at his instrument panel and looked at his gas gauge needle. It was just above ¼ tank.

"Um, s-s-sir, I-I don't think I have enough gas to get us all the way to the c-coast. I'm g-gonna have to stop and get gas somewhere," Joey said fearfully.

Earl leaned over from the passenger seat to look at the gas gauge, bringing the beer and cigarette and sweat smell with him. "What da…why 'nt y'all gas up 'for ya got heah?"

"I-I-I didn't think about it. I figured I'd do it on the way home," Joey mumbled.

"Git on da I-10 an head west. We'll git some gas down da in'erstate."

As Joey approached Interstate 10 he noticed the signs for the Exxon and Shell stations on the other side of the highway were also dark. Not much open at this hour in the small towns of north Florida. He started to get more nervous as he thought about driving around the panhandle looking for an open gas station at 2 o'clock in the morning with a dead body in his trunk and the inside of his car smelling like beer.

Turning right onto the ramp to the interstate Joey accelerated and eased onto I-10. They were the only ones on the road. About 20 minutes ahead right off the interstate was Defuniak Springs. Joey would turn off the highway there for gas and then continue south toward the coast if he was going home. He wondered if that was where Earl wanted to head.

"S-Sir, wh-where are we headed? And wh-what are we going to do when we get to the coast? I mean, where are we going to put the body?"

"Doncha worry none 'bout dat. Jus' git on o'er ta 'funiak Spring. We'll git some gas an' go on down da coast from thar."

Twenty minutes later Joey eased off the gas pedal and exited the interstate. There were a couple of gas stations just south of the highway but they were both dark. The only lights south of the interstate came from the golden arches just south of the exit ramp. He knew there wasn't much else that way so he turned right off the exit ramp to head north into the town of Defuniak Springs. As he was driving on the off ramp Joey started wondering how the town got its name and where the springs were. He wondered if there was another cave there like the one at Eddy Spring and what it looked like. *Was it bigger? Deeper? Did it have a grate in it too?*

The bright lights of a Waffle House and a couple of gas stations came into view to the right as Joey came to a stop at the end of the ramp and snapped Joey out of his daydreaming. He turned onto 331 and turned into the gas station on his right, pulling up to a pump. Joey got out of his car and walked to the pump. He pulled out his wallet and found his gas card, the only credit card he had, and removed it from his wallet. Just as he was about to insert the card into the pump Earl jumped out of the car.

"Whoa kid, whacha doin'?!?" he yelled. "Put dat thin' away. We can't have ya runnin' a card an' leavin' ev'dence we bin heah."

Earl took out his wallet and pulled a bill out of it.

"Heah. Git inside an' pay wit dis." Earl handed Joey a crisp new $20 bill. "I'm gonna take a leak."

Earl lit another cigarette as he walked off to the side of the building while Joey headed inside to pay for the gas. When Joey stepped inside he noticed the snack cakes on the end cap of one of the shelves They were only 99 cents each. Joey nervously glanced outside to see if Earl was back yet. No sign of him. Joey grabbed an apple pie snack cake and stepped up to the cashier. He held up the snack cake and placed the $20 bill on the counter.

"Um, this snack cake and the rest on pump 2 please."

"Ya need a receipt?"

"N-no, that's okay."

Joey turned and walked quickly out the door as he shoved the apple pie snack into a front pocket of his shorts. He hoped Earl wouldn't ask for change or a receipt. He started pumping gas and was about to pull the snack cake out of his pocket when Earl appeared behind him causing him to nearly jump out of his shoes.

"Bout ready ta git on da move agin kid?" Earl said from behind Joey.

"Um, just about. The g-gas is still pumping. I have to g-go to the bathroom." Joey said as he turned and walked quickly back inside the store to use the restroom. Joey stepped into the bathroom and pulled the snack cake out of his pocket. He took a big bite out of it eating almost 1/3 at once. Less than a minute later he had eaten the entire pie and was washing the stickiness off his hands.

As Joey returned to the car he noticed Earl leaning against it with his arms crossed waiting for him. Joey nervously looked around wondering why Earl was standing there like that. As he got closer he glanced at the fuel pump and saw it had only pumped $18.94 worth of gas. *Uh oh*, Joey thought. He had forgotten about that.

"Why's they only give us 19 dollas a gas kid? Y'all buy anything while's ya in thar?" Earl asked in an accusatory tone.

"Uh-uh-uh, I was hungry and got a snack cake. It was only 99 cents. I can pay you back. I promise." Joey cried out.

Earl stood there and stared at him for a moment, looking him up and down from head to toe. Then he smiled showing his crooked yellow stained teeth and said, "Nah kid. Nex' time jus' tell me. Don' try t' rip m' off. You an' me, we keep truthful wit each otha an' we'll be okay. Less git outta heah an' git dis done 'for da sun come up."

13

Back on the road again, Joey and Earl rode quietly for the next 25 minutes. This area of the drive was pretty desolate. They drove past an RV park and the occasional mobile home but mostly fields of trees lined the road. Most of the houses were dark at this hour. A few had porch lights on over a front or side door. The only street lights were at the intersection of a small town between Defuniak Springs and Freeport. Joey wanted to know what Earl intended on doing with the body but after what happened back at the gas station he was afraid to say anything and get Earl even more mad at him. By the time they got to the bridge that crossed the Choctawhatchee Bay over to Santa Rosa Beach Earl's head had fallen back against the headrest and he was snoring loudly. Joey wasn't sure what to do. Earl hadn't said anything more than they were heading to the coast. They were approaching the traffic light at the intersection with Highway 98 where Joey would have to turn left or right. He didn't know which way Earl wanted him to go.

The traffic light came into view and it was red. Joey started to step on the brake gently to bring the car to a stop at the light as Earl continued to snore in the seat next to him. He glanced at Earl for a moment but he wasn't waking up. He decided to pull into the parking lot of the Tom Thumb at the intersection. As he turned right into the parking lot he saw a black and tan Florida trooper car parked on the south side of the building in front of the main door. Through the glass doors on the east side of the building Joey could see the smokey bear ranger hat of the trooper who was standing in front of the counter talking to the clerk. He felt panic rise up in him.

He looked around the parking lot wondering what to do. He couldn't just drive through the parking lot and onto highway 98. That might make the trooper suspicious and he didn't need a cop coming after him. Especially with a dead body in the trunk.

He glanced down at the gas gauge. They had only driven about 30 miles so he didn't need gas. He looked over at Earl again and to the right of the car he noticed a tire air machine at the edge of the parking lot behind the Tom Thumb store. Joey turned the steering wheel and eased the car in that direction parking it in front of the air machine. He unbuckled his seatbelt and reached over to open the car door. As he opened the door and started to step out he felt a hand grab his shoulder.

"Where ya think y'all's goin' kid?" Earl whispered from behind him, "y'all ain't thinkin' 'bout talkin ta dat cop?"

Joey started off nervously, "I-I-I'm just checking the tire pressure. I didn't know where we were going so I pulled into this parking lot to wake you up and ask you but I saw the police car parked on the other side of the store so I pulled over here to make it look like I was getting air for my tires so he wouldn't come over." By the time he was done talking he was practically running his words together again.

Earl stared at him as if he was trying to read his mind for a moment. Then he smiled and said, "Good thinkin' kid. Y'all's a smart un aint ya. A'ight, git out an' check dem tires soes we can git on da way agin. We're almos' thar."

Joey stepped out of the car and walked around to the air machine. He grabbed the air chuck, uncoiled the hose from the hanger, and went through the motions of checking the tire pressure in a couple of the tires on his car. He was checking the front right tire when he noticed the side door to the Tom Thumb open and the trooper step out with a cup of coffee in his hand. Joey thought that was strange. The Tom Thumb had two doors, one facing 98 and the other facing 331, the road Joey had just come in on. The trooper's car was parked around the other side of the store outside a different door but for some reason he chose to exit through the door closest to Joey and Earl.

Joey looked back down at the air chuck but he was so nervous his hands were shaking and he couldn't get it on the tire valve. He glanced back up in the trooper's direction. The trooper just stood there with the steam from his coffee cup wafting up into the cool night air looking back in Joey's direction. Joey quickly dropped his eyes back to the tire. If the trooper walked over to the car he didn't know what they were going to do. There was a dead body in the trunk of the car!

He kept his eyes focused down on the tire, afraid to look back up, and hoped the trooper wouldn't walk over. A minute later he heard a car engine start and stole a glance in the direction of the store. The trooper was no longer standing outside the door. A few seconds later he saw the black and tan sedan pull out of the parking lot and head east on Highway 98. *That was close.*

Joey finished with the tires, coiled the hose back around the hanger on the pump, got back in the driver's seat of his car and pulled his seatbelt on. He looked over at Earl but it didn't seem like he had even noticed the trooper coming out and looking toward them. Joey put the car in reverse and backed up several feet so he could turn the car toward 98. He shifted the transmission into drive and turned to Earl.

"Wh-which way do I turn sir?"

"Go ta da right an' head ta Destin. We're gonna turn off 'fore we cross o'er ta Walton so don't git too fast."

Joey was relieved they were heading in the opposite direction that the trooper went. He drove west on Highway 98. As they got closer to Destin he started seeing more buildings. They passed an apartment complex on the left with lights turned on inside a couple of the windows. After the next intersection Joey saw a Krispy Kreme with the HOT sign turned on. His stomach started to grumble loudly at the thought of eating a fresh hot donut.

"Ya hungry kid? Wasn't that snack pie ya had back in 'funiak enough?" Earl must have heard his stomach.

"I-I-I didn't eat any dinner tonight. I didn't have much of an appetite then. I-I'll be okay though."

"Damn right y'all 'll be okay. We got ta git dis done. Sun's 'bout t' come up in couple hours."

Joey glanced at the clock on the dash and saw it was almost 3:30 am. The sun would be coming up pretty soon. He still had no idea what Earl had in mind but they better get it done fast. Joey's parents would be waking up at 6 to get ready for work and Joey needed to be back home and in bed before that. If he wasn't, there was no way he would be able to explain where he had snuck off to in the middle of the night.

"Pull off right heah inta dis parkin' lot," Earl said as he pointed to an empty parking lot to the left.

Joey drove up to the next break in the median and made a U-turn. He brought the car back around to the parking lot entrance and turned off Highway 98.

"Drive on 'roun' dat dar buildin'."

Joey continued to follow Earl's directions and eased the car around an old building. As they drove past the building Joey saw several boats tied up to some docks in the Destin Harbor.

"Cut da lights an' git as close as ya can ta da water o'er dar. Make sure ya back it in" Earl pointed at the space where he wanted Joey to park.

Backing in the car as he was told, Joey parked it where Earl had directed him to. Earl jumped out of the car and Joey watched through the rearview mirror as he quickly walked over to the boat that was docked directly behind them. Earl stepped on the boat and disappeared inside the cabin. Joey didn't move. He sat in his car watching for Earl to return. He couldn't wait to just get the dead body out of his trunk so he could go home and go to bed.

A couple minutes later Earl emerged from the cabin and stepped off the boat. He approached the car on the driver's side and stopped right outside of the door. Joey rolled down the window and looked up at Earl.

"Whachya waitin' fer kid? Git on outta dar so's we can git da body outta da trunk."

Finally, Joey thought to himself. He opened the door as Earl stepped back and stepped out of the car. They walked to the back of the car and Joey unlocked the trunk.

"We're gonna hafta carry 'im t' da boat. I aint got a barrow heah. I'll git da arms an' y'all's git da legs." Earl ordered.

Earl grabbed the body around the shoulders and pulled the torso out of the trunk. As he pulled the body out Joey stepped next to the legs. He quickly glanced around to make sure no one else was in the vicinity and then grabbed the legs with one leg resting on each hip. It was about 20' from the trunk to the back of the boat. They slowly struggled with the body in the direction of the boat with Earl walking backwards and Joey following him. Earl stepped off the concrete pavement onto a narrow boardwalk that extended out in between the boats. That's when Joey noticed the boat was too far out from the pavement to enter from the back.

Joey followed Earl onto the narrow dock, slipping as he stepped down onto it. The dock was so narrow Joey thought he was going to lose his balance and fall into the water between the dock and the boat. He immediately reached out to grab the side of the boat to keep himself from falling and in doing so dropped the legs of the body. Joey kept himself from falling in the water but he didn't keep Earl's wrath from falling on him.

"What da hell ya doin'?!? We aint dumpin' da body heah. Y'all's tryin' ta make me fall in da water?" Earl barked in a loud whisper.

Joey grabbed for the legs and stammered, "S-s-s-sorry sir. I s-s-slipped."

He pulled the legs up and he and Earl swung the body onto the side of the boat. Earl moved down along the body and when he got to the middle of the back he gave the body a shove and it rolled over onto the deck of the boat with a loud thump.

"A'ight, go git doze tanks o'er heah." Earl barked.

Joey walked carefully back to the car and pulled the tanks out of the back seat. He picked one up and carried it to the boat and gently placed it on the dock careful not to step onto the dock and risk slipping again. He walked back to the car, retrieved the second tank, carried it to the boat and set it down next to the first one.

Earl was already in the boat doing something on the upper deck. He was flipping some switches. Lights were turning on and a humming noise was coming from the boat. Joey stood there wondering if he could leave. He was afraid to try to put the tanks in the boat by himself after almost falling in. They were heavier than the legs had been. He thought about just getting in his car and heading home but was afraid to leave without Earl saying it was okay.

The boat motors started to turn over, caught quickly and came roaring to life. Earl revved the motors a couple times and a thick white smoke poured out from around them reminding Joey of the clouds of silt that had plumed up around him in the cave several times. Joey could smell the acrid exhaust fumes of the marine fuel burning in the motors. Earl eased back on the throttle and left them idling. He climbed down onto the deck and looked over at Joey.

"Whatcha waitin' fer kid? Git doze tanks in da boat an' le's git goin'"

Did Joey just hear him right? Let's get going? "Uh-uh-uh, I'm afraid I might fall in if I try to carry the tanks on the dock. Can I just hand them to you from back here?" Joey asked nervously.

"Tha's fine. Jus' han' me one 't time. Den git in."

Joey handed Earl the tanks one at a time and again just stood behind the boat hoping Earl wasn't really planning on making him go with him. It was almost 4 am and Joey just wanted to get home and into bed.

"Com'on kid. Git in!" Earl ordered. "We aint got all night. Sun'll be up in a couple hours."

"Do I h-h-have to sir?" Joey started but Earl quickly cut him off.

"Yeah ya hafta! I can't toss da body maself. Git in! We'll be back in no time 't all." Earl jumped out of the boat and started to untie the ropes securing it in the slip between the docks.

Joey carefully stepped onto the narrow dock and held onto the side of the boat. He eased his right leg over the side of the boat and stepped down but quickly pulled his leg back up. The body was on the deck right where they had dropped it. Joey was going to have to balance himself on the side of the boat and jump onto the deck over it. The boat was rocking side to side a little and Joey wasn't sure he could do it. He eased his right leg back up on the side of the boat and kneeled there as he pulled his left leg up onto the wall next to it.

As soon as he was balanced on the boat's side, Earl jumped in the boat from the other side causing it to rock even more. Earl climbed the ladder to the top deck and placed the boat in gear. Joey frantically looked around trying to figure out how he was going to get down off the side of the boat onto the deck. Earl pulled the boat out of the slip and turned right toward the pass. Joey started to lose his balance and opted to fall forward into the boat rather than back into the water. But a forward fall also meant falling on the dead body that was laid out on the deck below him.

He crashed onto the deck with his legs hitting the body. The body rolled over so it was facing up staring directly at him. The eyes were open! Joey scrambled backwards like a crab across the boat as quickly as he could trying to get as far from the body as possible. He got to the other side of the boat and turned himself around so he was sitting up and leaning on the cabin wall. Breathing hard, he remained in that position as Earl steered the boat between the marker buoys denoting the dredged channel in the pass out into the dark night into the Gulf of Mexico.

14

August 5, 2011 sometime after 4am

Fortunately, the seas were calm that morning. Once they were out of the pass Earl set the motors to full throttle heading south away from land. Joey saw the lights from some early morning fishing boats off in the distance. Earl made sure to steer clear of them.

Joey sat on the deck on the side opposite from the dead body. There were dim lights on in the cabin and out on the deck where Joey and the body were. He stole a glance toward the body about five feet away. It was face up on the deck. Fortunately, the scuba mask was still on his head and Joey couldn't see the eyes from this angle. Not that Joey wanted to see the eyes again. Once was more than enough. And just being on the deck five feet away from a dead body was freaking him out.

Even though the seas were calm Joey was starting to feel nauseated. Being on a boat always did that to him. It was a combination of the motor exhaust and the rocking. He still hadn't been diving anywhere but the freshwater springs. He wanted to go out on a dive boat but knew his stomach couldn't handle it. His father owned a boat and had taken him out on it a few times when he was younger but he was always miserable and got sick. His father got tired of having to clean up the vomit off the side of the boat and stopped taking him on those trips. He hadn't been on a boat in over five years.

Less than ten minutes on the boat and it was starting already. Scrambling to his feet, Joey pulled himself up and hung his head over the side of the boat…just in time. As soon as his head cleared the side he puked the apple pie snack he had eaten at the gas station. Earl was probably thinking Joey was getting what he deserved for sneaking the pie using his twenty dollars.

Wiping his mouth with the back of his hand Joey remained in the same position over the side of the boat for a while longer letting the wind from the movement of the boat hit his face. He didn't have anything left in his stomach but the nausea was still there, although it was easing off. He looked back behind the boat. The lights of Destin were barely visible. Joey wondered how far from shore Earl planned on going.

He stood and looked up at the upper deck where Earl sat. Earl was staring straight ahead, the wind blowing his hair back away from his face. He had been oblivious to Joey puking behind and below him. Joey glanced in the cabin and saw a sink on one side. Opening the door he stepped inside the cabin and walked to it. He turned the faucet handle and heard a pump turn on followed by water sputtering out. Joey splashed some lukewarm water on his face and felt better. He looked around the cabin and noticed a cushioned bench against the other wall. Joey felt so tired. He just wanted to go home and crawl in bed. As it was he didn't know if he was going to make it back home before his parents woke up and figured out he was gone. He walked to the bench and sat down. Listening to the hum of the motors he closed his eyes and leaned his head back.

* * *

Joey woke with a startle as the hum of the motors cut off and he was surrounded by silence. A moment later he heard Earl climbing down the ladder from the top deck and then the door to the cabin opened.

“A’ight kid, le’s git dis done.”

Joey stood up, walked toward the door, and asked, “Wh-what are we doing sir?”

“We’re tossin’ da body o’er. We’re ‘bout ten mile out. We weigh ‘im down an’ no’ne’ll e’er fin’ ‘im.”

Joey followed Earl out onto the deck. It was still dark. He looked around. The gulf water looked even more menacing than the water in the Eddy Spring basin. At least at Eddy he knew it was only 20 feet deep in the basin. And it was only a couple hundred feet across. The gulf was endless. He had no idea how deep it was and there weren’t any lights anywhere in sight except the ones on Earl’s boat. Joey wondered how Earl would find the way back to the dock and his car. Earl grabbed the scuba tanks and moved them by the body.

“Le’s put ‘im up on da side da boat heah. Whens we git ‘im up dar we’ll clip deez tanks on ‘im an’ push ‘im o’er da side.”

Earl grabbed the shoulders again and Joey moved over to grab the legs. They pulled the body up and flipped it over on its back on the side of the boat.

“Hold ‘im dar whiles I grab a tank. Don’t let ‘im fall yet.” Earl ordered.

Joey did as he was told, holding the body as he looked away. He didn’t want to chance seeing those eyes again. Earl grabbed a tank off the deck as well as a rope out of his back pocket that he began to wrap around the valve of the tank. He set the tank on top of the body and fed the loose end of the rope under and around the body, back over the scuba tank, and around the body a second time. He then rolled the tank slowly over the body until it eased off and was hanging just a couple feet above the water. The body started to shift and follow the tank in. Joey grabbed the BC and leaned back into the boat to brace himself. As the body started to slide off the boat Joey leaned back even more to try to keep it from falling in the water. Earl was reaching down for the second tank when he noticed what was happening.

Earl dropped the second tank and grabbed the body to help Joey keep it from falling out into the water. In his haste, he dropped the tank on Joey's foot and it fell against the shin Joey had injured twice going down the chimney at Eddy Spring earlier in the day. This caused Joey to lose his grip on the body. Earl didn't quite have a hold of the body and it slid into the water with a splash. Meanwhile Joey was sitting on the deck cradling his foot.

"What'd y'all go an' le' go of 'im fer?" Earl yelled.

"The t-t-tank fell on my f-foot. I couldn't help it." Joey cried out.

Earl climbed up the ladder to the upper deck. A few seconds later the boat was lit up all around. Joey saw Earl come to the edge of the upper deck and look around the boat at the surface of the black water.

"Dare 't is," he said as he pointed off the back of the boat. Sitting on the deck Joey was too low to see anything. And his foot and shin were still throbbing too much for him to try to stand up and look. Earl climbed down the ladder and walked around the side of the boat. He came back carrying a long pole which he stuck out the rear of the boat. After a couple minutes of poking the pole around in the water Earl yelled out, "Got 'im!"

Pulling the pole back in, Earl brought the body in next to the boat. "Git up kid an' hold dis stick heah," Earl ordered.

Joey stood up and took the pole in his hands. His foot still hurt a little but he didn't think it was broken. At least he could put weight on it. Joey glanced over the side of the boat and saw the right side of the body barely sticking out of the water. The first scuba tank was hanging from the left side and weighing the body down. As Joey held the body close to the boat Earl grabbed the second tank again and tied a second rope around the tank valve. He then lowered it over the side of the boat kneeling down on the deck and leaning over the side of the boat so he could reach down and attach the scuba tank to the body. He slipped the loose end of that rope through a D ring on the BC and pulled it through, tying it back to itself. He tried to route the loose end back through the D ring again but the body started sinking rapidly. Joey tried to stop it with the pole but it was impossible. The body was too heavy with the two scuba tanks tied to it. Joey tried to unhook the pole but that was snagged onto the BC and he ended up having to let go of it.

They stood on the deck of the boat and watched as the pole sank down below the surface of the water in the middle of hundreds of bubbles popping back up where the dead diver's body had just been. Joey felt a small sense of relief. It was done. Maybe he could go home now. It was still dark and because he fell asleep earlier he had no idea what time it was. Hopefully it wasn't too late.

"Dammit kid! Y'all's lost ma stick! Those ain't cheap!" Earl yelled at Joey.

Then quickly changing his demeanor. "Well, le's git outta heah kid. He's shark bait now," Earl said laughing as he climbed up the ladder to the upper deck.

A moment later the boat was engulfed by darkness and the motors roared to life emitting the same acrid odor they always did. Joey felt the boat lurch forward as Earl put the motors into gear. Earl swung the boat around and opened the throttle up. Joey looked around and decided to go back in the cabin and get a little more sleep while they headed back to land.

* * *

Joey was startled awake again as the hum of the motors quieted and the boat started to slow down. He sat up and looked out the cabin windows toward the front of the boat. He could see the lights of Destin ahead in the distance. It looked like they were just approaching the Destin Pass into the bay. Looking to the right he could see the hint of dawn just over the horizon.

Standing up Joey stretched. He could feel his arms and legs already starting to get sore from all the activity over the past 20 hours. Three dives, two which didn't go very well, and then moving a dead body around. Joey couldn't remember ever having done that much physically in such a short period of time. Scuba diving was the most active thing he did, and he'd only been doing that for a few months.

He yawned, rubbed his face with his hands, remembered the sink and decided to splash some water on his face. He stepped out of the cabin onto the rear deck of the boat as Earl slowly steered the boat out of the pass and around to the right toward the marina where the boat had been docked earlier that morning. A few minutes later Earl eased the boat just past his space and put the motors in reverse. He expertly maneuvered the boat backwards into the slip.

"Kid, grab dat rope an' hop out 'an tie it t' da dock." Earl called down from the upper deck.

Joey stumbled to the rear of the boat and picked up the loose end of a rope that was coiled neatly in the corner. He raised his leg over the side and stepped onto the narrow dock between the boats. He pulled his other leg up out of the boat and balanced himself carefully as he pulled the rest of the rope until it was taut. He scanned the dock for the cleat to tie the rope to but didn't see anything. He stepped forward and something caught his foot, the one that the tank was dropped on. Joey stretched his arms out as he went flying forward. His palms hit the dock hard, scraping along the old worn wood. He could feel splinters digging in as his hands slid along the boards.

"What more could go wrong?" thought Joey as he lay there on

the dock with blood slowly oozing out of his throbbing palms. He didn't know how he would explain this to his parents. They had seen him the night before and he hadn't mentioned anything about accidently hurting himself.

"Whatcha layin' aroun' fer kid? Git up an' tie dat rope off so's I can cut da motors." Earl yelled down.

Joey looked up at Earl briefly and then faced forward so he could stand. He placed the edges of his hands against the dock careful to avoid using his injured palms and pushed himself up. He searched for the end of the rope but it had fallen into the water. Grabbing the section that was hanging over the boat he pulled the end up. He looked down at the cleat that had caught his foot and caused him to fall down. Joey kicked at it and hurt his toe. The same toe the scuba tank had fallen on. That was the third time hurting that foot. And in doing so he almost lost his balance and fell in the water. He was tired and just needed to get home. Fortunately he only lived about 20 minutes from the marina. Earl would have to find his own way back.

With the boat tied around the cleat he turned and signaled up to Earl. The boat motors cut off, the lights went dark, and Earl climbed down the ladder. He grabbed a second rope from the opposite side and secured it to a cleat on that side. He then came over to check the rope Joey had tied in. Apparently Joey had done it wrong because Earl untied the rope and looped it around the cleat in what looked like figure 8s.

"C-c-can I go home now sir? I'm really tired and my parents are about to get up soon. I-If I'm not home and in bed before they get up they're going to want to know what I was doing all night."

"Shor' kid. Jus' soon as ya drop me off 't home. I don' live far from heah." Earl responded.

They walked across to Joey's car and got in. Joey started the car, put it in gear and pulled out of the parking space steering it around the building toward Highway 98 using the tips of his fingers because his palms were throbbing from the fall. He stopped at the highway and dejectedly looked over at Earl.

"Head tha' way." Earl said as he pointed to the right.

At least Joey was heading toward his home.

* * *

Finally having dropped Earl off Joey was on his way home. It was 5:45 am. He was still almost ten minutes from home and his parents would be awake in fifteen minutes. That was cutting it really close. He sped down the road careful to keep his speed at no more than five miles per hour over the speed limit to avoid getting pulled over. He didn't know how the cops were at this hour but during the day when he was usually out driving he always saw them waiting to pull someone over.

A few minutes later he turned into his neighborhood and glanced down at the clock on his dash – 5:51 am. A couple minutes later he shut off the headlights, shifted the car into neutral and cut the engine when he saw his house. The car coasted quietly down the street and Joey turned the steering wheel guiding the car into the driveway into his usual parking spot. Coming to a stop he put the car in park, pulled the keys out of the ignition and almost screamed out when one of the keys scraped against the abrasions on his palm. He quietly stepped out and looked toward his house which was still dark. His parents hadn't woken up yet. At least they hadn't made it over to this side of the house where the kitchen was. He shut the car door gently and walked around to the back of the house.

Opening the door to the house careful to not make any noise Joey snuck inside. All was quiet in the house. He moved quietly through the kitchen and down the hall to his room. He slowly opened his bedroom door careful to use just his fingertips. As he slipped inside his room he saw the light shoot out from under his parents' bedroom door. He gently closed the door behind him and let out a sigh of relief. He had made it. Stripping out of his clothes he eased himself into bed in between the covers.

Lying in bed Joey's hands were throbbing. Or the adrenaline that had been coursing through his body had eased off and he was noticing it more since falling. He hadn't even had a chance to wash them. He would have to keep them hidden under the covers if his parents came into the room. They shouldn't though. They knew he wasn't scheduled to work today. He had told them he was going scuba diving but they weren't too keen on him doing that so they probably would let him sleep in.

Once they left for work he would get up and take care of his hands. Then he'd get some sleep. After the day and night he had he'd be sleeping all day today. He could go scuba diving again tomorrow. He would need to so he could relax and forget about the horrible day he just had.

Joey lay in bed waiting for his parents to leave the house. He watched the light of the new dawn creeping in through the blinds of his bedroom window as the sun slowly rose over the horizon. He imagined those were the rays of sunlight shooting through the surface and into the water in the Eddy Spring basin. Joey drifted off to sleep dreaming about being under the water blowing bubbles from his scuba regulator. The events of the past 18 hours forgotten for the time being.

PART 2

15

August 5, 2011

Joey woke up screaming. He looked around his bedroom - his desk just to the left of the door, his open laptop resting in the center, the flat screen television mounted on the wall above his dresser which was to the left of the desk, and the window on the adjacent wall with the blinds closed. The familiar site calmed him a bit. The sun's rays were no longer shooting through the slots in the blinds like they had been when he had first gotten into bed. He must have fallen asleep before his parents left the house. From the way the light was coming in through the blinds it looked like it was afternoon. Looking toward his nightstand he saw the red glow of numbers stating is was it was 3:06. He had slept nine hours!

He pulled his hands out from under the blanket and looked at the palms. He had dozed off before he had a chance to wash them. There was blood encrusted on the palms of his hands from the abrasions he got when he clumsily tripped over the cleat at the dock. He tried wiggling his fingers. They were stiff and painful to move. That small attempt at movement made the throbbing in his palms return.

Joey carefully pinched the edge of his blanket between his thumb and index finger and threw it off of him. He eased his legs over the side and planted his bare feet on the floor. The soreness in his fingers and hands suddenly felt minor compared to the soreness creeping up the muscles in the rest of his body as he started to move. The events from the day and night before were taking their toll on him. He slowly stood up and stretched causing a sharp pain to shoot through his arms and legs. He started to rub his eyes with his hands and stopped himself just short of touching his palms to his face.

Joey shuffled to his bedroom door and slowly cracked it opened. Listening for any noise in the house as he cautiously peeked down the hall. He didn't hear anyone. He opened the door and darted across the hall to the bathroom. *Ouch! He felt that in his muscles!* After emptying his bladder he turned on the faucet and set the water to come out lukewarm. Tentatively, he eased his right hand under the stream of water. The water hitting his palm caused the abrasions to sting and Joey pulled his hand back quickly. He tried again but the pain was too much for him to handle. Reaching over the faucet Joey pulled up the chrome colored ball behind it causing the stopper to drop and seal off the drain.

The sink quickly started to fill with water. With it about two-thirds full Joey nudged the faucet into the off position with his elbow. Slowly, he lowered his right hand into the warm water bath he had created in the sink. He felt a sting and yanked his hand up. He tried again, more slowly, and was able to get his hand a little deeper. This reminded him of a Bugs Bunny cartoon video he had seen as a child where Bugs was trying to get into a bathtub filled with hot water and he kept pulling his feet out. Joey chuckled to himself at the thought of the cartoon.

He returned his attention to the sink of water. The sting was still there but it was becoming much more tolerable than it had been with the water pressure from the faucet blasting at his palm. He lowered his left hand into the water next to his right hand. The initial sting almost caused him to yank it out just like he had his right hand but he forced himself to keep it submerged and the pain started to ease off as well. Eventually the water bath was making his hands feel better.

After a few minutes the water started to turn pink from the dissolving blood that was encrusted on his palms. Joey carefully put his palms together and tried to rub them and remove the remaining blood but that hurt too much. He decided to soak his hands longer. He shook his hands around in circles to try to create a small whirlpool and knock some of the blood off by the motion of the water.

After another five minutes or so Joey tried to rub his palms together. It still hurt but wasn't as bad. Carefully and slowly rubbing his hands together he was able to get the remaining dried blood off. He pulled his hands out of the sink and looked at them. They were wrinkled from being in the water for so long but they didn't look as bad as he thought they would. The blood had made them appear in worse shape than they really were.

He popped the stopper up and watched the pink tinged water drain out of the sink. Nudging the faucet back on with his elbow, Joey used the backs of his hands to splash water around and clean up the hardened blood and pink ring that had formed in the sink. He turned off the faucet and reached for the white towel hanging on the wall next to the sink, then thought better of it. He pulled a washcloth out of a pile on the shelf and patted his hands dry careful to not pat the palms too hard and make them hurt or bleed again. Joey thought to himself that he should have splashed some water on his face. He couldn't bear the thought of putting his hands back in the water again so he took the damp towel and rubbed it over his face careful to not put too much pressure against his palms.

Next, Joey headed to the kitchen. He was starving. It had been over twenty-four hours since he had anything to eat. Well, there was that apple pie he had bought with Earl's money but then threw up later. He opened the refrigerator door and stood in front of it for a few minutes trying to decide what he wanted. Finally deciding on some pasta and chicken, probably leftovers from the previous night's dinner, he pulled the bowl out and dumped it onto a plate. He stuck the plate in the microwave and set it to three minutes and returned to the refrigerator to pour himself a cola.

After finishing the leftovers Joey looked at the clock in the kitchen – 3:32. He had a couple hours before his parents would get home from work. Remembering his scuba gear was still in the backseat of his car he thought he better move it into the trunk. He hoped his parents hadn't looked in the car and noticed it this morning. He hadn't told them about it because he still owed them money from the scuba class, and he didn't want them to find out just yet. Returning so late to his house this morning he hadn't even thought about putting the gear in the trunk. He opened the kitchen door and walked outside to his car in his bare feet. He walked around the back and stood in front of the trunk, staring, afraid to open it. He knew he and Earl had removed the body of the dead scuba diver but he was still freaked out just thinking about a dead body having been in there.

Finally he inserted the key in the lock and turned it. He heard the trunk latch click and felt the trunk lid pop up as the lock released from the catch. Slowly raising the lid he peeked in the trunk and saw it was empty. He let out a sigh of relief and walked to the back door and opened it, carefully grabbed his scuba gear putting his arms through the straps so as to not hurt his palms and tossed it in the trunk. Slamming the trunk closed with his elbow he returned to his room and pulled some clothes out to change into. He needed to shower and get dressed before his parents got home. They would be really concerned if they knew he had slept all day.

* * *

Feeling much better in clean clothes after a long hot shower Joey headed back to the kitchen. He was still hungry. He poked around in the refrigerator for a few more minutes but didn't find anything else that looked appetizing. In the pantry he found some pop tarts and decided they would do. It was already past 4 anyway so he shouldn't eat too much. It was Friday which meant his father would be bringing home pizza or Chinese or some other takeout so the family would be eating in a couple hours.

After warming the pop tarts in the toaster for a couple minutes Joey moved into the living room to eat and watch television. He sat on the couch, grabbed the remote and flipped through the channels. Nothing but talk shows on. Usually being at work during the week Joey didn't watch too much daytime television. Even when he was off every other Friday he took that opportunity to head to Eddy Spring and dive.

He thought about streaming something but he didn't have the energy to even think about choosing a show. So he settled on a talk show about some scantily dressed women who cheated on their boyfriends and wanted to know who the baby daddy was. Lots of loud and obnoxious screaming and yelling but Joey wasn't really interested in what was on anyway. He just needed some mindless background noise to disturb the silence in the house. He was trying to keep his mind off of the events of the last twenty-four hours but was having a really difficult time doing so.

Joey still couldn't believe he had found a dead body while diving in the cave at Eddy Spring. Not only that but he had been forced to pull the body out of the cave in the middle of the night and help Earl dispose of it! This was all so overwhelming. All Joey had wanted to do was take his newly purchased gear on a couple of dives to see how it worked. And now he was an accomplice to something. He wasn't sure to what. He didn't kill the guy. He didn't even know who he was. But there had to be something illegal about tossing a dead body over the side of a boat in the gulf.

* * *

"What are you doing, Joey? You don't usually nap on the couch." Joey woke up to his mother standing over him in the living room. He must have dozed off. The napkin he had used to carry the pop tarts was still in his hand which he quickly turned palm down so his mother wouldn't notice the abrasions. The television was still on but the talk show had ended and the local news was on. He had been asleep for about an hour.

"Um, I just had a long day I guess."

"Well, I'm glad you're doing something active, Joey, but I think you're over doing it with that scuba diving. You can't spend every free minute you have in the water. And with all the money you're spending on gas to get back and forth to that spring it's taking you a lot longer than you promised to pay back the money you borrowed from your father and me. You need to be more responsible and set your priorities, Joseph." Joey was still trying to clear the cobwebs from his head while his mother was going on and on lecturing him about responsibilities and priorities. He really didn't feel like listening to this at the moment.

"I know, mom. I'll pay you a back as soon as I can. I promise. We just haven't been getting as much in tips at work. I think some of the waitresses are holding back." Joey whined.

"Well, you should talk to your boss then. You should be getting what you deserve. It does you no good to sit back and let them walk all over you." Joey's mom continued with her lecture. "Now go wash up. It looks like you have dirt on your hands and your father will be home soon with dinner. I don't know how someone who spends so much time in the water can get so dirty." His mother exclaimed while shaking her head.

Joey quickly looked down and noticed his other hand on his lap palm up. His palms were starting to bruise a little and that's what his mom must have thought was dirt. He would have to be careful to keep his palms hidden from her for a while. He was lucky this time. The blinds were closed and the room was darkened so she couldn't get a good look at them. He might not be so lucky next time.

In the bathroom with the door closed Joey turned the faucet on and stood in front of the sink for about a minute so his mother would think he was washing his hands. His palms were still sore from his shower earlier. As he opened the bathroom door and stepped out into the hall he heard his father walk in through the side door. He also instantly smelled dinner. Ribs. While Joey absolutely loved ribs this was not a good night for them. His father usually got ribs that were dripping in sauce. And the only way to eat ribs were with his hands, which still hurt a lot. Why couldn't his father have gotten Chinese or something else that required utensils, Joey thought to himself. He would have to wipe his hands down before touching anything else at the table. Dinner was going to be a big test of his pain tolerance.

Joey ended up making it through dinner fairly easily. His mother had an eventful day at work and was so busy talking about her day that she didn't even notice Joey wincing every time he wiped his hands so he could take a drink. And the rib sauce did a pretty good job of hiding the bruises forming on his palms.

16

August 6, 2011 7am

Saturday morning had Joey up early. He was still dressed in his clothes from the day before and sleeping on top of his covers. After dinner the night before he excused himself, went to soak the remainder of the sticky rib sauce off his hands in the bathroom sink, and then closed himself off in his bedroom for the rest of the evening. He fell asleep with the television on again but his mom or dad must have turned it off because it was not on when he woke up.

Looking at the clock he saw it was just after 7 am. He looked at his palms and noticed the bruising was much worse this morning. This was going to be difficult to hide. He started to jump out of bed and instantly felt the soreness shoot through his entire body again. It felt much worse than it had the previous day. He took a minute to try to stretch the soreness out of his muscles but it didn't do any good. Every little movement sent aching pain throughout all of his muscles. Creeping to the door he slowly opened it and heard the television on in the living room. His parents must be up and having breakfast already. Joey wanted to head to Eddy Spring to go scuba diving but after the lecture from his mother the evening before he knew he was going to have to deal with more of that this morning before he could leave.

Darting across the hall into the bathroom again Joey went through his morning routine. This time he remembered to splash water on his face before patting his palms dry. They were still sore but it didn't feel as bad to put them in the water this morning. Quickly back to his room Joey changed clothes before heading to the kitchen for breakfast. He wanted to be ready to walk out the door as soon as he ate. He might even just take a couple of packages of pop tarts and eat on the go so he wouldn't have to listen to more lectures from his mom.

As soon as he walked into the kitchen his mom said, "Good morning, Joey. You must have been tired yesterday. First I catch you napping in the middle of the day and then I find you passed out in your room with the television on. You need to stop over doing it. What do you have planned for today?"

Well, if that wasn't a loaded question, Joey thought. She knew he was planning on heading to Eddy Spring to scuba dive today. "Um, I was just planning on heading out for a few hours."

"You're not going scuba diving again this weekend, are you, Joseph?" his mom asked accusingly.

"I'm not sure, mom, I haven't really thought about it." Joey tried to evade her questions. "Why does it matter anyway? You always say I need to be more active and now you're telling me I'm over doing it?"

"It's just there are a lot of other things you can be doing. Things closer to home and that don't cost as much. I saw your gas card bill the other day. That's a lot of money for one month of gas, young man. Driving an hour each way every weekend, sometimes both days, is expensive. And then there's other expenses I'm sure." his mother continued to lecture.

Joey went to the pantry, grabbed a couple of packs of pop tarts and headed toward the door going outside. "Where are you going? That's not a proper breakfast."

"I'm just tired of hearing it, mom. That's all you talk about. I'll be home later." Joey said as he walked out the door and slammed it shut. He got in his car and backed out of the driveway before his mother could alert his father so he would come out to stop Joey and maybe even ground him. He was 19 years old but he did still live under their roof, as they so often reminded him.

And there he was, right on cue. Joey saw the door open and his father step outside, newspaper folded under his arm and a coffee mug in his hand, just as he shifted the car into drive and took off down the road. The last thing he saw was his dad standing at the door shaking his head. Joey was certain to hear it later when he got home. But for now it was time to go scuba diving.

17

As Joey turned onto the dirt road to Eddy Spring he saw a sheriff's car heading the opposite direction away from the scuba park. He continued his drive up the road wondering what a cop was doing at Eddy. He rounded the bend and drove the last couple hundred yards to the shack at the entrance. That's when his question was answered.

Joey saw several more sheriff's cars in the parking area. There was a barricade set up across the entrance and a deputy standing next to it. As Joey pulled up to the barricade the deputy approached the driver's side window. Joey reached down and cranked his window open careful to not hurt his hand. He sure wished his parents had bought him a car with automatic windows.

"Park's closed today."

"Um, wh-what's going on?"

"Diver went missing and we got search teams in the cave looking for the body."

Joey broke out in a sweat despite the vents blowing cold air directly on him. How had they found out? He wondered if Earl had decided to confess to getting rid of the body. Had he told the cops about Joey helping him? Joey suddenly felt sick to his stomach. He was pretty sure the pop tarts he had eaten on the drive up were about to reintroduce themselves to his mouth.

"Oh, okay." Joey said quickly as he shifted the car into reverse so he could get out of there before he threw up in front of the deputy. He backed the car onto the grassy shoulder pointing it perpendicular to the road. As he shifted back into drive he saw one of the dive shop employees running toward the deputy at the barricade. When she got close to the deputy Joey saw her say something to him as she pointed toward Joey. *That couldn't be good*, thought Joey. He pressed the gas pedal down a little too hard and his wheels spun in the grass before finally gaining traction and setting his car in a forward motion. Joey eased off the gas pedal and slowly drove down the road trying hard to resist the urge to floor it and get out of there fast. He hoped the girl was pointing at something behind him and not at him but he doubted that was the case.

Rounding the bend in the road, and finally out of site from the entrance, he let the urge to speed up take over and he increased his speed a little. It must have rained the night before because Joey could feel small washboard ruts shaking his car as he quickly drove over them back toward the asphalt road a half mile away.

This only made the urge to throw up even greater but Joey was afraid to waste any time pulling over to puke on the side of the road. The girl must have known Joey helped Earl get rid of the body and the cops would be coming after him. He had to get out of there fast. He got to the end of the dirt road, stopped briefly for the stop sign, saw it was clear and quickly stepped on the gas pedal, causing the tires to spin again, this time on the dirt road. He turned left, leaving behind a couple of plumes of dust, and headed south. Once on the paved road Joey leaned forward and rolled his window back up. Maybe blocking off the warm air and just letting the cold air conditioning blow in his face would help him feel better.

By the time he saw the Tom Thumb store the nauseous feeling was starting to pass. With no cops rushing up behind him he began to relax. Maybe she was pointing at something else.

Joey wondered what he was going to do and how long Eddy Spring would be closed. What if they kept it closed until they found the body, which they never would because he and Earl had dumped it in the gulf. He could head down to Morrison Spring. He had heard about it from other divers but he had never been diving there. He was supposed to go there with his open water scuba class but it had been flooded. Joey wondered how a spring already full of water could flood.

The problem with going to Morrison Spring was he didn't have a scuba tank. He usually rented one from the dive shop at Eddy Spring. Morrison Spring was a county park and didn't have a dive shop located there. He had wanted to check out Morrison Spring for a while though.

From what he had heard Morrison Spring had a slightly larger basin than Eddy Spring. And the cave entrance at Morrison was in the middle of the basin rather than on one end. It was kind of like a bowl. Morrison was also free to get into because it was a county park, not a privately owned park like Eddy. Joey hadn't been there yet because by the time he got to Eddy Spring he was too excited to get in the water and scuba dive as soon as he could and didn't want to drive another 25 minutes back down the road to get to Morrison. So he always just went scuba diving in Eddy.

He was curious about Morrison though. He had heard that back in the 1960s a couple of scuba divers had gone into the cave there and died. In order to prevent anyone else from ever dying in the cave again the local sheriff at the time sent divers into Morrison with explosives and blew up the tunnel so it caved in on itself. Joey had heard there was still a really pretty cavern at Morrison, and much bigger than Eddy. Morrison also had lots of freshwater eels and he had heard there were even freshwater flounder there. He didn't know there was even such a thing.

Maybe he would head there just to get in the water and cool off. He wished he owned a scuba tank. There was no way he could buy one after the lecture he got from his mother this morning. He would have to wait.

As Joey was approaching interstate 10 he heard the *bwooop bwooop* of a police siren. He looked in his rearview mirror and saw a sheriff's car behind him with the lights on. Suddenly the nausea returned full force and Joey tasted the vomit in the back of his mouth. Those pop tarts sure didn't taste the same coming back up. He swallowed back the acidic taste of the partially digested pop tarts and pulled off the side of the road. He shifted his car into park and watched the sheriff's car roll in behind him. Joey waited for the deputy to approach his car but he wasn't getting out of the cruiser. He was looking at something in the center of his console. Joey sat in his car watching the deputy behind him through the rearview mirror for at least three minutes feeling worse and worse. Why wasn't the deputy at least getting out and letting him know why he had been pulled over?

At that thought, the sheriff's car door opened and the deputy stepped out. He put on a brown ballcap with large gold colored capital letters forming the word DEPUTY embroidered on it, then looked around, and started walking toward Joey's car. As he slowly approached Joey's car door, Joey broke out in a sweat again and the urge to throw up came back with a vengeance. When the deputy got to Joey's door he just stood there. Joey sat in his car wondering why the deputy wasn't saying anything when the deputy suddenly knocked on his window, made a circular motion with his hand and pointed down. Startled, Joey jumped up and started cranking the window down.

"Joseph Simmons?" asked the deputy.

Joey sat there and stared at the deputy, who didn't look much older than him, in his brown and tan uniform wondering how he knew Joey's name.

"Are you Joseph Simmons?" the deputy repeated his question.

"Um, uh, yessir."

"You mind turning your car off and stepping out, please. I have some questions I need to ask you."

"Um, okay, officer. D-did I do something wrong?" Joey fearfully asked.

"Just shut your car off and step out, please. I'll explain in a few minutes."

"Y-yes officer." Joey did as he was told. He turned the key in the ignition and removed it. The deputy stepped back from the door as Joey opened it to step out. Joey's legs felt rubbery as he swung them out of the car and stepped onto the hot pavement. He pulled himself up using the car door for support and stood there staring at the deputy while the deputy stared back.

"Go ahead and shut the car door and let's get out of the road and step back to my car, son," the deputy ordered.

Joey shut the door and turned to walk toward the deputy's car. *Son?* The deputy couldn't be more than five or six years older than him, Joey thought. Joey could feel the deputy following right behind him. Joey walked around to the passenger side of the police car and the deputy stepped around him to open the back door.

The back?!? Joey thought as he began to panic even more. The deputy was making him sit in the back behind a cage where criminals sat. He looked in the back seat and saw there was hardly any room between the back seat and the front seats. He would have to cramp his legs into the small space. Joey looked pleadingly at the deputy and the deputy just nodded his head in the direction of the back seat. Joey climbed in and sat down, his knees crushed up against the back of the front seats. The deputy closed the door on Joey and walked around to the driver's side and sat down behind the steering wheel.

"Hi Mr. Simmons, my name is Deputy Michaels."

"Um, hello Deputy."

"First, let me tell you, you're not in trouble. I just need to ask you some questions and rather than stand out in the hot sun dodging traffic going by I brought you back here. Besides, I take better notes on my computer here," he chuckled. "Sorry about making you sit in the back but as you can see this is my office up here and the passenger seat is my file cabinet."

Joey looked over to the passenger side and noticed several

file folders stacked on the seat. In the center of the cruiser was a laptop computer mounted to the console. That must have been what the deputy was looking at earlier when Joey was waiting for him to get out of the car.

"Oh, okay, sir. C-can I ask what this is about?"

"You were just back at Eddy Spring, weren't you?"

"Y-yes sir."

"I'm sure the deputy at the entrance told you we're searching for a missing diver in the cave and that the park is closed today."

"Y-ye---" Joey started to respond but the deputy cut him off and continued.

"Well, one of the dive shop employees recognized you and told him that you had been at the park diving on Thursday. We were planning on contacting you anyway since they had your name on the sign in sheet but you saved us the trouble of hunting you down," the deputy said with a grin. "You scuba dive at Eddy Spring a lot?"

"I-I go there pretty regularly. I try to go at least twice a month."

"How long you been diving there, son?"

There he goes with the son again.

"Only a c-couple months, sir. I-I just did my scuba diving class in May and finished the checkout dives in June."

The deputy's smile disappeared and the discussion turned serious at this point. "Did you notice anything unusual at the park when you were there Thursday?"

Joey almost threw up again and had to swallow it back to keep from soiling the deputy's car. Although he had heard it wasn't uncommon for criminals to throw up back here as well as leave other fluids. Joey glanced around the backseat hoping to only see clean surfaces. At least the seat had a plastic lining on it that should be easy to wipe down.

Why was the deputy torturing him like this, Joey thought. Why didn't he just tell him he knew what he and Earl had done and get it over with? Arrest him and put the cuffs on and bring him to jail. Stringing him along like this was so much worse.

"I-I-I don't think so. I was the only scuba diver there but that was my first time at Eddy Spring during the week and I-I don't know if that's unusual or not."

"Did you notice any other cars parked there that day?"

Joey suddenly remembered he had noticed the truck parked on the other side of the fence. It must have belonged to the dead scuba diver. He wasn't sure if he should tell the deputy that he saw it or not. After a moment of thought Joey decided it couldn't hurt to say he saw it and he admitted to seeing the truck.

"Um, yeah, I think there was a truck parked on the grass on the other side of the fence."

The deputy quickly typed something into his laptop and continued. "Did you see anyone around that truck at any time?

"N-no. B-but I wasn't really paying much attention to it either. I-I thought someone might already be scuba diving but I didn't see anyone in the basin and I forgot all about it after that." That was good. Technically Joey wasn't lying since he didn't see anyone else in the basin, only in the cave.

"So you were the only scuba diver there on Thursday. Are you sure you didn't see anyone else walking around or maybe scuba diving in the basin or the cave?"

"N-no sir. I-I'm positive there was no one else in the basin and I'm only open water certified and not allowed to go in the cave," Joey made his mind up to lie on this point about going in the cave. There was no one else in the water that day and the only person that knew he had been in the cave was Earl. He was hoping Earl hadn't said anything. For all he knew Earl hadn't even been back to Eddy Spring since Joey dropped him off yesterday morning. Either way it was too late. He had already committed himself to the lie.

"So you didn't go anywhere but in the basin? You didn't even peek into the cave?" the deputy asked suspiciously..

"N-no, sir. I was just in the basin. I-I bought some used gear last week and I was trying it out for the first time." Joey offered.

"How about any scuba diving equipment? You notice any equipment laying around anywhere, either in the water or around the park?" the deputy continued his interrogation.

Joey thought about this. He did see those two scuba tanks clipped to the air box. Should he tell the deputy? He didn't see any harm in that and if they already had scuba divers in the water looking for a body they probably already saw the scuba tanks anyway. "C-c-come to think of it, I did see a couple of scuba tanks clipped off to the air box down there. I-I thought they belonged to the guy who fills the air box every day."

"That's good. That helps us out quite a bit." The deputy seemed to relax a little once Joey had offered some useful information. "Do you remember what time it was when you saw those?"

"Th-they were there when I did my first dive Thursday morning. Th-that was around 9 o'clock." Joey wondered why that mattered. Every diver had to sign liability release forms and the sign-in sheet in the dive shop before getting in the water. And, from what he understood, the dive shop had the only keys to the lock on the grate so anyone going in the cave would have had to sign a key out at the shop. Didn't they have all that paperwork already?

Suddenly Joey again remembered the truck that was parked on the other side of the fence. Anyone who parked over there had bypassed the shop and not signed any forms. So they wouldn't be able to sign out a key either. He remembered Earl had even told him the only two keys were still in the shop. So how had the dead scuba diver gotten past the grate without a key? His thoughts were interrupted by the deputy.

"Is there anything else you can think of that you might have seen that looked unusual?"

"N-n-no sir. Other than being the only scuba diver there. That was the first time I-I've been at Eddy Spring without seeing any other divers around."

"Alrighty then. That's all the questions I have for you. Lemme see your driver's license so I can put your contact info in my report. If we need anything else, myself or one of the detectives on the case will get in touch with you."

Joey squirmed around in the back seat to try to get to his wallet. After a brief struggle he had his wallet in his hand and pulled his driver's license out of it. He handed the driver's license to the deputy through a slot in the grate separating the front and back seats of the cruiser, making sure to keep his palm facing down away from him. The deputy dug out a small scanner from the pile on the front passenger seat and inserted the driver's license into it. The license fed through and the image appeared on the screen of the deputy's laptop. The deputy pulled Joey's license out of the other side of the scanner and handed it back to Joey through the same slot. "I'll also need a number to get in touch with you. A cell phone would work best."

The deputy typed the cell number into his laptop as Joey recited it for him. The deputy quickly typed some more things into the laptop that Joey couldn't make out and then opened the driver's door. Joey reached for the door handle on the door next to him but it was missing. The door and window handles had both been removed. He sat there and waited as the deputy stepped out and around to the door next to Joey and opened it for him.

Joey carefully unfolded his cramped legs and stepped out of the back seat almost falling to the ground. The muscles in his legs screamed out in protest at having to be used again after being tortured in the cramped quarters of the back seat of the cruiser. It felt worse after having sat back there for the past 20 minutes or so. Joey started to worry that the deputy would notice and suspect something

The deputy did notice Joey stumbling and made a comment as Joey feared he might. "Sorry about that. It's pretty cramped back there. I wish we had a better setup, especially when I'm just interviewing witnesses."

Joey was relieved the deputy hadn't thought it was anything more than from being cramped. "Th-that's okay. I understand.

I-I suppose you don't want criminals to be too comfortable back there anyway." Joey said with a slight grin.

The deputy smiled back and said, "I can't say I'm too concerned about their comfort. Anyway, thanks again for your cooperation." The deputy reached out his hand to shake Joey's. Joey quickly wiped his palm on his shorts to dry any sweat that was on it before shaking the deputy's hand and instantly felt a sharp pain shoot from his palm up his arm. He winced a little and carefully held his hand out with the palm slightly down hoping the deputy hadn't noticed. The deputy grabbed his hand and squeezed it firmly while shaking it up and down a couple times. Joey did his best to keep a straight face and not let the pain he was feeling from the deputy grabbing his hand show. The deputy reached into his chest pocket, pulled out a business card and handed it to Joey.

"Give me a call if you remember anything else unusual about the other day. Otherwise we'll be getting in touch if anything else comes up."

Joey walked back to his car as quickly as his sore legs would allow and slid into the driver's seat. His hand was really hurting from the deputy grabbing it so firmly. He was feeling nauseated all over again but this time it was from pain rather than anxiety. He inserted the key into the ignition and sat there for a minute before turning it to start the engine. The pain wasn't subsiding yet and Joey was afraid the deputy would walk back up to see why he was still parked there so he started the car and shifted it into drive. He checked his rearview and side mirrors to make sure the road was clear and slowly pulled out into the lane. Joey drove past interstate 10, past the couple of gas stations and the motel on the left side of the road south of the highway and continued south toward Morrison Spring.

There wasn't much beyond the motel except an occasional house among the trees. A few minutes later Joey saw a wooden sign with a faded scuba diving flag painted on it and the words "Morrison Spring" in a faded white paint with an arrow underneath them pointing to the left. Joey took the next left and continued along a narrow tree lined windy road. A couple miles later he saw another sign with "Morrison Spring" and an arrow pointing to the right. He followed it onto a road named Morrison Spring Road and continued past a few mobile homes and farm fields until he came to where the road ended in a parking lot. There were cars and people everywhere. This was a big difference from the way Eddy Spring had been just two days earlier. He wondered if it was like this because Eddy was closed or because Morrison was always like this.

Joey saw scuba divers setting up gear behind their cars and trucks, scuba divers walking to and from the water on the other side of the parking lot, and a lot of guys walking around shirtless in swim trunks and girls walking around in skimpy bikinis. This might not be so bad after all, Joey thought to himself.

18

Joey saw the white backup lights on a car turn on ahead and to the left. He carefully guided his car around the flock of people scattered about in the parking lot and those in various stages of setting up or tearing down scuba diving gear. He stopped with his left blinker on a couple dozen feet from the soon to be vacated parking space.

After parking his car, he walked along the sidewalk toward the water. Joey was impressed with what they had done with the park. There was a scuba rinse station next to the parking lot with a bench just tall enough for a scuba diver with a BC and scuba tank to back up against and set the tank on for easy removal. At one end of the bench was a PVC pipe with a shower head at the top and a hose coming out a couple feet up from the boardwalk where the rinse station was located.

Continuing down the boardwalk Joey noted a large pavilion with several rectangular green metal picnic tables with attached benches and a couple of round shiny silver colored metal tables with attached stools. About a dozen divers were standing and sitting around the tables working on their scuba equipment. One table had a few plastic tubs with some scuba gear on it but no one nearby that seemed to claim it. The divers must be in the water. Joey thought it was cool that they could leave their equipment there and not have to worry about anyone taking it. He also thought it was cool how here at Morrison the various groups of scuba divers all blended together rather than being in their own cliques. He attributed that to the land area around Morrison being smaller than at Eddy but it seemed to encourage more camaraderie among the scuba divers.

There was a set of stairs with about a dozen steps leading down to a sandy beach about eight feet below the level of the pavilion. The small beach was packed with people sitting in beach chairs, laying out on beach blankets, having picnics, or just sitting around more of the round metal tables that were located on the sand. A couple of those round tables were even set in the water and people were keeping cool by sitting on the attached stools that were just under the water's surface.

Unlike Eddy Spring the sandy beach at Morrison gently sloped into the water and there were people keeping cool while standing throughout the shallows with the water at waist level. At Eddy Spring, most of the area just off the shoreline was too deep to stand in.

There was also a boardwalk to the left of the beach at the same level as the pavilion. It started next to the gear rinsing station near the parking lot and continued adjacent to the beach about eight feet above the sand until it split off in two directions. Straight ahead it continued over the beach and then around to the right and down several steps leading to the sand. The water level was high enough that the bottom couple of steps were submerged. To the left, the boardwalk continued over the water among the plentiful tall cypress trees that grew out of the water. The trees provided a nice cool shade for the people hanging out along the edges of the boardwalk and leaning against the rail looking down below them at the clear shallow water.

Joey had to weave his way through several people standing on the boardwalk looking out to the water and up into the cypress trees. Several swimmers were climbing up on the railing and then up some wooden planks that had been nailed to the side of one of the taller cypress trees. There was a branch large enough to hold a small person's weight about twenty feet above the water. These people were climbing up the side of the tree, stepping onto the branch and stepping out about arm's length from the trunk. They would then jump down into the cool clear water below. Joey watched as someone jumped off the branch and dropped down quickly into the water with a giant splash. The water was so clear Joey could see the jumper drop through the water and hit the bottom with his feet. He bent his knees and then popped back up to the surface. Joey thought that was crazy. The water wasn't nearly deep enough for people to be jumping into it from that height and someone was bound to get hurt. It seemed none of them had thought that through.

Continuing on past the crazy tree jumpers, Joey saw another scuba diving station at the end of this boardwalk. This wasn't a rinse station but rather a set up area. There was a tall bench on the right about the same height as the rinse station where scuba divers could place their BCs and scuba tanks and back up against to put them on easily. Whoever designed this had even included scuba tank holders like the ones he'd seen on dive boats down at the marina.

On the left was a shorter bench where divers could sit and put their fins on. At the end of this area was a metal ramp leading down to a floating metal dock. The floating dock was anchored to a couple of large metal posts and it slid up and down along those with the change in the water level. Joey could tell the metal ramp would also change its slope depending on the water level in the basin. Maybe that's what was meant about Morrison getting flooded. Apparently, the water level changed frequently enough that they had to designed the boardwalk to deal with the changes.

Across the basin from the boardwalk was another floating dock. This one appeared to be chained to some anchor weights in the water. There was no boardwalk leading to it so the only way to get on it was by swimming to it. There were about fifteen or twenty people from young kids to teenagers and even some in their twenties standing on it. Some of the teenage boys were laughing and running back and forth on the small dock and causing it to rock as they shifted their weight from one end of the dock to the other. This was causing some of the girls standing near the edges to scream out as they tried to maintain their balance and keep from falling into the water. Every now and then one of them would fall in, usually assisted by a push from one of her friends, and shriek from the shock of the cold water against her skin.

Joey looked around the basin and saw three red and white diver down flags floating on the surface indicating scuba divers were below. He could see a large hole underwater in the center that disappeared among thousands of scuba bubbles that were rising out from it. He could barely make out a long tree trunk that looked like it was precariously balanced on the rim of the bowl from one end to the other. The trunk dissected the bowl so it was about one-third to one side and two-thirds to the other. Some people had also pulled their boats into the basin and anchored them along the shoreline. People were just relaxing on the boats drinking beer. Others were floating around the boats enjoying the cool clear water.

Overall, it looked like a really fun place. Joey wished he had visited sooner. And he really wished he had a scuba tank so he could go explore the basin underwater with all the other scuba divers and maybe even take a peek into the cavern. Instead Joey returned to his car to retrieve his mask, snorkel, and fins so he could at least swim around on the surface and check out the basin from there. Just from what he could see while standing on the floating dock the visibility was great, even with this many people in it. That was rarely the case at Eddy Spring on the weekends, probably because there were always a lot more scuba divers there. Joey knew he'd be able to get a better look at what was in the basin once he got in the water with a mask on.

* * *

Back at the floating dock at the end of the ramp with his snorkeling gear in hand, the events of the past 48 hours temporarily forgotten, Joey prepared to jump into the clear refreshing water and cool off. He lowered himself down and sat on the edge of the dock with his feet dangling in the water. The metal surface of the dock felt hot against his bottom and the back of his thighs but the cool water on his feet and ankles felt really good. He leaned over and pulled his scuba fins on over his feet and brought the mask with the snorkel clipped to the strap down over his face. Reaching around with his right hand he grabbed the smooth hand rail of the ladder that was to his left. He felt a sting on his palm from the scrapes and quickly pulled his hand back causing him to lose his balance. His body rotated and he fell into the water.

His entry didn't end up being quite as graceful as he wanted. He hit the water hard causing a huge splash that sprayed everyone standing on the dock within ten feet. Joey sheepishly looked up at the half dozen or so people standing on the dock and murmured a sorry before turning away from them and quickly swimming in the opposite direction of the dock toward the middle of the basin. The initial sting of his hands hitting the water was gone and the cool water actually felt good on his palms and his sore muscles. As he swam along the water's smooth flat surface he placed the mouthpiece of the snorkel into his mouth and lowered his face into the water. Joey was once again instantly amazed at the clarity of the water in the Morrison Spring basin. He looked around the basin and took in the vast scene below him.

To his right was a wooden dock anchored in the sand with the surface of it probably two or three feet above the bottom and about fifteen feet below the surface. There was a class of scuba divers on each end kneeling in semi-circles facing other divers who were probably their instructors. It looked to Joey like they were doing skills for their open water scuba certification. There were about a dozen divers total on the platform and room for more.

At the farthest corner of the platform from where Joey was a thick rope was tied to it. The rope lead away from it along the gently sloping sandy bottom toward the center of the basin where it appeared to be tied around one of the ends of the tree trunk that dissected the top of the bowl. Joey followed the line from 15 feet above toward the bowl where he saw several more scuba divers, too many for him to count, all over the place. Three of the scuba divers were straddling the large tree trunk holding onto it with their legs.

He saw a skinny teenager wearing just a wetsuit, a set of really long fins, and a mask and snorkel on one end of the tree trunk also straddling it and carving something into the bark with a long dive knife. A few seconds later the skinny teenager put the knife into a sheath strapped onto the lower part of his left leg, swam to the surface, took some breaths, and headed back down to the log where he pulled the knife out to continue his carving. Joey floated on the surface and watched him do this over and over while he continued to carve letters into the bark. He envied him for being able to swim so far underwater while holding his breath and stay there for as long as he did.

Positioned just above where the rope wrapped around the trunk and the edge of the basin closest to the beach entrance Joey could tell the tree log was deeper than the platform by at least ten feet. That would put it at about 25 feet deep. And the teenager was spending at least 30 seconds straddling the log and carving it with that dive knife. That was something else on Joey's list of scuba gear to buy. Joey thought the calf knife looked really cool but he didn't know how practical that would be for him. Not being in the best shape Joey didn't think he was flexible enough to be able to get to a knife strapped to his calf very easily.

Moving on, Joey tried to get a look down into the dark cave opening at the bottom of the bowl in the basin. The bowl was not symmetrical. The cave opening was on one side of the bowl and the bottom steeply sloped up from there out to the surrounding basin. Even the walls of the bowl were asymmetrical. It looked more like a lopsided funnel than a bowl.

His eyes followed the slope of the bowl to the dark opening positioned under the wall to his right. Joey swam to his left so he could try to get a more direct look down into the opening. When he reached the top of the slope he turned around and looked toward the dark opening. He could just make out a white rectangular sign like the one inside the Eddy Spring cavern but there were so many bubbles coming out of the cave that Joey couldn't tell for certain.

From this vantage point Joey had a better view of the side of the bowl he had been floating over, the one closest to the beach. It was more of a wall. The wall rose from above the dark opening almost straight up to the rim of the bowl 25 feet below the surface. In that wall was another cave opening that was shaped similar to an hour glass and was much larger than the one at the very bottom.

Joey scanned the bowl and his gaze followed the sloping floor down to where it disappeared into the dark opening and the cave beyond. He started kicking his fins to swim around the bowl and get a better view of the shallower cave opening. When he was over the far end of the tree log he used his hands to turn himself around and he could almost see directly into the large hour glass opening. Joey saw a couple of divers in the top part of the hour glass heading deeper into the cave. A shudder suddenly moved through his body as he thought about finding the dead scuba diver in Eddy Spring a couple days earlier.

Joey started kicking his fins again so he could swim around the basin and check out the rest of it. It got shallow pretty quickly once at the top of the bowl. The farther away he got from the bowl in the center the shallower it got. There were areas where Joey could stand up. He tried that at one point and felt the soft mushy bottom underneath his fins and feet. He quickly stuck his mask in the water and saw a huge cloud of muck and silt bursting up toward him from the bottom. It was so thick he couldn't even see his fins. He pulled his feet up and put himself into a floating position on the surface as soon as he saw what he had done and started kicking away from the area. The water was so clear Joey didn't want to be the one who silted it up and ruined the visibility for everyone else.

He continued to snorkel around the basin but kept coming back to the bowl and the opening to the caves. Joey really wished he had a scuba tank so he could go underwater and check out the openings down there more closely. He had heard that Morrison was an easy dive. Lots of open water divers went diving in the Morrison cavern without having any problems. Joey had been in a really bad silt out in the Eddy Spring cave, twice! And he still made it out alive. Morrison should be a piece of cake.

Speaking of cake, Joey felt his stomach start to grumble. It was probably getting close to lunch time. Unfortunately, he had stomped out of the house in a huff so quickly this morning because his mother had started in on him so early and he forgot to grab something to eat for lunch. There was a sub shop right off the interstate, Joey thought, and since he wasn't going to be renting a tank or getting any air fills today he had enough money to get something to eat.

Joey turned toward the beach. He swam over the platform where the classes were still doing their open water skills and felt the rush of exhaust bubbles tickling the skin on his belly and legs as they detoured around him quickly rising to the surface. He continued to watch the bottom slope up toward him and the surface. The sand below him was such a pure white it was almost blinding. Occasionally there would be a dark cypress root that stuck out in a sharp contrast to the white sand. One of the roots looked like a large dark brown lizard laying on the bottom. Joey had to look twice to make sure it wasn't a lizard. He was in such awe at the beauty of the sand that he didn't notice the crowd of people surrounding him. He had reached the shallow area just off the beach where everyone was standing waist deep to stay cool on the hot August morning.

Bumping his head on something Joey popped his face up out of the water and saw a smooth bikinied hip directly in front of him. Quickly dropping his knees down to the sand beneath him he anchored himself so he could lift his face out of the water and apologize and make sure he hadn't hurt anyone. As he pulled his mask off he noticed who the hip belonged to. It was the cute blond girl from the dive shop where he did his open water class. *How embarrassing!*

19

It had been a couple of months since Joey had last seen her. It wasn't that he didn't want to see her but he couldn't keep returning to the dive shop without an excuse. After the embarrassment of not being able to pay for his mask, fins, and snorkel the first night of class Joey had returned the following day but she had been helping another customer so Joey dealt with the shop owner instead. He returned to the shop a couple times after finishing his class and getting his scuba certification card but since he couldn't afford new gear he never bought anything.

He would enter the shop and look at the gear and she always came over to him immediately and asked if he needed any help. Joey would ask some questions but always got tongue tied in front of her. The last time he was there he couldn't even think of anything to ask so he told her he was just looking. She went back to restocking the displays and Joey slipped out the door quietly.

Now here she was standing in front of him and all she had on was a bikini. Joey realized he was staring at her bikini, and her body, and quickly averted his eyes hoping she hadn't noticed. He looked back at her making sure to keep his eyes on her face. She stood there with a huge pearly white smile.

"Hey! Joey, right?"

"Uh, u-um, yeah. H-how are you?" *How are you?? How are you??? What kind of greeting was that?* thought Joey.

"I'm fine. You remember me, doncha? Lindsey Carter, from the dive shop."

Joey stood there for a minute just thinking about her voice and that cute southern accent. Lots of people in the Florida panhandle spoke with a southern accent, actually more of what some would describe as a redneck accent, the panhandle coast was known as the Redneck Riviera after all. Lindsey had more of a southern belle accent, which practically made Joey melt right in front of her.

"Y-yeah, I remember you, Lindsey. Of course I remember you!"

"How ya been? I haven't seen ya in the shop in a couple months. Still scuba diving?" Lindsey asked.

"Uh, yeah, I'm still diving. I-I was supposed to be diving today but Eddy Spring is closed and I don't have my own tank." Joey couldn't believe it. That was the most he had said to Lindsey in one breath.

"Eddy is closed?!?" Lindsey exclaimed with a shocked look on her face. "What's going on? They're never closed."

"Uh, they s-said a scuba diver is missing and they have s-search teams in there l-looking for him." Joey's nervousness was increasing the longer he stood in front of Lindsey and talked to her. He kept trying to look at her eyes or away from her but it wasn't very easy.

"Wow! I can't remember ever hearing of someone dying

there!" Lindsey said, the corners of her mouth turned down into a frown. Joey suddenly became even more nervous. He hadn't said anything about anyone dying. He just said the scuba diver was missing. What made her think a diver was dead?

"U-Um, I don't know if anyone is d-d-dead. They just said s-someone was m-missing," Joey stammered as he looked away from her.

"Oh, well sweetie, if there's a diver missing at a cave diving site then I'm sorry to say he's probably dead. That's usually why they're missing," Lindsey explained. "I hope his dive buddy is okay. That's gotta be tough. Oh, and his poor family. They must be devastated!"

"I-I don't know. Th-they wouldn't even let me in when I got there this morning. So I d-decided to come check out M-Morrison. This is my first time here."

"Oh, it's really beautiful here, isn't it sweetie? This is one of my favorite places to come on hot summer days. I usually come out here and do a couple of dives in the spring but my dive buddy stood me up today so I'm just hanging out with some friends and enjoying the water."

Lindsey pointed to a couple of other girls lying on towels on the sandy beach sunning themselves.

"Hey, wait a minute! Did you ever buy any scuba gear? I have a couple of tanks from the shop and I'd love to get a dive in."

Joey couldn't believe it. Lindsey was asking him if he wanted to scuba dive with her. "Um, y-yeah, I-I bought some used gear about a week ago. I-I wanted to get new stuff but I couldn't afford it." Joey said sheepishly as he looked down at the water embarrassed.

Lindsey looked around, then leaned in toward Joey and in a low whisper said, "Oh, I know it. Scuba diving gear is so expensive. I don't know how they expect anyone to buy gear with such high prices. I had to get a job at the dive shop just so I could get a discount and afford to get my own gear."

Joey could feel her sweet warm breath against his ear. He could feel the hair on the back of his neck stand up and goose bumps form on his arms. He practically melted into the water in front of her.

She pulled away and said in a louder voice, "Well, let's go get our gear and those tanks and go check out the beautiful cavern here. You're not going to believe how amazing it is in there."

* * *

Half an hour later Joey and Lindsey had their scuba gear set up and were walking back toward the water along the boardwalk. Joey took a little longer than Lindsey setting up his gear but he gave her the excuse of not being completely familiar with the new gear. In reality Joey was going through a mental checklist of everything he had to do to make sure he didn't forget anything and look like a fool in front of her. With all the times he had recently forgotten his weight belt and looked foolish in front of Earl, he didn't want to leave Lindsey with a bad impression of him. And the walk back from the water at Morrison to his car was a lot farther than it was at Eddy Spring!

"Do you want to walk in on the beach or jump in off the

dock?" Lindsey asked as they approached the split in the boardwalk.

"Let's jump in," replied Joey. "It l-looks easier than having to c-climb down those steps and walk through the sand, especially with all the p-people on the beach and in the shallows."

"Good point! It's a busy day here today. There's almost no room to walk on the beach."

They got to the scuba bench and Lindsey backed against it to rest her scuba tank on it and get the weight off her shoulders. Joey did the same next to her. He looked over at Lindsey but had to look away quickly. She was wearing a shorty wetsuit and even though that was not as revealing as the bikini she wore underneath it, the wetsuit was snug so he could still make out the shape and curves of her body.

He couldn't believe he was about to go on a dive with Lindsey. She had always been nice to him but girls like her usually didn't hang out with guys like him. He suddenly became very self-conscious. *I need to lose weight,* he thought to himself. This dive might not mean much to Lindsey but she was really friendly and Joey was enjoying it and hoping he could spend more time with her, even if just as friends.

Lindsey interrupted Joey's thoughts. "Let's do our buddy check up here. It'll be easier with the tanks leaning on this bench."

Joey nodded in agreement.

Lindsey started going through the buddy check which Joey remembered learning in his class. He had been pretty good about doing it for the first several dives after he finished class but he was diving with the same people every weekend and they just stopped doing it because it was the same every time. And over the past week he had been diving alone so there was no need to do a buddy check. Although, Joey thought, he would have saved himself the weight belt embarrassment had he gone through the check with himself before heading to the water.

They finished their checklist and everything was in order. Joey had even remembered to put new batteries in his dive light the day before. He wasn't sure why he did that because he had no interest in going back into the Eddy Spring cave but he was happy he did because Morrison Spring sounded really cool. Lindsey had told Joey about the Morrison cavern as they were setting up their gear.

She told him the story about the sheriff having explosives set off in there and causing part of the passage to collapse. Even though Joey had heard it before he loved listening to Lindsey's sweet southern belle accent and let her tell the story as if he hadn't heard it before. What Joey didn't know was that before the explosives were set the cave had been explored and was known to be pretty deep.

Sheck Exley, someone who many cave divers considered the founder of cave diver training, had done some dives in there and gone to over 200 feet deep before the passage was blown up. He had even drawn a map of the cave. Lindsey told Joey there was a lot of water pumping out of the Morrison Spring. It was so much that it was nearly impossible to silt it out. But it was also difficult to get in because all of that water was flowing out of the small entrance. Once inside though it was easy to get out of the water flow and just enjoy the beauty of the cavern.

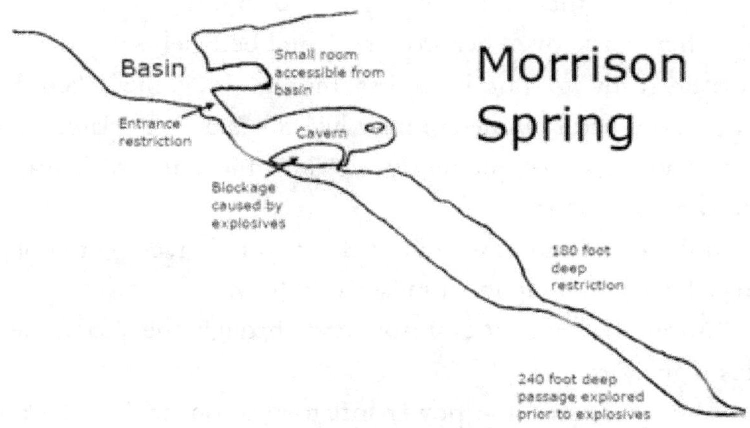

Joey couldn't wait to see it for himself.

They walked down the ramp to the floating dock and stood next to each other near the edge. Lindsey put a hand on Joey's arm to steady herself while she pulled one of her fins onto her foot. Once again, Joey could feel goose bumps pop up all over his skin and the hair on the back of his neck start to tingle. Lindsey turned around and held onto Joey with her other hand and pulled her other fin on. She turned back to face the water, held out her right arm and said, "Okay, your turn."

Joey faced away from the water and reached out and touched Lindsey's right forearm gently with his right hand. Her tan skin felt so smooth and soft under his palm. He hoped she couldn't feel the roughness of the scabs that were beginning to form on his palms. He pulled his right fin on and turned to face the water. He held onto Lindsey's arm with his other hand while pulling his other fin on.

Finished donning their fins they stood on the edge with the paddle part of their fins sticking out over the water. Lindsey pulled her mask over her eyes and grabbed her second stage regulator ready to put it in her mouth. Joey mimicked her motions. He hadn't done an entry like this since his class. Eddy Spring had steps descending directly into the water so it wasn't necessary to jump in.

"I'll go first and move out of the way and give you the okay signal. Then you jump in." Lindsey told Joey.

"Mmm-hmmm," Joey responded through the mouthpiece in his regulator..

Lindsey pressed the power inflator button on her BC and filled it with air. She then placed her hand in front of her face to hold her mask and regulator in place. She gracefully dropped into the water barely making a splash. Her head dropped underwater a couple of feet and she popped to the surface, turned around, and signaled Joey with a big okay signal she made with her left arm over her head. Joey waited for her to back away from the dock a bit before doing anything.

He followed the same steps as Lindsey had before she stepped in. He inflated his BC with air, put a slight pressure on his mask and regulator, and stepped off the dock. He also went underwater a couple of feet. When he popped back up to the surface he could see everyone that was on the dock backed up with their arms stretched out in front of them. Apparently Joey had caused another big splash when he jumped in. Not quite as graceful as Lindsey.

Joey looked around and found Lindsey a few feet away from him floating at the surface. He kicked his feet and paddled with his hands to get closer to her. Her blond hair was plastered to her head with the ends stretched out along the surface of the water around her. He could see her bright blue eyes jump out at him from behind the lens of the scuba mask. Even in a scuba mask with her hair wet she looked beautiful.

"Ya ready?" Lindsey pulled him out of his daydreams again.

"Sure."

"Follow me and make sure to stay close. When we get to the grim reaper sign you want to let the air out of your BC and get negatively buoyant 'cuz the water flow right there is pretty high. If you're not negative it'll just blow you out of there." Lindsey explained.

Joey nodded as she explained the entry technique but he was still thinking about how she had told him to stay close to her.

"Let's go," Lindsey said as she grabbed her scuba regulator and placed it in her mouth. She then raised her BC inflator hose and depressed the exhaust button. As she dropped under the surface Joey watched her hair rise up above her head and remain on the surface briefly until it was yanked down into the water after her. Joey grabbed his own scuba regulator and once again mimicked Lindsey's actions. He was soon underwater beside her.

Joey descended through the water and followed Lindsey as she placed herself in a horizontal position and started swimming toward the entrance to the cavern. Joey watched her in awe. Most of the divers here were swimming around in an upright position moving like they were riding bicycles. Lindsey was the only one that was swimming like she was flying through the water. She was also doing a strange kick. Her knees were bent and she was almost clapping the bottoms of her fins together rather than keeping her legs straight and doing the flutter kick he had been taught in class. He would have to remember to ask her about that kick after the dive. Joey tried to get into the same position as Lindsey but it was difficult for him to stay like that. No matter how hard he tried, his feet kept sinking below him. He'd have to ask her about that too.

They swam past some divers who had just come out of the cavern. They were all vertical and kicking up the sand on the bottom. Joey watched the sand swirl around and settle a few feet away higher up on the sloped bottom. The water flow was keeping the visibility pretty good in here even with everyone kicking the sand up. Joey was relieved by that. He had his fill of silt already. He saw the white sign that he had seen earlier from the surface. It was located under a wall and on a ledge just over the entrance. It looked identical to the one in the Eddy Spring cavern. That sent a shiver up his spine.

Looking down at the entrance he could see particles of sand swirling around like they were in a blender. *Was that the flow doing that?* he thought. As Lindsey approached the edge he saw her reach back and pull on the string of the exhaust valve on the bottom rear of her BC and saw several bubbles rush madly out of the valve and up at an angle away from her. She grabbed a large rock on the bottom with both hands and disappeared over the edge. Joey thought back to the instructions Lindsey had given him. She had said something about the BC inflator and the water flow. They were going deeper and usually that meant putting air in the BC to compensate for the increased depth. But he had just seen Lindsey let air *out* of her BC. Maybe she had inflated too much and reached back to let some out.

Joey grabbed his inflator as he approached the edge Lindsey had disappeared over and pressed the inflate button. He reached down to the same rock Lindsey had grabbed but it was getting farther away from him. Joey was going up not down like he wanted. As he ascended he caught a glimpse of Lindsey's golden blond hair splayed out away from her head which was peeking out from behind another ledge. He reached back to find his exhaust valve and dump air from his BC before he got too far out of control. Luckily, he found it right away and yanked on it. He felt the bubbles caress his hand as they rushed out. He held onto the string until all the air was out of his BC and waited to start descending but that never happened. He was still ascending. The flow was pushing him away from the cavern entrance and up the slope of the bowl.

Reaching down with both hands Joey sank his hands into the sandy bottom and anchored himself. He could feel the coarse, grainy sand digging into his bruised palms but he held tight. He stopped his upward movement but felt his legs being pushed up above him. He kicked trying to get them down so he was at least horizontal. After several kicks he felt the sandy bottom under his feet. He pushed up with his hands to even out his body and came face to face with Lindsey.

20

They were close enough to kiss if they didn't both have scuba regulators in their mouths. That was the thought that had entered Joey's mind. He immediately pushed that thought out of his head as he realized Lindsey had just witnessed him losing control of himself.

Lindsey's hand popped up in front of his face with her thumb and index finger in a circle, the scuba hand signal for okay which could be used as a question or an answer. In this case, Lindsey was asking Joey if he was okay. He held up his right hand with the same signal letting her know he was, if only a little embarrassed. Alright, a lot embarrassed.

Lindsey then bent her index finger forward into what was the question mark signal and pointed to the cavern entrance. She did the question mark signal again and pointed up. She was asking him if he wanted to go in the cavern or end the dive. He had embarrassed himself enough and firmly pointed toward the cavern. He wasn't ready to end this dive just yet. Lindsey signaled okay again, this time as an affirmative, and turned to head toward the cavern entrance again.

This time Joey paid closer attention to the way Lindsey

negotiated the entrance. He noticed she never put air in her BC. She hadn't overinflated earlier and had to let air out of it. She had just let it out so she would be heavier in the water and allow that to help her get through the heavy current pouring out of the entrance.

As Lindsey disappeared over the edge a second time Joey reached back and let all the air out of his own BC and felt himself drop onto the sandy bottom. He reached down and dug his hands into the sand again, pulling himself toward the entrance. He reached the edge and looked down. About six feet below him was a flat hard limestone bottom with some rocks scattered around it. He could see pea-sized gravel rocks flying around in circles, as if they were in little tornadoes. He looked toward the right and saw Lindsey's fins disappear under the ledge into a horizontal slit leading into the darkness beyond. He pulled himself over the edge and down the wall to the floor below him. It felt like he was rock climbing, only upside down. Not that Joey had ever been rock climbing. But he imagined that's probably what it would have been like.

Once on the bottom he looked to the right and saw Lindsey waiting for him. She was holding onto another ledge. Her body was below it and her head was sticking up just above it. Her golden blond hair was streaming toward him framing her face and mask. He could stay there all day and just look at her. Except the current was trying to push him away from her and out of the cavern again. *This cavern really didn't want him in there,* Joey thought. He shoved his fingers inside a crack in the floor and pulled himself toward Lindsey and into the flow of water. Lindsey moved back and to the side to make room for Joey.

The entrance was wide and low at this point. As Joey pulled himself through he could feel the resistance easing off. His body was finally through the opening and inside a large room and Joey could barely feel the water movement anymore. He swam in a few feet and then pushed off the floor to turn and look for Lindsey. As he turned Lindsey appeared directly in front of him, again close enough to kiss, and Joey almost jumped out of his skin. He hadn't expect to see her right there. And he had to stop thinking about kissing her. They were just diving together. Joey was snapped out of his daydreaming once again when Lindsey waved for him to follow her. He made the okay signal and she turned around and swam deeper into the cavern.

Joey fumbled around for his dive light which he had clipped to his BC so he could use both hands to pull himself in through the entrance. He found it hanging below him from a D ring. He grabbed it and found the power switch. A dim yellow thin beam of light emitted from the bulb. Even with new batteries the light wasn't very bright. Joey had heard about new LED lights that were supposed to be really bright. He'd have to look into that soon.

Following Lindsey, Joey noticed she had a small light in her hand. It was much smaller than his own light. But it was also a lot brighter than his light It must have been one of those LED lights he had heard about. Lindsey pointed out several freshwater eels swimming around in the cavern along the floor. She approached one and pointed her light in its face. Joey held his breath as he waited for the eel to snap out and bite off one of Lindsey's thin, delicate fingers. The eel stopped swimming and appeared to look at the light, and Lindsey's fingers. Joey started swimming faster toward her to pull her, and her hand, away from the eel and its dangerous mouth full of sharp teeth. But before Joey got to her the eel turned and swam in a different direction, uninterested in Lindsey and her fingers.

Lindsey continued to swim around and light up different areas of the cavern. Joey did the same thing with his pitifully dim light. As he moved around the cavern he noticed he was about eighty feet deep and areas of the floor were still about a dozen feet below him. Being in the water with a ceiling over his head was deceiving. He would never have guessed he had descended eighty feet below the surface.

He saw more of that blender effect in one area of the floor. The small sand pieces looked like popcorn popping. Joey dropped down to take a closer look. As he got closer he could feel the water flow getting stronger. The water appeared to be coming out of the floor. Joey thought that was strange. There was no hole there. It was sand and gravel.

The floor where the water was coming from looked like it was moving. Joey placed his hand above it and felt a strong current of water pushing against it. Slowly he placed his palm against the floor and could feel the sand and gravel tickling it as it danced beneath his hand. He could feel a little bit of a sting where he had hurt his hands the day before but it wasn't as bad as it had been. He pushed his fingers into the sand and watched as his hand started to disappear into it. There *was* a hole in that sand! The water flow must be holding the sand up. He pushed his hand farther in but the sand and gravel was too dense and he couldn't push it any deeper than his wrist.

Joey looked around and noticed a huge rock next to the

area he was in. This must be part of the collapse from the explosives. Pulling his hand out of the floor he started swimming around the rock. He saw a small passage to the left that was below the huge boulder under the entrance to the cavern. As he got closer to it he suddenly felt himself being pushed up and to the side. He tried to stop himself but couldn't overcome the force. A few seconds later he felt himself being pushed against the wall located opposite the small passage. He quickly looked around and found Lindsey behind him watching him. *Not again!*

Pushing himself off the wall he swam toward Lindsey careful to avoid the passage with the strong flow of water coming out of it. As he got closer he could see about a dozen freshwater eel squirming around the floor just behind her. *Those things were everywhere down here!* He looked back toward the small passage that was blowing water out like a fire hose and could see how it curved around from his current vantage point.

Dropping to the floor, Joey grabbed at some big rocks with the tips of his fingers careful to not rub his injured palms against their hard sharp surfaces and carefully pulled himself closer to the passage. As he approached it he could feel the current getting stronger. There were rocks about the size of golf balls and baseballs on the floor in this area of the cavern and leading into the passage. Joey pointed his light down there. He could feel the water flow pushing the big light back into his hand. He watched the passage bend away to the right and out of sight. He tried to pull himself in a little farther to see where this passage went but felt the scuba tank on his back hit the rock above him. The passage was too low for him to go any farther and he still couldn't see where it went. This was apparently also part of the collapse that happened back in the 1960s. Joey wondered what the cave looked like beyond this giant rock that covered the passage.

He felt something tug at one of his fins and almost screamed into his regulator. He pushed himself out of the small area he was in and turned around to find Lindsey giving him the okay signal again. He was okay. But a couple of seconds ago he thought one of the eels had grabbed his fin in its mouth and had flashbacks to his childhood memories of monsters under the bed. Joey signaled an okay signal.

Lindsey grabbed her submersible pressure gauge, pointed to it, and then gave Joey the question mark sign. Joey looked down at his pressure gauge and noticed he only had 800 psi left in his tank. *Wow! That went fast!* Looking at his depth gauge he looked for the deepest depth indicator. He had gone to ninety-five feet at one point. He turned back to Lindsey and gave her the thumbs up sign to end the dive and begin their ascent. He had only been in the cavern for seventeen minutes. He was going to have to figure out how he could stay longer on his dives. He was breathing through his air way too fast.

They began their ascent out of the cavern. Joey went first with Lindsey following behind. He tried to get her to go first so she wouldn't see him blunder his way out but she insisted he take the lead. He guessed she wanted to make sure he got out okay. He felt the current pushing him from behind as he was ascending. He looked around and noticed a large rope hanging in the middle of the cavern leading from the opening to the opposite wall. *How had he missed that before?* Grabbing the rope he slowed down his ascent and used it to ease himself out of the cavern. The rope was tied onto a chain near the entrance and the chain looked like it wrapped around a boulder the size of a car, the same boulder he had just been underneath attempting to see where the water flow was coming from. He wondered if someone had tried to pull the collapsed rocks out at some point and just left the chain behind.

A smaller rope was tied to the end of this rope and lead out of the cavern. Joey slowly continued to follow it, using it to control his speed. A couple times his hands slid along the rope and the feeling of the rope sliding over his scabbed palms caused them to sting again. Once he was through the low wide opening he discovered there was no more rope. He still had to get through the area that had pushed him out the first time. This wasn't going to be easy. And Lindsey was right behind him watching.

Joey slowly approached the limestone wall in front of him. This was the same wall he had "rock climbed" down to get in. It was only about four feet tall and then he'd be at the ledge above where the current had kicked him back earlier. He pulled himself up the wall carefully trying to anticipate when the current would grab him and flip him over the ledge above him and up the sandy slope. His hands reached over the ledge and he carefully pulled himself up so he could see just over it. As his eyes cleared the ledge Joey could see the small gravel swirling around in front of him. He pulled himself farther up. So far so good.

Suddenly the current grabbed his fins and he felt his legs rising up from below him. Joey held onto the ledge as tightly as he could and started kicking his feet to try to keep them down but that only propelled him feet up even faster. Still holding onto the ledge he felt his feet continue to rise behind and above him. Before he was flipped upside down Joey let go of the ledge and his body went flying up the slope away from the cavern. He tried to kick his feet down under his body to regain control but it was useless. The water current was too strong for him.

His upward motion was arrested by a crash into the top of the sandy slope where it merged into the limestone wall that surrounded the bowl leading to the cavern. Joey could see a big silt cloud forming around him as he disturbed the sandy bottom. Actually, obliterated would be a better description of what he did. Fortunately, it settled down and cleared quickly. Unfortunately, just as it was clearing Lindsey swam gracefully into view behind Joey. She easily and effortlessly came to a stop just above him and put her hand out in the okay sign again. Joey held his hand up and signaled he was okay. *How many times was this going to happen to me,* he thought. He regained control of himself and looked down at his pressure gauge to see how much air he had left – 400 psi. Not very much, and he still had a three minute safety stop to do.

He quickly shot Lindsey the thumb up sign to signal he was ready to end the dive and surface. He then began an ascent to the top edge of the bowl at twenty feet depth. Looking around the basin he focused in on the end of the tree trunk that had the rope tied around it and swam toward it. He followed the rope to the platform he had seen earlier when he was snorkeling and stopped just short of it. He looked at his pressure gauge again – just over 300 psi. He was at fifteen feet and had to stay there for three minutes to off gas the nitrogen that had built up in his body while he was ninety feet deep in the cavern.

Looking back he saw Lindsey following him along the rope. She stopped with him and they both remained there for three minutes. Joey concentrated on slowing his breathing so he could stretch the little remaining air in his tank out as long as possible. He took in a breath and held it until he couldn't any longer. Then he exhaled and held his breath as long as he could. He had been taught to never hold his breath underwater but he was concerned if he didn't he wouldn't have enough air to last the entire three minutes.

When they finally cleared their safety stop Lindsey swam around the platform toward the beach and Joey followed her. Joey stole a glance at his pressure gauge and saw he had about 100 psi left. *This was getting really close!* Just on the other side of the platform the bottom of the basin started getting shallow quickly. Joey could see the slope ahead. As they got to the top of the slope Joey looked at his depth gauge and saw he was only 7 feet deep. He glanced at his pressure gauge again – the needle was somewhere between 50 and 100 psi. He was beginning to question whether it was a good idea to join Lindsey on a dive. She probably wouldn't want to dive with him ever again.

At Eddy Spring he had never had problems like he had on this dive. There was a little water flow coming out of the Eddy Spring cave. Joey had felt it, but it wasn't nearly as bad as the current coming out of Morrison Spring. Could it also be that he was nervous diving with Lindsey? He knew he was, but that shouldn't make him such an awful diver.

They continued swimming along the white sandy bottom toward the beach. Joey saw the lizard looking thing in the bottom that he had seen earlier. He reached out to touch it. It was a large buried branch, or possibly a cypress tree root.. He glanced at his depth gauge again. They were four feet deep.

"Well that was so much fun! What did you think Joey? I just love that cavern. It's so beautiful." Lindsey exclaimed as they broke the surface and stood up.

"Th-that was beautiful. S-s-sorry about all the trouble I had in there. I-I'm not usually that b-bad."

"Oh sweetie, don't worry about it. You did great for your first time. The water flow coming out of Morrison can really mess a person up. I've seen divers come out of there upside down and crash into the other side of the bowl with their tanks. Next time I know you'll do better. You did better the second time going in."

Joey could feel his cheeks heating up. He was blushing. He didn't expect Lindsey to compliment him. She actually thought he did good. He was happy he had decided to let go when he did, otherwise he could have been one of those divers she just commented on.

"I-I didn't expect the water to be moving that fast. It's nothing like that at Eddy."

"No it's not. And Eddy isn't nearly as pretty either. I'd been to Eddy a bunch of times before I ever came here. After my first dive in Morrison I just knew I had to see more of the caves. Morrison is the reason I became a cave diver."

21

Joey couldn't believe what he had just heard. This young, pretty, petite blond standing in front of him was a cave diver?!? He thought cave divers were all big muscular, macho guys.

"Y-you're a cave diver?" Joey blurted out.

"Well, not a full-fledged cave diver yet. I took my cavern and intro cave diver classes. That means I can go beyond the daylight zone into the caves but I'm limited on how far I can go into the caves. Now I'm just saving up money so I can take my decompression diving classes and then finish the cave diver training. It takes a lot of time and a lot of money. Even with my shop discount it's expensive. I had to buy almost all new equipment for my intro cave class. At least now I have most of the gear. I just have to save up to buy a decompression cylinder and regulator so I can take the decompression diving classes."

"Wow! I'm really impressed. I would never have guessed you were a cave diver."

Lindsey tilted her head to the side as the corners of her mouth turned down into a frown. "Now why not? Don't ya think a girl can be a cave diver?" she asked as she fluttered her eyelashes.

"N-n-no! That's not what I meant." Joey stammered. "I just

meant, um, well…"

Lindsey's frown quickly reversed itself into a big smile. "I'm just teasing you sweetie. Not many people would guess that. Most cave divers tend to be men but that's changing. I know quite a few women who cave dive. What…"

Lindsey was interrupted by a couple of divers walking by them. One of them bumped into Joey and said, "Nice exit from the cavern."

They both started laughing loudly at Joey's expense. Joey tried to think of a response but he drew a blank. He had never been very good at coming up with retorts. But he didn't have to this time because Lindsey stepped right in.

"Well, aren't y'all precious," she said to them with a sarcastic tone.

"What do…." the other diver began to say.

"Why don't y'all quit being ugly? We were all new to diving at some time. Rather than being insulting how about offering up some helpful advice? Or are y'all too good for that?"

The divers looked at each other, dropped their chins to their chests and continued walking toward the beach. If they were dogs they would have had their tails between their legs.

Joey didn't know whether to be embarrassed or feel honored that Lindsey did what she did. She didn't even give him time to respond before she stepped in.

Lindsey turned back to Joey, "Don't pay no mind to people like that, sweetie. Most divers are friendly and helpful but occasionally you come across someone who thinks he's highfalutin. Just ignore those people. They aren't worth a minute of your time."

Then before Joey could respond to that Lindsey asked, "What are you doin' for lunch?"

That took Joey by surprise. "Um, I didn't have any plans. Actually, with Eddy Spring closed today I've just kind of been going with the flow."

As soon as the words came out of his mouth Joey realized how fitting they were after his experience on the dive they just did. Apparently, Lindsey thought the same because she let a giggle escape at that response.

She looked back toward the beach. Her two friends were still laying out on their towels on the sand.

"Well, those two don't look like they're going anywhere. You wanna head up the road to get something? There's a little restaurant just north of the interstate that's pretty good."

"S-sure! I wanted to ask you about the way you fin and how you keep your feet up off the bottom."

* * *

Later that night Joey lay in his bed recounting the events of the day. After what he had experienced the previous couple of days he couldn't believe he had the good fortune to run into Lindsey and not only go scuba diving with her but also have lunch with her. He wasn't sure if what they had was a date or not. He could only hope. He had been attracted to her since he first saw her at the dive shop three months earlier but didn't think he had a chance. Maybe he didn't and she was just being nice. She did jump right in and defend him against those bullies at Morrison. So maybe she really did like him.

After packing their scuba equipment into their cars Lindsey walked over to Joey's car. She wanted to ride to the restaurant together in his car. Joey had been so nervous he almost turned the wrong way a couple times. They finally got to the restaurant and went in for lunch. He had been careful to not order his usual amount of food. First, he wanted to be able to pay for Lindsey's lunch and he couldn't afford to do that if he ordered appetizers, a burger, and dessert. But he also didn't want to look like a glutton in front of Lindsey. He had been wanting to lose weight for some time. Now was as good a time as any to start.

They ate slowly and talked about scuba diving. Joey found out the fin kick Lindsey was doing was called the modified frog kick and it was the kick most often used in caves because it directed the movement of water caused by fin kicks back behind the diver rather than down into the silty bottom. Joey would have to try that kick next time.

Lindsey also gave him pointers on how to keep his feet up off the bottom. She told him he was positioning his scuba tank too low on the BC. This put most of the weight lower on his body and made him off balance. By placing the tank higher he could balance the weight on his body and be horizontal with very little effort. Joey couldn't wait to get back in the water and try out these new things he was learning from Lindsey.

When lunch was over Lindsey tried to pay for her lunch but Joey insisted he pay. He told her it was repayment for letting him use her scuba tank and diving with him and for sharing her knowledge with him. Her response had been, "Oh, alright sweetie, I guess that's fair."

He wished she had resisted a little more because he wasn't

sure whether it was a date or just repayment for using the tank. Either way, they had not only exchanged phone numbers and she had told him to give her a call anytime he wanted to go scuba diving, but they had also planned to meet again the next day. He couldn't wait to see Lindsey again and spend the day with her. Joey fell asleep with a smile on his face dreaming about diving with Lindsey.

22

August 7, 2011

The next morning Joey woke up with a startle. His mother knocked loudly on his bedroom door as she walked in holding the Sunday paper, a concerned and almost angry look on her face.

"Joseph, what do you know about this?" she said as she jabbed her finger at the headline at the top of the front page.

GRIM REAPER CLAIMS ANOTHER: DIVER MISSING FROM EDDY SPRING!

"I-I-I don't know anything, mom," Joey lied.

"It says here he went missing this week and they've been searching for his body all weekend. Weren't you diving there yesterday?"

"U-u-um, no." Joey stammered. He tried to clear the cobwebs from his head so he could think about how to respond before he got himself into trouble with his mother. This was not a good thing. She already didn't like that he had taken up scuba diving and then an article appears in the newspaper about a diver dying somewhere she knows Joey has been diving. And the day after he did his first of what he hoped would be many dives with Lindsey. "I-I went to Morrison Spring instead."

"Well, it says here this boy was last seen sometime Wednesday and he hasn't been seen since. They think he died in that cave at Eddy Spring but they can't find his body. You've done a lot of diving there, Joey. I don't think I want you going back to such a dangerous place anymore."

The cobwebs were suddenly clear and Joey sat straight up in his bed. "Mom, that's not fair. Eddy Spring is not a dangerous place. That's where I did my training dives for my open water class. Do you think instructors would take students there if it was so dangerous? Every weekend there are hundreds of people diving there without dying. They didn't even find the body so maybe he didn't die in there. You can't keep me from diving there just because of this one thing."

"You're right Joseph. Maybe you shouldn't dive at all anymore. It's too dangerous. I can't believe people go underwater so deep with only a small tank of oxygen on their backs. That just can't be safe."

"Mom, you can't do that. I really like scuba diving! And I've already spent a lot of money to learn how to scuba dive and get my certification card. I'm not even done paying you back and you're going to keep me from doing it?!?" Joey was almost in a panic. She couldn't do this to him. It wasn't even about the money but he couldn't tell her about Lindsey. That was not a subject he wanted to discuss with his mother. "Besides, I'm 19. I'm an adult and I can scuba dive if I want."

"Young man, you will do as your father and I say as long as

you live under this roof. I know you've spent a lot of money on this already but sometimes life's lessons are expensive. This just doesn't seem like a very safe activity, especially around those caves. I've heard of other people dying in caves. Those cave divers are crazy."

"Mom, I'm not a cave diver. I'm just an open water diver. That means I can always go straight up to the surface."

He was technically telling her the truth but Joey's past experiences in the Eddy Spring cave flashed in front of his mind's eyes. He thought back to being in the cloud of silt and hitting the ceiling on those dives. And then he thought about Lindsey telling him she was certified as an Intro Cave diver. He knew he would at least take a cavern diver class at some point, which meant he would still be able to see daylight from wherever he was in the cave. He really liked the cavern at Morrison Spring and wanted to see other caverns. But after what he'd experienced this past week he wanted to get trained properly so he could do it safely and without getting himself killed. For now, he couldn't even bring that up to his mother. He might never be able to tell her. She still didn't know about the used gear he had bought.

"We'll talk about it later, Joseph. This just upset me so much. Now get up and I'll fix you some breakfast."

She turned and exited the room just as quickly as she had entered. Joey lay in bed shaking his head and thinking about their encounter. That was close. And it probably wasn't over. He'd have to tread carefully around his mother when it came to his scuba diving.

* * *

Ten minutes later Joey was sitting at the kitchen table eating some pancakes and reading the article in the paper about the missing diver. According to the article one of the employees had reported an abandoned vehicle on the property Friday morning after arriving at work. Apparently, a couple hours after he had dropped Earl off on Friday and gone home to bed one of the employees at Eddy Spring must have arrived at work and noticed the truck Joey had seen on Thursday. According to the article the sheriff's office had checked the tag records and the person they were registered to hadn't signed in to dive the spring that week. The article stated one of the employees had noticed the truck there when they arrived Thursday morning but forgot about it until getting back to work Friday morning and seeing the truck hadn't moved from that location. The employee called the sheriff's office to report the truck.

The sheriff's office shut down Eddy Spring Scuba Park and called on a group of recovery cave divers to go search for the body. They had four different dive teams search the cave Friday and Saturday with no body found. The article said the recovery divers were putting their lives at risk to go back into the cave beyond the grate and look for the body. They had called off the search dives for the time being but they might try to get more teams in there at some point to continue looking for the body.

Thinking about that made Joey feel guilty but he didn't know how to get them to not risk their lives searching without crossing Earl and risking his own life. He also didn't know if they would lock him up or not if he told them he found the body and helped Earl get rid of it.

There wasn't much else in the article. After being closed all day Friday and Saturday, the scuba park was reopening that morning. Although Joey doubted there would be many people there. Most instructors planned on being at the park the whole weekend with their students. If they couldn't dive Saturday, or even camp out there Friday and Saturday like they usually did, they would probably go somewhere else.

Joey thought about this. Earl wanted to dispose of the body quietly so no one would find out a diver had died at Eddy Spring and have it affect business. He hadn't considered someone reporting the truck. In his haste to get the body out and get rid of it he had forgotten about it being parked on the other side of the fence.

Joey wondered what Earl was thinking. He had told Joey, "I cant'ave no'un find'in dat body in thar. It'd be bad fer bizness. People'd be a'scared t'come dive heah."

Well, now, not only had the place been closed all day Friday and Saturday, two of the busiest days of the week for the scuba park, but the story of an abandoned truck and no body found was the headline in the local paper. It was also bound to be a hot topic on the internet groups dedicated to scuba diving. At least if the body had been found and retrieved people would only know someone died there. But now divers might not go there because they would be afraid of coming across a dead body while they were diving.

Earl's plan had completely backfired on him. Well, Joey didn't feel sorry for him. However, he did find himself worrying about how Earl would respond to this and what it might mean for Joey.

* * *

After breakfast, Joey dressed and left to meet Lindsey. While they were talking at lunch the day before, he had mentioned never having done a salt water dive. Lindsey suggested they head to Panama City Beach the next day and do a dive at the St. Andrews Jetty.

"The tide schedule is perfect to do an early afternoon dive there sweetie. You need to see what it's like to dive in the ocean. I like diving the springs and all but you can't see damsels and sea stars and grouper in fresh water. Can you make it? Are you free tomorrow sweetie?"

Joey couldn't believe Lindsey was asking him to dive with her again. Even if he had other plans he would have broken them just to spend more time with her.

Since Joey had never been to the St. Andrews State Park they planned to meet at the entrance to the park at 10:30 in the morning so he could follow her to the dive site. He looked at the clock on the wall – 8:33. He still had time. It would take about an hour and a half to drive there. It should take less but it was a summer Sunday morning and the beach traffic would be horrible.

By 9 he was dressed and heading out the door.

"Joey, where are you going? You're not going back to that spring today, are you?" his mom interrogated.

"No mom, I'm heading to the beach. I'm meeting a friend there."

"The beach? You don't usually go to the beach. What friend are you meeting there?"

"Just someone I met a few months ago and saw again yesterday. No one you know. I'll see you later." Joey said as he rushed out the door before his mother could ask any more questions. If she found out he was meeting a girl the questions would never end.

* * *

It was a straight shot to the east once he got onto U.S. 98. An hour later Joey was approaching the resort hotels on Front Beach Road in Panama City Beach. This was where the traffic got bad. It was another hot blistering day in the Florida panhandle and there were a lot of tourists out visiting the Emerald Coast. Cars were parked all along the road and it was bumper to bumper traffic just like he expected. He was only a few miles away from the state park entrance and he still had 25 minutes before he was supposed to meet Lindsey. It would probably take him that long to drive those last few miles. He started sweating despite the air conditioner blowing on him full blast. Even though he couldn't wait to see her again, he was nervous about spending more time with her.

He slowly moved through the traffic on U.S. 30, known as Front Beach Road in PCB, having to stop at almost every crosswalk to let tourists walk across. Twenty minutes later he drove past a dive shop on the right side of the road and then saw a brown sign with white lettering announcing the state park entrance 1000 feet ahead. As he passed the sign he saw Lindsey's car parked on the side of the road in a small pull off right before the park ranger office at the entrance. He eased his car in behind hers, rolled down his window and waved. Lindsey stuck her arm out her window and waved for him to follow her as she merged back onto the road and pulled up to the park ranger office. He watched Lindsey and the ranger talk. The ranger looked back at Joey and smiled. Lindsey then handed the ranger some money and got a receipt back. She pulled up enough for Joey to move his car to where the ranger was standing.

"Hey there young fella', how are you this beautiful Sunday morning?" a woman with a huge crooked smile about the age of Joey's grandmother said as he pulled up. "I'll bet you're wonderful if you're meeting that lovely young lady in the car ahead of you." She said as she nodded her head in the direction of Lindsey's car.

"I-I'm doing great ma'am. Yes, we're headed to the jetties."

"Well, the young lady paid your entrance fee. Take this receipt and place it on your dashboard so it can be seen by the other rangers. Here's a map of the park and you're all set to go. Have a great day!" grandma ranger said as she handed Joey the receipt and winked at him.

"Th-thank you ma'am." Joey took the receipt and continued to follow Lindsey to the jetties. *Why had she paid the entrance fee,* Joey wondered. It was a nice gesture but he was a little concerned about it. Joey wasn't a chauvinist but he felt the man should pay for things. It's how he was raised. And Lindsey paying his entrance fee only confused him more about how she might feel about him.

Joey followed Lindsey as she turned right onto the first road they came to. They drove along a winding road, past a small parking lot that was about half full. They continued down a more or less straight stretch of road with sand dunes blocking the view of the gulf to their right. After a couple of minutes Joey followed Lindsey into a much larger parking lot than the one they had passed earlier. This one looked like it was already full. They drove up and down the rows looking for available parking spaces. Joey saw other scuba divers at some tables under pavilions located at one end of the parking lot. They were in different stages of setting up their gear and getting ready to do their own dives.

Joey and Lindsey got lucky and found a couple of spaces right next to each other only two rows back from the pavilions. It was already in the high 90s and humid and would have been miserable if they had to park all the way at the other end and haul their gear and tanks across the parking lot to the pavilions.

"Hi Joey. I'm so happy to see you!" Lindsey exclaimed as she walked up to him and gave him a big hug. Joey was taken aback by the hug and it took him a few seconds to react and hug her back.

"H-hi Lindsey. I-I'm happy to see you too." Joey stammered. "Th-thank you for paying for my entrance but you didn't have to do that."

"Aww, I know sweetie. But after you were so insistent on paying for lunch yesterday I had to do something. It just came to me when I was paying for myself. No big deal sweetie."

"W-well, thank you."

"Are ya ready to go dive?"

"Sure!"

"Well, we have a little time before high slack tide so let me show you around the place before we get all that heavy gear out. We actually got pretty lucky getting these parking spaces here. I've had to park several rows back from the pavilions and it's never fun having to carry all that gear and tanks across the hot parking lot." The edges of Lindsey's mouth turned down into a frown as she said that last part.

They walked together across the parking lot toward the pavilions and the sand dunes beyond that separated the parking area from the beautiful white sandy beach. Lindsey walked beside Joey and a couple times her soft tanned arm brushed against his arm. Every time this happened goose bumps rose on Joey's arm and he could feel the hair on the back of his neck standing up again. Despite the heat from the sun beating down on them and reflecting off the dark asphalt parking lot, he also felt a chill move through his arm and body. Joey wondered if Lindsey was feeling the same thing.

They climbed the steps leading up over the sand dune and Joey got his first glimpse of the beautiful clear water. He grew up on the gulf coast of Florida but he still never got tired of seeing the deep emerald color of the water contrasted against the pure white sand on the beach. He could definitely understand why this area of Florida was called the Emerald Coast.

Joey realized they had stopped walking to admire the view when they reached the top of the steps and they were blocking the path. Someone came up behind him and Joey reached out and gently grabbed Lindsey's arm to nudge her aside so the family behind them could pass. Lindsey moved over and back into him so her back was right up against him. Joey could smell the scent of oranges in her hair, probably from the shampoo she had used that morning in the shower. He took in a big breath and filled his nose with the citrusy scent of Lindsey and held it in so he could memorize it.

"Isn't it beautiful Joey. I just love looking out to the sea and thinking about all the beautiful coral reefs and marine life that live under the surface. Just wait until you see it!" Lindsey exclaimed.

Taking a step forward, Lindsey stepped away from Joey and toward the beach and the water. "Com'on" she said as she grabbed his hand and pulled him across the wooden walkway and down the steps on the other side of the dunes. They walked across the white sand beach toward the water hand in hand. His palm didn't even hurt against the soft touch of her hand. Joey hoped his palm didn't feel sweaty and wished she had given him a little warning so he could have wiped it on his shirt before she grabbed it. She was still holding his hand so it mustn't be too bad.

They reached the water and Lindsey kicked her flip flops off. Joey did the same and they stepped in ankle deep. The cool water felt really good on such a hot day. It didn't feel nearly as cold as the 68 degree water of Eddy and Morrison Springs though but that was okay with Joey.

"This water is pretty warm," said Joey.

"It should be somewhere in the mid-80s today. It stays warm all summer. This area right here is called the Kiddie Pool. It's just a shallow sandy area that's protected by the surrounding jetty. It's about 7 feet deep at its deepest during high tide. That area is over by the jetty rocks over there," she said as she pointed across the water to a line of rocks sticking up above the surface.

"We usually enter here and head toward the area where you don't see any rocks. The rocks are there but they're submerged. They're low enough right now that we can swim right over them. Be careful though sweetie. There are usually sea urchins in the rocks and they are shallow enough that you'll be able to touch them. So when we cross over into the channel keep your BC inflated and stay on the surface because if you accidently touch a sea urchin you'll be picking out pieces of their spiny needles the rest of the day. Alright sweetie?"

"I'll be careful."

"Just on the other side of the jetty it drops down to about 30 feet deep to the sand. We usually swim to the right out toward the gulf along the rocks. It gets to about 60 feet deep or so and there's a lot of life among the rocks. Then we turn around and swim back along the rocks until it gets to be about 15 to 20 feet deep or so. Since this is the channel between the bay and the gulf we want to stay close to the rocks. Sometimes boats will come close to the rocks too but divers are out here enough that most of them steer clear of our dive flags. Just make sure you don't surface away from the dive flag and you look up to make sure there isn't a boat near it."

"There shouldn't be any current in the channel right now because it's almost high slack tide. During high tide the water flows north into the channel toward the bay. During low tide it's flowing out to the gulf. During the times in between it doesn't do much of anything which is why it's called slack tide. The reason we dive during high slack is because the visibility is clearer at that time since all the water in the channel is coming from the gulf and not the bay."

She paused for a few seconds and Joey tried to take in everything she had just told him.

"Are you ready to go gear up and see what's under there sweetie?"

"I sure am," replied Joey.

They retrieved their flip flops and walked back through the beach taking a roundabout path to avoid walking over the beach blankets and towels spread out every few feet. As excited as Joey was to do his first salt water dive and see the life along the jetty he wouldn't mind just sitting out on a beach blanket with Lindsey for the rest of the day. Maybe after the dive they could relax on the beach before heading back home.

Back at their cars Joey grabbed the scuba tanks from Lindsey's trunk and carried them to a table under one of the pavilions. The heaviness and the pressure of the valves on his palms didn't feel very good but he wasn't about to let her carry the tanks over after her comment earlier. Lindsey followed shortly with her bag of gear. Joey returned and grabbed a bag of weights from Lindsey's trunk and his gear from his own trunk.

They set up their gear at the table under the pavilion while Lindsey continued on in her southern drawl about everything they were about to see on the dive. Joey positioned his scuba tank a little higher on the BC like Lindsey had recommended the day before. He was hoping that would help him get into a better position in the water.

He thought about the time he had spent with Lindsey since swimming into her at Morrison Spring and was still confused as to how Lindsey really felt about him. She was very friendly, had held his hand, and seemed to enjoy spending time with him but he didn't know if that was how she acted with all her friends or if she had a romantic interest in him. He hoped it was the latter. But either way he planned on just living in the moment and enjoying her company.

They finished assembling their scuba equipment and put it on. Joey actually remembered to put his weight belt on. Because the water was so warm Lindsey wasn't wearing a wet suit today. She just had a bikini with a tight rash guard shirt on that hugged her figure quite nicely. Joey was wearing his usual swim trunks and t-shirt, which he hoped was enough to hide the fat on his belly. They walked toward the beach up the steps over the dune and back down to the sand. Soon they were in the water cooling off.

The water felt good, nothing like the cold water in the springs creeping up and shocking certain parts of the body. They waded out to where the water was deep enough to float their scuba tanks and get most of the weight off their shoulders and backs. When the salt water hit Joey's palms he almost screamed. The salt really stung the wounds. Fortunately he was behind Lindsey and she didn't notice. He slowly eased his palms back into the water and waited for the stinging to subside. They did their buddy check and afterwards headed to the low spot in the jetty. As Joey swam over the rocks he did see a few sea urchins but they were nestled in deep enough that he wasn't concerned about them. They got past the rocks and began their descent into the clear emerald water.

23

The dive at the jetties was very different from anything Joey had experienced in his short time as a scuba diver. The descent was a lot easier than any of his descents in the springs had been. He was able to maintain better control and he didn't crash into the bottom like he did on most dives. He had heard buoyancy control was not as difficult in salt water but hadn't really believed it until this point.

Moving his tank higher on his back also helped his body line up in a more horizontal position. His feet no longer wanted to sink below him. He didn't think his form looked quite as good as Lindsey's did in the water but he felt much better than he ever had. The suggestion she gave him made a world of difference.

They had dropped down alongside the jetty rocks until they were just above the sandy bottom, about twenty-five feet deep. Lindsey towed a dive flag and tied off the line attached to the dive flag buoy to a small protrusion from one of the boulders below them. She then signaled Joey to follow her south along the jetty.

There were fish everywhere! Black and yellow striped fish, silver colored fish, large purple and yellow fish almost as big as dinner plates, sea stars strapped to the rocks, and sea urchins sticking up out of the nooks between large boulders. As they got down to about sixty feet deep a large grouper appeared right in front of them! Joey couldn't believe everything he was seeing. He had thought the eel in the springs were cool but this was like an aquarium with all the different fish and different colors. And he was a part of it!

After watching the grouper for a few minutes they swam along the boulders until they came to the end where the sand continued on into the vast underwater desert. Joey felt intimidated by the view. There didn't seem to be anything out there beyond the boulders but Joey knew there was something there - the dead diver he had helped dump overboard a couple days earlier.

He wondered what happened to the body. Was it on the bottom where they had thrown it over or did the tides move it closer to the coast. Joey wondered if it would ever wash up on shore and how long that would take. Lindsey had mentioned the tide brings water from the gulf into the bay. What if the body had drifted east from Destin and ended up here in the St. Andrews Pass?

Joey pushed that thought out of his mind. Destin was at least 50 miles away and it had only been a couple days since they had tossed the body into the gulf. But the water current did seem to be moving from west to east. He continued to stare into the abyss thinking about the dead diver out there all alone.

Joey felt something touch his arm and practically bolted to the surface. He quickly realized it was just Lindsey trying to get his attention. He must have really fallen into his daydreaming haze because she was holding her hand out in front of him with her index finger and thumb in the circular okay signal. If he could see the expression on her face he's sure it would be a look of concern. He quickly returned the signal and turned away from the open ocean and faced back toward the boulders that were teeming with marine life.

They started swimming back alongside the jetty toward where they had come from. The white sand below gently sloped upward. Lindsey ascended above one of the boulders and moved closer to the jetty and away from the sand. Joey followed and saw that the boulders were not all stacked on top of each other. There was a small field of large boulders laying on the bottom and sloping up toward the wall that rose to the surface forming the west wall of the channel.

Lindsey and Joey eased up to about 35 feet deep and swam around the boulders and smaller rocks looking at all the different marine life living among them.

Suddenly Joey felt something pushing him away from the jetty. He looked around but couldn't see anything. A current seemed to have come out of nowhere and he was being pushed toward the gulf, the abyss he had been so mesmerized by earlier. Joey started to kick his fins to keep from being pushed back but the current was stronger than his fin kicks. He was slowing his movement but not stopping it. He looked around and saw some boulders passing by quickly to his left that were just beyond his reach. He turned his body toward the boulders and kicked his fins harder. The current was still winning the battle and pushing him out to sea. He continued to kick as he watched the boulders getting farther away.

As he was being pushed back by the current a large boulder appeared beneath him. Joey reached down and grabbed it. His fingers slid over the soft slippery surface and he could feel the pain shoot back into his hands. His fingers continued to slip along the top of the boulder. He frantically looked around for something else to grab onto when he felt a flat edge of the boulder under his hand. It wasn't much but it was enough for Joey to grasp and hold himself against the raging current. He had no idea what was going on. He thought about the current he had fought at Morrison Spring but this was at least ten times worse. Lindsey had mentioned the water moving back out toward the gulf at the end of high slack tide but it was still an hour before that was supposed to happen. It shouldn't be doing this.

Lindsey! Joey suddenly realized she wasn't next to him. Where was she? He looked around and above him but didn't see any sign of her. The visibility wasn't as good as it had been at the beginning of the dive though. There was a lot of particulate in the water and visibility had cut down from 40 feet or so to less than 10 feet. High slack tide must have ended early. Had the current taken Lindsey out to sea? How could he have forgotten about her and let the current push her away?

Maybe it didn't, Joey thought. She was a good diver. Maybe she was able to get to a boulder and hold herself against it. Or maybe she was able to kick against it. The flow at Morrison hadn't seem to bother her at all.

As he was holding on for his life Joey saw a dark object off in the distance. It was getting bigger. It looked like it was moving closer to him. He didn't know what it was and started to get a little concerned. He had heard of hammerhead sharks being seen in the Kiddie Pool. The last sighting hadn't been too long ago. And he was stuck holding onto a boulder. If he let go he could be blown out into the vast sea desert behind him. Or he could have to contend with whatever it was that was about to be on top of him.

The object continued to get closer and he saw it was moving. Joey realized it wasn't an object. It was Lindsey. She was kicking her fins and while she was able to slow herself down better than Joey had been, she was still no match for the current. She also looked like she was too far from any of the boulders to reach them. When she was about ten feet away from him Joey let go of the boulder with his right hand and reached toward Lindsey keeping his left hand firmly planted on the surface below him. She was approaching quickly. He reached out and grabbed her leg but Lindsey recoiled from his grasp.

As she flew past him Joey turned to look at her. Lindsey saw him and stretched her arms out toward him. Their fingers brushed each other briefly but Lindsey was moving too fast and they had gotten too far apart. Joey looked down at the boulder he was holding onto and back at Lindsey. He looked back down at the boulder and let go of it to chase after her. He didn't know what he was going to do once he caught up to her but he couldn't stay there holding onto a jetty rock while Lindsey was in trouble.

Being bigger than Lindsey the current pushed Joey along slightly faster and with a few kicks of his fins he was able to catch up to her within seconds. He reached toward her and grabbed her hand. Lindsey grasped his hand and held it tightly.

This caused the pain in his hand to get worse but he didn't even flinch this time. He wasn't about to let go of her. Joey turned around into the current and they both started to kick with all their might.

Joey turned toward the jetty like he had earlier. It was still to their left and they might be able to get to it before they were pushed out of the pass. They kicked as fast and hard as they could. They started to make some headway against the current and were inching up on the boulders. Joey reached one of the boulders and stretched his left arm down toward it. He managed to find an area jutting out that he could hold onto. With his right hand he pulled Lindsey next to him so she could grab the boulder with her right hand. They settled in together and tried to catch their breath.

After a couple of minutes the shock started to wear off a bit and Joey let go of Lindsey's hand so he could find his pressure gauge to see how much air he still had left. Only 900 psi. He wasn't sure that would be enough to get him back to the surface, especially with having to swim against this current. He looked at his depth gauge and saw they were back down to sixty feet. Joey stole a quick glance behind him. They were at the end of the jetty. If he hadn't grabbed this boulder they would be flying out over the barren sea floor.

Looking back at Lindsey Joey noticed she appeared to be more calm now that they were no longer fighting the current. He grabbed her hand again and gave it a gentle squeeze. Lindsey squeezed back. She then gestured in front of them toward another boulder just a few feet away. Joey nodded and they released hands and started to kick and pull toward it. They made it to the boulder and settled in to look for another one.

Joey saw one a few feet ahead and above them. This one was positioned so it was blocking the current from hitting them directly. They swam and pulled toward it careful to not put their hands down on any sea urchins. A few seconds later they were on the next boulder. This continued on for several more minutes looking for boulders that were blocking the current and above them so it would be easier to swim to them and they could get shallower and breathe less air from their scuba tanks.

They made it back to the boulder Lindsey had tied their dive flag to. That meant they were back at twenty-five feet depth. Joey stole another glance back to his pressure gauge – 400 psi. There were several boulders in front of them blocking the current and making it much more manageable in this location.

Joey was concerned that if they ascended along the line to the dive flag the current would whisk them off to sea again. Lindsey must have had the same thought because she was quickly untying the line from the protrusion she had anchored it to so they could move the flag along the boulders and up the jetty wall. Lindsey spooled the line in as Joey held onto the boulder with one hand and onto her with the other to make sure the current didn't pull her away from him again. They slowly ascended along the wall until they saw the top of the submerged rocks just below the surface. They quickly pulled themselves over the rocks into the Kiddie Pool.

Joey began to relax until he realized the current was still pushing them south. He reached down and dug his fingers into the sandy bottom with one hand and held onto Lindsey with the other. The coarse sand jabbed into his wounds and sent searing pain through his palm and up his arm. He kept his hand there anyway and held on.

They pulled themselves along until it was shallow enough to stand. When they stood up they were still in chest deep water and saw they were over 100 feet south of where they had crossed over the jetties to the Kiddie Pool. They tried to remove their fins and walk north but quickly gave up. The current was too strong to even pull their fins off. They left their fins on and walked west toward the beach. A couple minutes later, the water surface at thigh level, it was much easier to anchor themselves to the bottom and pull their fins off. They could finally walk against the current.

They exited the water, crossed the beach, and walked in silence up and over the sand dune to the table under the pavilion. When they got there they quietly removed their gear and collapsed on the table next to each other.

Joey turned toward Lindsey. "What happened?? What was that?!?"

"The tide charts must have been wrong." Lindsey breathed out. "I've never felt such a strong current. We almost got swept out into the gulf Joey."

She turned toward him and draped her arm across his chest. Joey brought his arm around her shoulder and they laid there on the table face to face holding each other while they both let the shock of the events of the dive pass through them.

Joey found the thought of Earl and the dead scuba diver out there somewhere in the gulf creep back into his head. Was what happened a sign? Was this some type of karma getting him back for helping Earl toss the body of that scuba diver into the gulf. Joey shook the thoughts out of his head. Whatever it was they had beaten it and gotten back to the Kiddie Pool and out of the water. He turned his thoughts back to Lindsey

Joey was having trouble believing what happened had affected Lyndsey so badly. She was a great diver. How could this shake her up so much? And why wasn't he more shaken up?

"A-are you okay?" Joey asked softly.

A moment passed before Lindsey said anything. "I think so. I'm just still recovering from that dive. High slack tide wasn't supposed to happen for another half hour. And then we usually have another half hour to an hour before the tide starts to go back out. I've seen the tide schedule be off a bit before but never by that much. It was impossible to swim against the current. If you hadn't been there to hold onto me I'd still be out there somewhere."

"I didn't do much Lindsey." Joey said sheepishly. "The current was pushing me out too but I got lucky and was able to grab onto one of the jetty boulders before it pushed me too far out. I tried to grab you but it must have –"

"I'm so sorry about that." Lindsey interrupted. "I didn't mean to pull away. I felt something on my leg and it scared me. I was swimming as hard as I could to try to move against the current and then I felt something touch my leg and got spooked. I didn't know it was you trying to save me."

"I-I didn't save you." Joey blushed. "I just reached out and helped you. You're a much better diver than I am. You would have eventually gotten out of the current."

"I don't think I would have sweetie. You saved my life."

With that Lindsey reached around Joey and hugged him tightly. Joey was more in shock over Lindsey's reaction than he was about the dive. After a moment he reached around her and hugged her back. It felt good to hold her in his arms. Joey could get used to this.

PART 3

24

August 7, 2011 around 6pm

When Joey got home later that evening his mother was sitting in the kitchen waiting for him. She didn't look happy. *This couldn't be good,* thought Joey. Not after the way she had lectured him all weekend, especially after that morning's news headline. She didn't even wait for him to step inside the house before addressing him.

"Have a seat at the table, Joseph," she told him as she walked out of the room. *Oh, this was bad.* After such a great weekend spent with Lindsey Joey couldn't believe this was happening. Was this still about his mom not wanting him to scuba dive anymore? Joey sat at the table with all the possible scenarios racing through his mind waiting for his mother to return.

She came back into the kitchen with his father following close behind.

"Joseph, your father and I want to talk to you tonight because something strange happened while you were out. A man came by looking for you today. His name is Earl Hewitt."

His mom became silent a moment and watched Joey,

probably to see if he had any reaction to what she had told him. He tried to remain calm and not show any response. He realized he didn't know Earl's last name but how many Earls could there be looking for him only three days after he had helped the Eddy Spring Earl get rid of a dead body in the gulf? Joey decided to remain silent and let his mother continue her interrogation to see if she would reveal anything else.

"Do you know an Earl Hewitt, Joseph?" Another moment of silence as Joey sat there with an expression on his face like he was trying to remember if he knew an Earl Hewitt. His mother got tired of waiting for a response.

"Well Joseph, I do know Earl. Or at least I knew him. We went to high school together. I didn't know him very well but we were in some of the same classes. He didn't have a very good reputation back then. I haven't kept touch with him since we all graduated but he doesn't seem to have changed much since those days. He comes up in conversation every now and then and it's never good. Now what on earth would Earl Hewitt want with you, Joseph? What are you doing getting involved with the likes of him?"

Joey didn't know what to say. He remembered the headline from the paper earlier that morning but what did Joey have to do with that? Earl should be chasing down the employee that called the sheriff's office not Joey. Joey did everything Earl had told him to. He had pulled the body out of the cave and then stayed up all night to help Earl get rid of it. Joey thought that would be the end of it.

"U-um, I-I don't know why he's looking for me mom. I-I met him at the scuba park, Eddy Spring, and t-talked to him for a little bit but that's all. I-I-I think he's the manager there." Joey stammered.

"Well, I don't like it. I don't like it at all, Joseph Simmons. What would a grown man, the same age as me be doing looking for a child your age? And especially someone with the reputation he has."

"I-I-I don't know mom. He d-d-didn't tell you what he w-wanted?"

"Of course not! If he had I wouldn't be asking you."

Joey looked over to his dad for help. His dad just sat there looking at him. He wasn't going to be any help. Joey wondered why he was even sitting in the room with them if he wasn't going to say a word.

"I-I don't know mom. M-m-maybe I left something behind at the park the other day –"

"Now why would he drive all the way down here to return something you might have left there? And why wouldn't he have left it with me then?"

"Mom, I-I don't know. I was just g-g-guessing –"

"Well, this isn't looking very good, especially after what happened at that scuba park this past week." She pulled the Sunday paper off the counter and slapped it down on the table in front of Joey. "First someone disappears and now the manager of the park comes here looking for you. You are not allowed to go to that park again young man."

"Mom, you can't do that. D-dad, help! I didn't do anything wrong. I-I can't c-c-control what other people do. Why am I in trouble because someone c-came looking for me?"

"Alison, Joey has a point." His father finally said. "We don't even know why Earl was here. Maybe he has Joey confused with some other young man. Joey isn't the type of boy to get mixed up in trouble."

Joey eased back in his chair and waited for the blow up. His dad rarely spoke up to his mom but when he did it wasn't always a pretty sight afterwards. To Joey's surprise, his mom just looked at his father, let out a *Hmmph!* and walked out of the room.

Joey looked at his dad and quietly said, "Thanks dad."

"No, Joseph, don't thank me. I'm not too happy about how things have been going with you since you started into this scuba diving thing. You're spending a lot of money and still haven't paid us back. You're spending a lot of time away from home on the weekends and not doing your chores, and you're making your mother upset all the time, which is making my life not so pleasant. I'm not taking your side, Joseph. I'm curious as to why this Earl Hewitt would be looking for you. But if you honestly don't know then I'm going to believe you…for now. But I want you to find out what that man wants from you and I want you to put your mother at ease."

"Yessir. I-I'll do what I can sir."

* * *

Joey stood up and went to his room. He noticed the light to his parents room was on. His mother was probably in there brooding because his father had stood up to her. It was rare he did that. Joey could understand why. He didn't like standing up to her either. It just made his life miserable. It was better to not disagree, at least not out loud.

He threw himself onto his bed and thought about Earl coming to look for him. What could Earl want from him now? Joey had already done more than he should have for Earl. Why couldn't he leave him alone? Joey didn't know what to do. He wanted all this business with Earl to be behind him so he could move on with his new relationship with Lindsey. He didn't know if he should go find Earl or if Earl would just give up.

No. He knew Earl wouldn't give up. Earl would keep coming by the house until he got what he wanted. Joey knew he had to go see Earl and find out what he wanted before he returned to the house and upset his mother again. Joey wasn't due into work until 10am the next day. He would get up early and go by Earl's house before work and talk to him. It would be better to just get this over with.

With that decision made Joey turned his thoughts toward Lindsey. He had really enjoyed his day with her. After getting over the shock of the tide charts being wrong they loaded their scuba gear back into their cars and decided to spend time on the beach for part of the afternoon. They grabbed their beach towels and laid them down on the sand next to each other. Lindsey sat on her towel and started spreading sun tan lotion on her arms and legs. When she finished that she asked Joey to rub some onto her back. Sitting there on his bed Joey could still feel the soft smooth skin of Lindsey's back. The lotion made his scraped up palms sting but he didn't care. He slowly rubbed the lotion onto her back until it disappeared.

Lindsey had then asked Joey if he wanted some lotion. He took some and rubbed it onto his arms and legs. When she asked if he wanted her to rub some on his back Joey declined.

His shirt was still on and he had been too self-conscious about his gut to remove it in front of Lindsey.

Joey definitely needed to start doing something to get into better shape and lose weight. He wouldn't call himself fat but he could definitely stand to lose 15-20 pounds. He had been thinking about it for the past couple months but now he had something to motivate him to do it.

He had already changed his diet the past couple days. He was eating smaller portions and cutting back on the junk food. He and Lindsey had gone out to lunch in Panama City Beach after they left St. Andrews State Park and he only had a burger and fries. Usually he would have ordered a lot more – onion rings, a milk shake, and even dessert – but he restrained himself. He was still hungry after lunch but he was able to push the thought aside by thinking about Lindsey instead.

He needed to start exercising too. In fact, this was as good a time as any to start. Joey got out of bed and headed out of his room. He saw the light to his parents' bedroom was on. His mom must still be in there. He quietly walked past the living room where his father was sitting watching television. He snuck out the kitchen door and headed down the driveway toward the street. Joey didn't know where he was going. He just wanted to exercise a little and walking was a good start. He also wanted to get out of the house for a little while.

Turning left out of his driveway Joey quickly walked down the street away from his house. Even though the sun had already set it was still hot out. It wasn't as bad as during the day when the bright sun was beating down on him but the humidity made the air pretty thick. He started sweating almost immediately. As he approached various intersections in the neighborhood he made random turns without even thinking about where he was going. About twenty minutes into his walk he was out on highway 98 heading west.

Joey realized he was heading toward Earl's house. Even though he had decided to go there in the morning, subconsciously he must have wanted to get this over with before turning in for the night. He was already halfway there so he decided to keep going. Might as well. He didn't know if Earl would even be there in the morning anyway. There was a better chance of finding him at home in the evening. And he didn't want to risk having Earl go to his house again.

Up ahead he saw the street turning into the neighborhood where he had dropped Earl off Friday morning. He quickened his pace and continued heading in that direction. The house was only a couple blocks from here, Joey thought to himself. He started getting a little nervous and having second thoughts about confronting Earl. He wasn't sure he wanted to know what Earl wanted from him. Joey almost turned around but then he recalled his mother standing in the kitchen yelling at him earlier. He decided it would be better to find out what Earl wanted and deal with that than to deal with his mother's wrath if Earl stopped by again.

He turned onto another street, the street Earl lived on, and saw Earl's house ahead. He could see lights on in the house. That was good. Someone was home. Hopefully it was Earl. He didn't remember Earl mentioning anyone else living there and Earl hadn't seemed too concerned about waking anyone when Joey dropped him off the other morning.

When Joey arrived in front of the house he stopped and just stared at it for a few minutes. There were lights coming from a couple of windows in the house but Joey didn't see any movement inside. He walked up the sidewalk to the front door, stopped in front of the door and took a deep breath. He could hear the sounds from a television inside the house. Ironically, it was *Unsolved Mysteries.* After another minute he took in a deep breath and reached out to ring the doorbell.

A couple seconds later the sound from the television was muted. Joey heard the locks in the door turning. He thought about turning around and running off but the door opened before he could even finish processing that thought. Earl stood just inside the door, unshaven and his hair disheveled, looking at Joey.

"Well well well, if t'aint good ol Joey agin. Long time no see m'friend." Earl said with a wink. "Com'on in boy."

25

Joey slowly stepped inside the doorway. He glanced around the room and took in the surroundings. The room was darkened with only the light of a single plain lamp on an end table next to the couch casting a dim light across the meager furnishings. Earl wasn't much of a decorator. He seemed to have the bare essentials for furniture in the room – a couch, end table, and large television. The only other piece of furniture in the room was a gun cabinet in the corner. Joey lingered on the cabinet and noticed several shotguns and rifles behind the glass door.

Across from the couch was the head of a large deer hanging on the wall over the television. Other than that, the walls were bare. On the floor in front of the couch lay this morning's newspaper with the same headline Joey had seen earlier in the day popping out at him. There was an empty beer bottle lying on the floor next to the paper.

"Ha' ya seen t'day's paper boy?" Earl almost snapped at him. "It ain't none too good. Dis whole thin' 'as caused me whole lotta trouble. I lost lotta money dis weeken' wit dat missin' diver thin'."

Silence.

"Ain't ya got nut'n ta say?"

Joey started shifting his weight from leg to leg nervously. "I-I-I-I don't know sir. I didn't tell anyone. I s-s-swear."

"I din't say nut'n bout it bein' y'all's fault. I know t' wasn't y'all. One of m'damn workers calt in dat truck. I'm gonna hafta figga out howda fire'm. He cost me lotta money. An' I don' like ta lose money. Damn dep'ties had me busy doin' nut'n all day yestaday. Jus' waitin' on 'em divers ta spend all day searchin' fer nut'n. Woulda bin easier ta jus tell 'em you pult da diver outta dare Thursday night."

Joey felt a panicked feeling rising at what Earl had just said. Earl was making it sound like Joey was responsible for the dead diver being in the cave. "Um, s-sir, y-y-you wouldn't –"

"Ah, don' worry kid. I'm not gonna throw ya unda da bus. We was both thar an' both jus' as 'sponsible."

Joey couldn't believe what he was hearing. Earl hadn't given him a choice. He was forced to help him.

"So now I gots ta figga out wut ta do ta fix dis whole mess."

Earl stumbled over to the couch and dropped down onto it. He sat glaring at Joey for a few minutes. Joey stood there wondering what he could say to get out of Earl's house and get out of this whole mess. He didn't even know why he had come to Earl's house to begin with. Then he remembered Earl's visit to his house earlier in the day.

"U-um, sir, m-my mom told me you came by looking for me earlier today. W-w-was this what it was about? Th-this whole thing with the cops and the body?"

"Ah, yeah, Al'son. Haven't seen 'er in years. Din't know she was y'all's ma." Earl paused for a few seconds, looking like he was reminiscing. "Yeah, dis is it. Din't mean ta get ya in trouble wit ole Al'son but I needed ta talk ta ya. I need y'all's services agin."

"W-what do you mean?"

"I need y'all ta do some divin' for me agin. An' y'all showed up jus' in time. We can head on out now."

"D-diving for you??? Head out now?!? W-Where?"

"Where ya think? We got ta fin' dat body an' put it back in da cave so dey can fin' 'im."

Joey's jaw dropped open in shock. He didn't know how to respond to that. How did Earl expect him to find the body in the gulf? Joey had just done his first dive in the gulf earlier in the day and looking out at the open sea from the edge of the jetties had intimidated him…a lot! And now Earl wanted him to dive in the gulf tonight, in the dark, and look for the dead body they had tossed over the side of the boat the other night. How would they even find it? And what would Joey do once they did find it? He couldn't go through anymore of this. He needed to figure out a way to get out of this and get as far away from Earl as possible.

"S-sir, I-I don't have my scuba gear with me. I-it's back home in my car."

"Well, dat's easy 'nuf. Les go git it. Y'all's ain't gots nut'n ta do tanight anyway. Otha'wise y'all wouldn't be sittin' here in ol' Earl's livin' room."

"S-sir, I-I can't just get my gear. I g-got in enough trouble with my mom because y-y-you stopped by earlier. If I-I went back home and left again with m-my car, I'd get grounded."

"Well, dat wouldn't do us no good. We might not fin' da body tonight an' I can't sit roun' waitin' for y'all to get ungrounded ta start lookin' agin. How 'bout tomorra mornin'? We can head out right afta y'all's parents head out for work."

"B-b-but I have to be at work tomorrow."

"Jus' call outta work. Tell 'em y'all's sick."

Joey was in a panic. It didn't seem Earl was going to let him get out of this. He had to come up with something. He had already played hooky from work last week. And look where that got him. He couldn't do it again. But Earl wasn't going to take another excuse.

Then it came to him. "S-sir, I d-don't have any scuba tanks. I always rent them from the shop at Eddy Spring."

"Damn, I don' have time ta be drivin' up ta Eddy an back." Earl thought for a moment. "A'ight, I gots it. I'll head on up ta Eddy tomorra an' get y'all's a couple tanks ta rent an' we'll head out tomorra night. What time y'all's folks head off ta bed?"

"I-I-I work all day tomorrow and I have to work all week. H-how are we going to find the body anyway? The g-gulf is pretty d-deep and it's pretty b-barren out there. I c-can't just swim around looking for him all night."

"Don' worry 'bout dat kid. I know whar we dumpt da body. S'only 'bout 110 feet deep dare 'ccordin' ta ma fish finder. Da body was purty heavy an' shoulda gone straight ta da bottom."

"But what if it didn't? 110 feet is really deep. I can only stay there for a few minutes before I have to come up."

"We'll figure't out."

* * *

Joey was just a couple feet off the bottom of a barren desert sea floor. At least the small area lit up by the dim yellow light in his right hand was nothing but sandy bottom. The light didn't punch too far through the water. There was a lot of particulate in the water that also obscured his view. He was holding on tightly to the anchor line from the boat with his left hand. He had to eventually let go of the thick rope and venture into the darkness if he was going to find the body they had dropped there a few days earlier. But he was even more afraid of losing the anchor and not being able to find it again than he was of the surrounding darkness swallowing him up.

He finally mustered up the courage and opened his left hand slowly. He felt the line pull away from his hand and could almost feel the sweat on his palm. That was a strange feeling – to feel sweat underwater. He swam around the anchor for a minute sweeping his dim light back and forth looking for any signs of the body. There was nothing but darkness. He turned to look for the anchor and found it a few feet away from him to his left.

He turned away from it and swam for a minute, continuing to sweep his light back and forth. He turned around and headed back in the direction he had come from. A minute later he saw the anchor line. *What a huge relief!* He turned and headed in a different direction and continued to sweep his light over the sandy bottom.

Earl had said he saw something on his fish finder about the size of a person on the sea floor. He had told him it wasn't too far from where the anchor dropped. Joey didn't know if he was going out far enough but he didn't want to get too far away from the anchor line and not be able to find it again.

He was able to find the anchor line again after his second

venture out from it. He glanced down at his pressure gauge and he still had 1600 psi in his tank. He had enough air for one more pass, maybe two. He started on his third pass. After a minute he turned around and headed back toward the anchor. As he was swimming back toward the anchor he felt something tug on one of his fins. Joey yanked his foot forward and quickly looked back behind him.

It was the dead diver. Only he wasn't dead. Or maybe he was, but he was coming after Joey! Joey could see the diver's eyes wide open staring at him through the clear lens of the scuba mask he was wearing. The diver was reaching for Joey and moving toward him. Joey screamed into his regulator and turned around to swim toward the anchor. He kicked furiously for a minute but never saw the anchor. He turned and swam in a different direction for another minute. Still no anchor. He looked back and the dead diver was still behind him. He started zigzagging along the bottom hoping to lose the diver and find the anchor. He was having no luck with either. He continued like this for several minutes until it started to get harder to breathe from his second stage regulator. He remembered this feeling from the first dive in Eddy Spring when he found the dead diver. He was really close to being out of air. He had to find that anchor soon or just head for the surface and hope he was close to the boat. He glanced back one more time and saw the diver a few feet away from him, his arms stretched out in front of him as if he were reaching for Joey's fins.

It was time to ascend to the surface. He didn't think he had any chance of finding the anchor and maybe ascending would throw off his chaser and he could get away from him. Joey made the decision and pushed himself off the bottom. He felt himself rising in the water column into the darkness above. The sandy bottom disappeared from beneath him and there was nothing but black surrounding him. He followed the bubbles from his regulator up until he could no longer get a breath from it. Completely out of air. He grabbed his depth gauge. Still 100 feet deep! He felt something pulling on his fin again and screamed out as everything went black.

* * *

Joey sat up as he was screaming out. It was completely dark. He couldn't even see the dim yellow glow from his dive light. He suddenly realized he no longer had his regulator in his mouth. Slowly the realization that he could breathe came to him and he took in a deep breath. Following that he became aware that he wasn't wet. He wasn't underwater.

He was safe in his bed in his bedroom. *What a relief!* It was just a nightmare. Looking over toward his clock he saw the menacing red glow of the numbers telling him it was 2:12 in the morning.

After leaving Earl's that evening Joey walked straight home. His father had still been up in the living room watching television, that same *Unsolved Mysteries* show. There must be a marathon going on that evening. His mother wasn't in her usual spot on the couch. She probably went to bed already, still mad at both of them. Joey headed straight for his room and went to bed.

Earl had decided they would meet the following night at

midnight and go look for the dead diver's body. Earl would get a couple tanks from the shop at Eddy Spring during the day. He made sure to let Joey know that if he wasn't at his house at midnight he would have no problem going and knocking on his door and waking his parents. Joey had no choice but to go with Earl even though he was terrified of the thought of diving in the middle of the gulf in the middle of the night. He fell asleep thinking about what Earl was making him do the next night and apparently had a nightmare about it.

Joey tried to get his mind off of the daunting task before falling back asleep. *Lindsey.* He pushed the thought of Earl and the dead diver out of his head and focused on Lindsey and the wonderful time they had the past two days. He couldn't wait to see her again. She had the closing shifts all week at the dive shop and Joey was working during the day so they wouldn't be able to see each other again until the weekend. Lindsey had promised to stop by the restaurant and have lunch with Joey sometime during the week before heading into the shop. And Joey was planning on stopping by at the shop after work to look at gear and spend time with Lindsey. She had offered to let him use her discount for anything he wanted there. Maybe he would get a new dive light.

* * *

Joey looked across the room at his alarm clock. It was blasting staticky country music from a local station from its small speaker and displayed 7:00 in dim red digits. Time to get up and start his day. At least he hadn't had any more nightmares.

He was glad he hadn't woken up his parents with his scream.

It was going to be a long day. He had to work until four this afternoon and he had told Lindsey he would stop by the shop after work. He had been hoping to stay there with her until closing if she wasn't too busy. That plan was no longer an option. He had to try to get some sleep before meeting Earl at midnight. He still had to work tomorrow and didn't know how long Earl was going to keep him out looking for the body. He wished he could think of a way to get out of it but he had already tried a few excuses on Earl and all it did was buy him a twenty-four hour delay. Maybe he would get lucky and find the body fast and be done with it.

No sense in dwelling on it all morning. Joey got out of bed and headed across the hall to the bathroom. It had only been three days since his fall but his hands were already beginning to feel better. They were still sore but he could at least get them under the faucet without pain shooting through them and up his arms. He splashed water on his face and headed to the kitchen to grab breakfast. His mother was already up and making pancakes.

"Good morning Joey."

"Morning mom."

"I decided to make some pancakes for breakfast this morning since you didn't have a very good breakfast yesterday. I apologize for all the things I said yesterday. I know you like to scuba dive. I was just worried all day long after seeing that article in the paper yesterday morning. All I want is for you to promise me you'll be careful and not do anything like that boy did. You're too young to have something like that happen to you."

She placed a tall stack of pancakes on a plate in front of him.

Joey thought about how beautiful Morrison cavern had been and how he wanted to go back. He quickly stuffed his mouth full of pancakes. His mother was always getting on him about talking with food in his mouth. He didn't want to make a promise that he might not be able to keep.

He quickly ate a few bites. With half the pancakes still on his plate Joey got up from the table.

"I have to get to work."

"But you hardly touched your breakfast."

That was part of the problem. His mother was always getting onto him about losing weight but she didn't do anything to help it. In fact, if anything, she only facilitated his eating problem.

"I'm not too hungry this morning."

Joey quickly walked out of the kitchen to his room before she could say anything else. He took a quick shower, got dressed and headed to work. Time to begin his long day.

26

August 8, 2011 4pm

It had been a long, busy day at work for Joey. The lunch service had been unusually crowded. Summer months were typically steady due to the tourists that visited the area but Joey couldn't remember having worked that hard any other day. On top of that he hadn't gotten very good sleep because of his nightmare. And he hadn't had time to take a lunch break. He was definitely not planning on having his usual two sandwiches but he hadn't even had one.

By the time he left work that afternoon he was exhausted. So exhausted he entertained the idea of going straight home to get some sleep before having to meet Earl at midnight. But the thought of spending more time with Lindsey kept him from doing that, even though it would have been the smart thing to do considering what Earl was making him do later that night.

Fifteen minutes after leaving the restaurant he pulled into the parking lot of the dive shop. The lot was empty, which meant Lindsey would be free to spend some time with him. He pulled into a parking space directly in front of the door and shut the engine of his car off. Exhaustion enveloped his entire body.

Joey leaned his head back on the headrest and closed his eyes. He just needed a few seconds to gather some energy.

Joey's eyes popped open and he felt hot and disoriented. He quickly looked at his watch and saw that twenty minutes had passed since he had arrived at the dive shop. He had fallen asleep! Hopefully Lindsey was busy restocking or cleaning or doing something and hadn't noticed him sitting in his car all that time.

He rubbed his eyes and quickly stepped out of the car. Even though it was hot it felt good to leave the mugginess of the car into the fresh air. But the rapid movement caused him to feel lightheaded and he had to steady himself on the car to keep from falling over. He didn't know how he was going to get through the night.

After a minute or so the lightheadedness passed and Joey got himself together and walked toward the glass door of the dive shop. He could see Lindsey in the back of the shop through the door. Maybe she hadn't noticed him in the parking lot all this time. He opened the door and felt the cool blast of the air conditioning of the shop as he stepped in. Lindsey turned toward him when she heard the chime from the electronic sensor that announced whenever a customer walked through the front door. As soon as she saw him a big smile appeared on her face. She ran over and gave him a big hug.

"Hi sweetie! I was wondering how long it would take you to come inside."

She had noticed! "U-um, sorry about that. It was real busy at work and I-I didn't get much rest last night. I-I guess it just caught up with me."

"Oh don't worry about it sweetie. I was just starting to get a little worried about you. It's hot out there today."

She paused for a few seconds and stared at him with a concerned look on her face.

"Are you feeling okay? You look tired and stressed. Did I wear you out too much this weekend?"

"N-No! You didn't wear me out! I'm okay. Like I said, I-I didn't sleep well last night. I g-guess I'm just tired." Joey smiled weakly hoping Lindsey would let it pass and not ask any more questions.

"I'm sorry you didn't sleep well. Hopefully you'll get much better sleep tonight."

"I sure hope so too." Joey said as he looked down at the floor and away from Lindsey.

He hated to lie to her but he couldn't drag her into the mess he had gotten himself into with Earl. He didn't think she would understand. And it was too early in their relationship - if that's what this was - for something like that. He couldn't believe a girl like Lindsey would even want to spend time with him. If she knew about the trouble he was mixed up in she would definitely keep her distance.

"So, how has work been?" Joey said to change the subject.

"It's been slow today, but that's typical for a Monday. In a little bit, once work lets out for everyone, there should be some customers returning scuba tanks that they rented over the weekend but I don't expect much more. We don't have any classes scheduled this evening. You're the first person to walk in here all afternoon. I don't mind though. Especially on a Monday. It gives me a chance to straighten up the place. It can get pretty messy and disorganized in here on the weekends. You mentioned your day was busy?"

"Yeah, it was a real busy day. N-no sooner did I clear a table and the hostess had more people seated there. I-I don't think we had an empty table from 10:30 until sometime after 2. I-I was glad to get out of there." Joey sheepishly looked away. "And I-I'm glad to be here talking to you now."

"Awwwww, that's so sweet. I'm glad you're here too. It sure was a fun weekend. I had a great time diving and spending time with you. And I'm real sorry about the dive yesterday. I'm still in shock about that."

"You d-don't have to apologize. Like you said, the t-tide charts must have been off. At least we got out of it alright."

There was silence for several seconds as they stood there looking at each other. Joey wasn't sure what else to talk about but in the short time he had known Lindsey he hadn't known her to be at a loss for words.

"Umm..."

"Are you..."

They both started at the same time.

"I'm sorry," Joey apologized. "Go ahead."

"Are you here to look at scuba gear? Or...did you stop by just to say hi?" A smile appeared on Lindsey's face as she asked the latter.

Joey looked away a little embarrassed. "I-I stopped by to say hi and s-see you."

"Well, then why are you looking away?" Lindsey teased. "Want me to show you around the shop? I know you've been here plenty of times but I'm sure you haven't seen the compressor room or regulator workbench. Let me give you the grand tour."

"Sure!"

Joey was at the shop a lot longer than he had planned. Not that he minded all that much. He was spending time with Lindsey. But it also meant he wouldn't have time to take a nap before having to meet with Earl. He should be able to sneak in a nap on the boat as Earl drove it out to where they had tossed the body overboard. If he wasn't too nervous to sleep that is. Regardless, they couldn't be out there too long. The area was pretty deep and Joey's dive wouldn't last very long. Maybe he could still get home in time to get a few hours of sleep.

When Joey got home he barely acknowledged his parents. He said hello and good night and went straight to his room. He only had about an hour and a half before he had to leave. Maybe he could sneak in a quick nap.

* * *

An hour and forty minutes later Joey's eyes popped open. He quickly glanced at the clock and saw he had slept far longer than he should have. He jumped up out of bed and slowly opened his bedroom door. He listened to the sounds of the house. He could hear the sounds of some sitcom coming from the television in his parents' bedroom. He looked down the hall and could see an occasional splash of light peeking out from beneath their bedroom door. It looked like they had retired for the night already.

Joey crept out of his room across the hall to the bathroom.

He turned the faucet so a slow stream of cold water poured out and splashed some water on his face to try to wake up. With that done he quietly stepped out of the bathroom and walked down the hallway toward the kitchen. He opened the back door and slipped out into the warm night, easing the door closed behind him.

He had thought about parking his car in the street when he got home an hour earlier but he was concerned his parents might ask him why he didn't park in the driveway and he couldn't think of a good reason to give them. So just like the night he was forced to pull the dead body out of the cave he put his car in neutral and pushed it out of the driveway and down the street a few houses before he started it. Ten minutes later he came to a stop in front of Earl's house.

No sooner had Joey cut the engine to the car and he practically jumped out of his skin to Earl opening the passenger door and hopping in, the smell of stale beer and cigarettes following him.

"Where ya bin boy? Y'all's late!"

"I-I-I..."

"Oh, quit yer stammerin'. I'm jus' messin' witcha. Y'all's got sleep lines on y'all's face. Take a little nap?"

"I-I-I…"

"Ne'er min'. Les git goin' ta da boat. Time's a wastin'."

"Wh-wh-what about the scuba tanks?

"They're awready in da boat. I brought 'em down earlier. Dontchoo worry boy! I ain't ferget'n nut'n. Git on now."

Joey started the car and backed onto the road. Although he wasn't looking forward to diving in the middle of the gulf at night he wanted to get this over with and have it behind him. He was tired of dealing with Earl...and just plain tired. He wanted some normalcy in his life again. Especially now that he had Lindsey in his life.

A few minutes later Joey backed his car into a parking space close to Earl's boat. Earl jumped out of the car and headed directly to the boat. Joey slowly climbed out of the driver's seat, still a little sore from the last time they did this. He walked around to the back of the car and popped the trunk open so he could grab his scuba gear and load it onto the boat. He was dreading this and looking forward to getting it over with at the same time.

As he carried his gear toward the boat Earl fired up the engines, revved them, and then brought them to an idle. Joey approached the boat and carefully looked over the side on the deck where the body had been just four days earlier. Obviously nothing was there so he tossed his gear into the boat and returned to his car to make sure he had everything. He didn't see anything else in his trunk. He lowered the trunk lid and returned to the boat. Earl was pulling the ropes from the cleats and getting ready to launch the boat.

Joey stood a few feet away watching Earl's hands working the ropes as if he was in a race. Earl pulled the last rope and turned to face Joey.

"Com'on boy! Git in!"

Joey climbed on board with Earl right behind him. Earl quickly climbed up to the top deck and then slowly pulled away from the slip. This was it. There was no turning back. Joey didn't know whether he hoped to find the body quickly or whether he didn't want to find it at all. He wasn't sure how long Earl would make him look, or how many times he would make him come back out to look if he didn't find it right away, so he thought finding it quickly would be the best outcome for him in the long run.

As they slowly made their way out of the marina, Joey decided he would try to get another nap. He stepped inside the cabin and stretched out on the padded bench. Not even a minute had passed and Joey fell asleep to the hum of the engines motoring their way out toward the open gulf.

* * *

"I'm awake mom. Just let me stretch a little." Joey said as he awoke with a start to being shaken by the shoulder.

His mom used to shake him awake like that when he was in high school. Joey wasn't much of a morning person and the alarm didn't always get him out of bed.

"Git up boy. We're heah."

That didn't sound like his mom, or his dad for that matter. Joey's eyes popped open and he saw Earl standing over him.

"Com'on! Les git goin'. Boy, yer a hard sleeper. I bin tryin' ta wake y'all fer five whole minits."

Joey reached up and rubbed his face. He wondered how long he had slept. He looked at his watch and saw he had been asleep for almost an hour and a half. It should have taken less than an hour to get to the location where they had dumped the body.

"Wh-what happened? What took us so long to get out

here?"

"I bin cruisin' roun' scannin' da bottom. I finally foun' sumtin' but y'all need ta git in da water quick. I din't anchor in. We prolly drifted off in da time I bin down here tryin' ta wake y'all. I'll have ta scan fer it sa'more. Y'all's gonna hafta drop in as soon as I fin' it ag'in."

Joey scrambled to his feet and headed toward the back of the boat where his scuba gear was piled up. Earl had already turned on the lights on the boat so Joey could see what he was doing. Slowly, he started to assemble his gear.

"Hurry up boy. We ain't got all night!"

"I-I'm trying sir." Joey stammered.

A few minutes later Joey had his gear put together and the BC and scuba tank on his back. Earl climbed back up to the controls and started his search for whatever he had seen earlier.

Several minutes passed before Earl yelled down, "It's right b'low us boy. Showtahm!"

Joey cautiously looked over the side of the boat into the black foreboding water. Even though he lived in Santa Rosa Beach, only minutes from the coast, he didn't spend much time at the beach. The gulf had always made him nervous. It just looked so vast and unknown. It was especially worse at night when it was dark.

It didn't help that when he was young his dad decided to give him swimming lessons. And his dad's version of swimming lessons consisted of carrying Joey out to where he could no longer stand, dropping him in the water, and walking back to the beach. Joey was terrified. His mother had hurried out to rescue him. His father didn't live that one down for a while.

Joey had only done the one dive at the jetties the day before and that was only because it was Lindsey who had invited him. He recalled looking toward the gulf and thinking about how big and empty it looked right before the massive current came and tried to push them out into it.

The Florida freshwater springs like Eddy and Morrison had banks all around them that could be seen. The bottoms of the basins could be seen from high on the banks on good days. During the day not much could be seen in the gulf waters and at night nothing at all could be seen. Joey stood there wondering what might be lurking beneath the surface waiting for him to jump in.

"Y'all's wastin' time boy! Whatcha waitin' fer? Git in so's we can git dat body an' git dis o'er wit."

"Ye-yes sir." Joey said as he sat on the side of the boat and swung his legs to the outside so they were hanging over the black water. He put his regulator in his mouth, took a few breaths from it and slowly eased himself closer to the edge. He continued to inch himself closer to the water while at the same time dreading the thought of dropping into the black abyss below him. Suddenly the boat motors, which had been idling quietly, roared to life. This startled Joey, causing him to jump. He lost his balance and plummeted into the cool dark water below him.

27

August 9, 2011 sometime after midnight

Joey was swallowed up by the blackness. He knew he was plummeting to the depths of the gulf because he could feel the pressure in his ears increasing. He reached up to pinch his nose so he could blow against it gently. He needed to equalize the pressure in his ears before it got so bad he would rupture an eardrum. It wasn't working. He had gotten too deep without equalizing and now it was too late.

Joey started kicking to try to get shallower. The kicking didn't get him shallower but it did slow his descent. He grabbed the low pressure inflator hose on his BC and pressed the button that would send air from his tank into the BC and slow his descent even more. Nothing happened!

In his sleepy haze he had forgotten to open the valve on his tank! And apparently he had also forgotten to breathe since he fell off the boat into the water. Suddenly Joey felt his lungs start to hurt. He needed some air soon. He reached back behind his head with his right hand. He felt the hoses coming out of the regulator attached to the valve but he couldn't quite reach the knob to open the tank valve. He tried to stretch his arm more but there was no stretch left.

Reaching back with his left hand Joey grabbed the hoses on that side and pulled up and forward on them. He could feel the ridged knob of the valve brush the fingertips of his right hand. He pulled up harder with his left arm while pushing on the knob with his right hand. As he did this he felt the knob give way slightly. Then his finger slipped off of it. He quickly moved his fingers back to the knob and pulled up even harder with his left hand. He felt the knob and was finally able to grasp it. He worked to turn it counterclockwise and open the valve. *Which way was counterclockwise?!?* Joey was usually standing behind the tank when he opened the valve. He couldn't remember with the valve behind him.

He tried turning the knob toward him and it didn't move. He turned it away and heard a whoosh as the air from the tank was released into the first stage regulator, hoses, and finally, to the second stage regulator in his mouth. He quickly took in a breath but got a mouth full of salt water instead. He forgot to purge the regulator. He violently coughed the water out of his mouth with what little air he had in his lungs and grabbed the second stage regulator, depressing the purge button while taking in a large breath and finally feeling air fill his lungs. *Relief!* He was suddenly very thankful that Lindsey had told him to move the tank higher on his BC. Had it been in the lower position he was used to he would never have been able to reach the valve.

With the burning in his lungs gone, Joey noticed the pressure in his ears again. He reached for the low pressure inflator and pressed the button again. This time he heard the air whoosh through the hoses and felt the BC tighten around him.

His descent eased off and he came to a stop. A few seconds later Joey started to ascend slowly and he felt the pain in his ears ease off. He tried pinching his nose again to equalize but he still wasn't shallow enough for that to be effective. As he continued to ascend Joey reached up and let some of the air out of the BC. He didn't want the air to expand too much in his BC and cause him to have a runaway ascent to the surface.

A few more feet and Joey was finally able to equalize his ears and the pain disappeared. He looked at the dive computer on his wrist. It had finally stopped its incessant beeping and returned to normal so Joey decided to use it on this dive. He pressed a button on the side of the dive computer to illuminate the display. The depth reading was 29 feet. The maximum depth reading was 54 feet. Joey was shocked he hadn't ruptured an ear drum.

Joey felt for his dive light, found it, and turned it on. A dim yellow light creeped out from the front of the canister. It didn't even penetrate a foot into the water but it comforted Joey a little to have some light and be able to see, even if it was only a few inches. He hoped he hadn't gotten too much off course during his ordeal. He reached down and grabbed his pressure gauge to see how much air he had in his tank – still 2800 psi. Well, he hadn't had the tank valve open for very long.

No sense wasting any more time. Joey lifted the low pressure hose up above him and released a little air so he could begin his descent. He had no idea how deep it was here. Earl hadn't bothered to tell him. He hoped it wasn't too deep and that he hadn't gone too much off from whatever it was Earl had seen on the bottom. He pointed the light down in hopes of seeing the floor of the gulf before he hit it but he wasn't too hopeful. A few seconds later he slammed against the sandy bottom into a cloud of dust that extinguished the light completely.

Pushing up off the grainy terrain below him Joey ascended out of the silt. He could see the faint yellow light again. He looked at his dive computer. His depth was 116 feet. He didn't have much time before he would have to begin his ascent. But he had no idea which way to go. Earl hadn't told him anything about what he had scanned on the gulf floor. Joey started swimming in the direction he was facing. It was as good as any. He would spend a few minutes going in different directions until it was time to ascend. At this point he didn't care whether he found the body or not.

Twelve minutes later Joey was heading in the fourth direction since he began the search. Still nothing. He swam about two minutes each way and turned around to head back to where he had started, which he only knew where that was because there was still a cloud of silt above the sandy bottom from his crash landing earlier. Looking down at his pressure gauge he noticed he had just over 1000 psi left in his tank. He would swim out this one last direction and then begin his ascent. Earl would have to be satisfied with that. After all, he hadn't told Joey anything about what he had seen or where.

Once again there was still nothing to be seen. It was just flat sandy bottom. As Joey was swimming back to his starting point he heard a beeping sound. He looked at the dive computer on his wrist and saw it was flashing at him again. He had violated his no decompression limits! Looking at his pressure gauge he saw he had about 800 psi left. He quickened his pace and returned to the cloud of silt a few seconds later. He immediately began ascending.

Looking at his dive computer again he read the numbers and tried to make sense of them. If only he had studied up on this stupid thing after the last time this happened. He understood what the display was telling him as long as he was doing everything right and staying within no decompression limits. But as soon as he overstayed those limits he was lost. The backlight on the screen just kept flashing at him making him even more panicked. *Why did they need to make it do that?!?*

Joey slowly ascended, trying to go slower than the smallest bubbles from his regulator just like he was taught. He also kept an eye on the depth readout on his dive computer. At least that was in the same location on the display. About three minutes after he began his ascent he reached 30 feet below the surface. He slowed his ascent even more. He needed to stop at 15 feet and stay there as long as the air in his tank would allow. He remembered something from class about 8 minutes but he doubted he had that much air left. He looked at his pressure gauge again – 300 psi. Not very much. He should have skipped that last search spoke and ascended. Joey looked back at his dive computer – 17 feet. That was close enough. He released a little more air from his BC and watched the number change to 18, then 19. He immediately put some air back in the BC, precious air he should be saving for breathing.

He hoped he wasn't too far from Earl's boat. As dark as it was out he doubted Earl would be able to see him once he surfaced. Joey tried to hold his depth in the water as close to 15 feet as he could. He was doing a pretty good job, if he didn't say so himself, especially considering he couldn't see anything around him. He also watched as the needle on his pressure gauge dropped closer and closer to zero. His dive computer was still flashing and beeping. At this point there was nothing Joey could do about it. He would stay underwater until he had no air left in his tank and then ascend the last 15 feet to the surface and hope Earl and the boat were close by.

That moment came all too soon. As Joey took his next breath he could feel the regulator becoming more difficult to pull air from. After four breaths like that it suddenly cut him off about halfway through an inhalation. His tank was empty. Joey did as he was taught and began the final part of his ascent to the surface while blowing out the half lung of air he had gotten with that last breath. His head broke the surface, he spit out his regulator, and gasped in a huge breath of air. *He made it!*

He exhaled and suddenly his head was back underwater. Joey began kicking his feet to get his mouth back above the surface. He felt the warm sea air on his head again and opened his mouth to take in another breath. This time he reached for his BC inflator and exhaled the breath into it. He quickly took another breath and exhaled that one into the BC inflator as well. Joey did this repeatedly until the BC was full and keeping him afloat. Then he relaxed, dropped his head back, and floated on the surface breathing in the warm salty sea air.

After catching his breath Joey realized he hadn't seen nor heard Earl. He picked up his head and looked around. There was nothing but blackness in front of him. He felt a panic rise inside him and started to spin around so he could see if the boat was behind him. Just as Joey felt the panic starting to get out of control he saw the lights from Earl's boat in the distance. It didn't appear too far but he knew it was too far for Earl to see him. If he hadn't been so far out Joey would just swim back to shore. But he had no idea how far they were. He didn't even know which direction the coast was. Reluctantly he began swimming toward Earl and his boat. Hopefully Earl wouldn't make him do another dive.

28

Back on the boat 20 minutes later Joey practically collapsed on the deck. He was exhausted from the swim back to the boat on top of the stress of the dive he had just done. He was definitely ready to crawl in between the cool crisp sheets on his bed and pass out. Earl had other plans though.

"Com'on kid! Swap out y'all's tank an' les git ya back in dare."

Joey couldn't believe his ears at first. But when he thought about it, he wasn't all that surprised. When Earl wanted something done he make sure it was done by any means necessary. He didn't care how it affected others. Joey thought about begging Earl to not make him do another dive. He knew it was futile though. Arguing, begging, anything other than just doing as he was told would only waste time. In the end, he knew he would give in to Earl's demands.

* * *

The result of the second dive was no better than the first. Joey had remembered to open his tank valve and inflate his BC before splashing in the water. And this time he jumped in without any help from Earl and the boat motors. Joey had even remembered to ask Earl where he was seeing something and Earl gave him some vague response. But there was still no body to be found during his search. The only thing Joey found was some old tires piled up under a bunch of sand. They were hardly recognizable. That must have been what Earl was seeing from the boat.

This time Joey cut off his search sooner. He began his ascent with plenty of air in his tank to make it to the surface before the tank was empty. He also surfaced closer to the boat and it only took 5 minutes to swim to it.

Earl was not happy that Joey hadn't found the body and he went off on a rant pacing back and forth on the deck of the boat. There was nothing he could do about it though. He had only brought two tanks from the dive shop and Joey had breathed one empty and the other almost empty.

Joey was relieved that they could finally head back and he would soon be in his bed. However, he also knew this would not be the last time he and Earl would be on the gulf in the middle of the night. He had only known Earl for a short time, less than a week, but one thing he already knew about him was that he was very stubborn and persistent and he always got what he wanted.

On the ride back to the marina, Joey tried to sleep a little more but he was too worked up about the thought of having to come back out to the gulf every night until the body was found. Earl hadn't said as much but Joey completely expected this to be the plan.

They arrived at the marina and Joey loaded his gear into the trunk of the car as Earl secured the boat to the dock. The ride to Earl's was quiet. Earl didn't say a single word on the way back. This scared Joey more than Earl's threats. Earl had become very talkative and always had something to say, especially when he was angry.

Joey pulled into Earl's driveway and Earl opened the door and exited the car without a word. He didn't even look back at Joey as he walked toward the house. Joey sat in the driveway and watched Earl unlock the door and disappear inside. He waited another minute to see if Earl would come back out to tell him he wanted to meet again the next night. He thought about knocking on the door and asking Earl what the plan was. Not that Joey wanted to continue these activities with Earl but he was afraid Earl might show back up at his house and set his mom off again.

He decided against knocking on the door. Earl was obviously not in his right mind and Joey didn't want to know what that might mean for him. He put the car in reverse and backed out of the driveway to head home. This complete reversal in Earl's behavior was concerning Joey. No, actually, it was terrifying.

29

August 17, 2011

It had been more than a week since Joey's last encounter with Earl. Joey had been full of nerves and jumpy the first couple of days. He regretted not knocking on Earl's door to question him about what was next. The anticipation of not knowing was worse than knowing he was in for a sleepless night on the gulf looking for a dead body.

Joey's days were fairly routine. He spent 8 hours at work bussing tables then headed over to the dive shop to spend time with Lindsey for an hour or so if she wasn't too busy. Lindsey had a couple of evenings off this week but Joey was put on the dinner shift those same days. They didn't even get to dive on the weekend because it was Lindsey's turn to work at the shop. It seemed Joey just couldn't catch a break.

And to top it off he wasn't getting great sleep because he was so worried about Earl showing up on his doorstep looking for him again. He considered going to see Earl so he could get some closure on things and move on with his life without being in constant fear of Earl popping back in whenever he decided it was time to look for the body again. He hadn't quite decided whether or not that was a good idea.

* * *

Joey and Lindsey's schedules finally lined up and they both had an evening off from work the same day. Even though he had been seeing her at work every chance he had and they would text back and forth throughout the day, Joey still wasn't sure about their relationship. They hadn't had any time together outside of work since their weekend of diving. He didn't know if they were just good friends or if there was a potential for a romantic relationship between them. Their schedules weren't lining up to allow him to find out.

When Joey learned they both had the same evening free from work he decided he would ask Lindsey if she wanted to go out to eat and maybe catch a movie. His self-esteem wasn't that great and normally he wouldn't be so forward with a girl but they had been seeing a lot of each other. He really liked Lindsey and she seemed to like him.. He thought if she wasn't romantically interested she would be nice about letting him down.

Joey was at the dive shop spending time with Lindsey one evening as was his usual routine. He had been there so much that he began helping her with her duties, mainly restocking, organizing, and cleaning. The owner of the shop didn't mind. She even joked that she was getting two employees for the price of one. While they were squatting down next to each other organizing a shelf of scuba booties Joey got brave and asked Lindsey about dinner and a movie.

"U-Um, s-so you don't have to work the next c-couple days?

"I've got them off. Clear and free to do anything I want."

"I-I was thinking. U-Um… W-would you want to go get d-dinner somewhere tomorrow. And then m-maybe a movie?"

This was it. The moment of truth. Joey held his breath in anticipation of a rejection.

Lindsey stopped what she was doing but didn't say anything right away. Joey examined her face but he couldn't tell what she was thinking. The pause and the silence was killing him. He immediately regretted asking her out. Then…

"I would love to sweetie."

Those were the most wonderful words Joey had ever heard. Joey almost fell back from his squatting position. If he hadn't grabbed hold of the shelf in front of him he would have been splayed out on his back.

"Do you have anywhere in mind, sweetie? Any particular movie you want to go see?"

Joey hadn't expected Lindsey to say yes so he hadn't thought out any of the details. His father had recently taken the family to a waterfront restaurant in Seaside, only about 15 minutes away from Santa Rosa Beach, and it had good food and a romantic atmosphere, but not too romantic. Joey suggested that restaurant.

"Oh, I've heard of that place," Lindsey responded, "I've been wanting to try it out. That sounds great!"

"I-I didn't have any particular movie in mind," Joey added. "We c-can look at the movie listings in D-Destin and pick something out together."

"Anything you've been wanting to see?" Lindsey asked as she pulled out her phone to bring up the listings for the Destin Commons movie theater.

* * *

Joey picked Lindsey up the next evening for their date, or whatever it was, he still wasn't completely sure, and they headed to Seaside. Joey had called to make reservations just in case it was busy. It was a weekday but Seaside had a lot of tourism and restaurants could be busy every night. They were seated a few minutes after they arrived and began looking through the menu. Joey hadn't noticed the prices when his father had brought them there. They were a little higher than he expected. He would be short on his payment to his parents this week. Just something else to deal with. He pushed that out of his mind and focused on the beautiful woman sitting across from him.

The waiter brought them their drinks as they looked over the menu. When the waiter returned Lindsey and Joey ordered their food. Thankfully Lindsey had decided on a selection that wasn't too expensive. The waiter left and they sat there sipping their colas, talking about how work had been over the past several days.

Joey was sitting at the table looking into Lindsey's striking blue eyes while listening to her sweet southern accent while she recounted a story about some divers that came in over the weekend acting like they were big shots, but in reality, had only a few dozen dives and didn't know what they didn't know. He was only half listening to the story. He was mostly thinking how incredibly lucky he was to be sitting across from Lindsey at that moment. Then his thoughts were interrupted.

The door to the restaurant was located behind Lindsey and it suddenly flew open slamming into the wall next to it. Joey looked up at the noise and saw Earl stepping through with a couple of other men. Joey's heart immediately sank. He was sure Earl would spot him and come over to talk right in front of Lindsey. Joey hadn't told Lindsey a word of anything that had happened at Eddy Spring or with Earl since the day he found the body beyond the grate. She was about to learn all about it because of Joey's sheer dumb luck in choosing the same restaurant Earl decided to visit on the same evening.

Lindsey had been in the middle of the story about the "big shot" divers when Earl came barreling through the door. The expression on Joey's face must have shocked Lindsey because she stopped mid-sentence.

"Joey, what's wrong?"

He didn't respond, instead staring straight at Earl dumbfounded at his horrible luck.

"Joey?"

He snapped out of his trance, "U-ummm, yeah?"

"Are you okay? You just turned white as a sheet."

"I-I-I'm okay. I just….." He didn't know what to say. He had never planned on telling Lindsey about what happened and now he might have to…on their first date…or what he hoped was a date.

Earl stood at the door and scanned the restaurant while waiting to be seated. That's when he noticed Joey sitting at the table with Lindsey. His face brightened into a smile and he turned toward the men with him, said something Joey couldn't hear, and walked directly to Joey and Lindsey's table.

"How ya doin' kid?" Earl bellowed out in the middle of the restaurant causing all of the patrons in the room to look over.

Joey cringed at Earl's roughness, "U-u-u-mmm, I'm okay."

"Haven' seen y'all in a while. Ya haven' e'en bin out divin'."

"I-I-I've been busy at work."

"Well, com'on by dis week. I need ta talk ta ya." Earl breathed down on them. Joey could smell the mixture of alcohol and cigarettes on his breath. And just as quickly as he had appeared, Earl briskly turned away and stumbled back to rejoin his friends.

* * *

"What was that all about, Joey? How do you know that man?"

" I-I met him at Eddy Spring. He's the manager."

"I know who he is. I also know he's a bad man. I've heard of him being involved in bad things. Why does he want to talk to you, Joey?"

"I-I don't know."

"Com'on, Joey," Lindsey said with a tone of skepticism, "you must have some idea of what he wants. Someone like that doesn't just walk up to people out of the blue and say they need to talk."

Joey didn't know how to respond. If he didn't tell her something she was going to know he was keeping things from her. That was no way to begin a relationship. But if he told her what happened and what he helped Earl do it could very well scare her off.

"C-c-can we talk about this later, in private? I-I'd rather not talk about it here in the restaurant. With him right there."

Lindsey nodded and picked up the dessert card that was sitting on the table. She looked it over until the food was served. They ate quietly, occasionally making small talk but nothing like their usual conversation. Lindsey didn't even finish recounting the story about the divers that came into the shop. She was definitely upset over the encounter with Earl. And Joey couldn't blame her one bit.

30

They finished their dinner, opting to skip dessert. Joey paid the bill and they headed out to the car. Joey opened the passenger door for Lindsey and then walked around to the driver's side and got in. As soon as he shut the door Lindsey immediately turned to him.

"Okay, mister, what was that all about in there? What did that nasty man want to talk to you about?"

"L-let's get out of this parking lot first. He's still in there and I-I don't want to ch-chance him coming out while we're still sitting here."

Lindsey huffed and turned away from Joey. He put the car in reverse, backed out of the parking space and drove up the street until he found an empty parking lot to a public beach access path. He pulled into a parking space and shut off the car. They sat in the car in silence for about a minute while Joey contemplated what he was going to tell Lindsey. He decided truth was the best option. If it scared her away there was nothing he could do about it. It was better than lying to her and having her find out down the road.

* * *

An hour later Joey finished recounting all the details of the past couple weeks, from the moment he found the body beyond the grate, to Earl threatening him if he didn't return that night to pull the body out, and getting rid of it in the gulf. He told Lindsey about Earl coming to his house and talking to his mother. He finally finished with a description of the dives he was forced to do in the gulf searching for the body they had gotten rid of. Lindsey sat next to him in silence the entire time he was talking. She never said a word or gave any indication to how she was taking it.

He silently waited for her reaction. He fully expected her to demand to be taken home and for him to never call her or come by the shop to see her again. He wouldn't blame her one bit. He wasn't sure he wouldn't do the same.

"Oh bless your heart, Joey!! It all makes sense now! How tired and stressed you've looked, falling asleep in your car outside the shop. You poor thing!" She took his hand into hers.

Joey couldn't believe his ears. Lindsey wasn't mad at him.

"I-I should have told you sooner but I didn't know how to bring it up or what to say. I-I just hoped it would go away. I thought it had after the first night. Then Earl came to my house and I was in too deep at that point. I thought it might finally be done because I hadn't heard from him in over a week. I-I don't know what I'm going to do now. I-I don't know how to get out of this. He just keeps demanding more."

"Well, sweetie, we will figure something out. That man is bad news. Everyone in the dive community knows that. When he became the manager at Eddy Spring a few years ago the dive shops in the area that use it for training were concerned with the changes he might make, and with due cause. He's raised the cost of everything – the entry fees, camping fees, and even tank fills. Maybe this will finally be what gets rid of him."

"Wait!! No, you can't tell anyone! What if I get in trouble?? I helped him get rid of a dead body! I even talked to the cops and lied to them about what I know!"

Lindsey paused for a moment. Joey could just barely see her face in the glow of the street lights coming through the windshield. He could barely make out the wrinkles on her forehead. She was in deep thought.

"You're right, sweetie, we can't tell anyone. We're going to have to figure something else out to get you out of this. We're going to have to deal with Earl ourselves."

31

Joey didn't know what Lindsey had in mind but he felt a lot better having gotten all of that off his chest. Even if she didn't think of a way to get him out of this mess he had gotten himself into it felt good just sharing the details with someone else. He had been bottling all this in for so long he didn't realize how much it was stressing him until he finally released it all like the vent on a pressure cooker.

He did notice that Lindsey was behaving a little strangely after learning about all that had happened. Not strange in a way that Joey felt she didn't like him. In fact, it seemed to bring them closer together.

After he finished getting Lindsey caught up on everything with Earl she suggested they pass on the movie and take a walk along the beach instead. She told Joey she needed to clear her mind after hearing about everything he had gone through the previous couple weeks and walking on the beach always helped. When they stepped on the sand, Lindsey kicked her flip flops off and ran to the water. Joey followed. When Joey caught up to Lindsey she was standing ankle deep in the water looking out toward the gulf. Joey stopped a few feet behind her and stared at the blackness of the gulf. He wondered if she was thinking about the dead diver being out there somewhere in that vast underwater void like he was.

She suddenly turned toward Joey, grabbed his hand in hers and pulled him along the shoreline. They walked along the beach with the warm gulf water gently lapping at their feet and ankles. The sound of the waves was soothing and relaxing. A few times the waves broke close to them and splashed up onto their shorts. Lindsey was closer to the water and jumped but then just laughed and kept walking. It was good to hear her laughing. They walked together hand in hand in silence for about half an hour.

Lindsey suddenly stopped walking and turned toward Joey. They stood under the moonlight facing each other. She looked up into his eyes. Joey looked back into her eyes and saw something different in them. He wasn't sure what. He thought she was going to tell him she didn't want to spend time with him anymore. After what he had gotten himself into he couldn't blame her if she told him that. Instead, she reached her hands around to the back of his neck, stood on her tiptoes, leaned into him and pressed her soft, full lips onto his. Joey wrapped his arms around her and held her tight. They stood there holding each other with their lips pressed together for what seemed like an eternity to him. A blissful eternity.

Lindsey slowly pulled back, took his hand in hers again and started walking back the way they had come. They slowly walked back with just the sounds of the surf hitting the beach, holding hands, enjoying the moment. Joey's stress completely gone for the first time since finding the body beyond the grate.

* * *

Back in the car Lindsey asked Joey in her southern drawl, "Do you have any plans this weekend, sweetie?"

"N-nothing in particular. I-I was hoping to spend some time with you."

"I have to divemaster for an open water class all weekend. Would you like to come along? You can dive while I'm with the class and we can spend time together during the surface intervals."

"Sure!" Joey was excited at the thought of spending another entire weekend with Lindsey.

"One thing though," Lindsey added, "the class is at Eddy Spring."

"Oh…." Joey wasn't sure he wanted to hang around Eddy Spring all weekend and chance being confronted by Earl. He knew he had to talk to Earl at some point, but at the same time, he didn't want to hear what Earl wanted.

"Hear me out, Joey. Earl wants to talk to you so let's get it done and over with. We'll ride in together in my car so he won't be able to get you to take him anywhere. And I'll be there for you."

Joey didn't want Lindsey to get involved in this mess. It was already bad enough she knew about it. But he really wanted to keep her out of it. On the other hand, Earl had seen Lindsey with him at the restaurant. It's possible he would recognize her at the scuba park and maybe confront her to get to Joey. So Joey decided it would be better if he were there with her to make sure Earl didn't bother her.

"Alright. I'll go with you this weekend. It is best to get this over with." Joey let Lindsey think she was helping him out, when in reality, he was going only to protect her from Earl.

32

August 20, 2011 6:30am

Joey ran out of his house at 6:30 Saturday morning. His parents were still in bed and he hadn't mentioned to them anything about his plans for the weekend. He scribbled a short note telling them he would be out with friends until dinner and left it on the kitchen table. His scuba gear was already with Lindsey so he wouldn't have to mess with it in his driveway and give his parents an opportunity to lecture him.

Lindsey pulled up in front of the house just as Joey stepped out of the door. He ran to her car and jumped in next to her. Lindsey quickly drove off. Joey had explained to her how his parents felt about him scuba diving and she was more than willing to do whatever she could to help him avoid another confrontation with them. She slowed the car as she approached the stop sign a block down the road, brought the car to a stop, and put it in park. She turned and surprised Joey with a hug and kiss. They held hands as she drove the rest of the way to Eddy Spring.

A little less than an hour later they turned onto the dirt road leading to the scuba park. It was the weekend so the gatehouse at the Eddy Spring entrance was staffed. Lindsey told the employee they were there to meet a dive class and they were directed to the main building to sign in and wait for the students and instructor.

As they drove the couple hundred feet from the gatehouse to the dive shop Joey noticed there were a couple of police cars parked in the area to the left of the changing rooms. There were deputies standing next to some divers at one of the picnic tables. Joey wondered what was going on.

Lindsey parked the car and they walked into the shop. She told the employee behind the counter she was there to divemaster for a class and was waiting for the instructor and students to arrive. The employee handed her a clipboard with some forms on it.

"You know what to do," she told Lindsey. "Oh, and by the way, I'm sure you heard about the diver that went missing here a few weeks ago. We have a couple of cave divers here today that are going to be in the cave searching some more. They shouldn't bother any of the classes in the basin, though. Just make sure you stay out of their way when they're going in or out of the cave."

Lindsey took the clipboard and nodded and walked off to a corner of the shop to wait for the class.

"This isn't good," Joey whispered. "This is only going to get Earl even more worked up."

"Maybe he already knew this was going to happen and that's why he wants to talk to you," she responded calmly. "Whatever happens, it'll all come out in the wash, sweetie."

While it was endearing to Joey when Lindsey used those

cute little southern phrases, this one meaning the truth will come out, it didn't make Joey feel any less anxious.

He had dealt with Earl enough to know this was going to upset him. If there were more divers searching for the body, they were probably planning on coming back until they found it. Earl was going to want to get it back and into the cave soon so they could eventually find it and stop coming to Eddy Spring. It couldn't be good for business to see police cars parked there every weekend. Joey had even seen talk in the internet groups about divers afraid to dive at Eddy Spring because of the possibility of a dead body in the cave.

And what did Lindsey mean by '*it'll all come out in the wash*'? Her demeanor was starting to worry Joey a little. He had been afraid to tell her because he was afraid it would scare her off. Instead, she seemed to be planning something, but he didn't know what. He was going to have to figure out a way to bring it up and ask her.

* * *

The students and instructor arrived and everyone signed in and paid their entry fees. Joey and Lindsey got back in her car and she moved it and backed it up against the chain barrier next to the Grande Vista Chalet. They unloaded their gear and started assembling it on one of the two picnic tables they had claimed for the class. Joey kept his distance so Lindsey could conduct her duties as divemaster but stayed close enough so if Earl showed up he could divert him away from her. Joey hadn't seen Earl yet since they had arrived, and he hoped he wouldn't see him at all, especially with the deputies present.

Lindsey was busy assisting the instructor getting the students ready for their first open water dive. Joey remembered that feeling as a student – pure excitement. It wasn't all that long ago but also seemed like it was ages ago.

He finished assembling his gear, put it on, weight belt not forgotten, and headed down the steep hill to the water. He wanted to do a self-check and make sure he had everything sorted before Lindsey got in the water with the class so he would be ready to dive when the students started their dive. He was planning on just swimming around and observing the class and Lindsey while they did their skills.

Once he was floating on the surface Joey noticed the divers that had been with the deputies were also in the water. They were standing in the shallows to the left of the steps that lead into the water. Their tanks were hanging on ropes tied to the railing. One of the divers already had a tank clipped onto his BC. They were diving sidemounts like the dead diver had been. Joey wondered just how small that cave was. What he had seen of it so far was a pretty decent size. He stayed close to see if he would hear them talk about the dive but they continued to get ready for their dive in silence.

Joey saw Lindsey, the students, and the instructor walking down the hill toward the water. He moved off to the side, a little closer to the cave divers, to wait for her. He noticed that in addition to the sidemounts the cave divers also had three extra tanks each, two 80cf tanks like Joey and the rest of the scuba divers here were using, except they didn't have them mounted on their backs. They also each had a smaller tank with a decal on the side with a large number 20 on it. He would have to remember to ask Lindsey about the small tanks.

The students stepped into the water and Lindsey led them to the buoy just above the cement platform. They did their last checks on the surface and the instructor told everyone to empty the air from their BCs and descend to the cement platform below. Joey did the same and followed them careful to stay out of their way. The platform was right next to one of the metal caverns so Joey decided to swim around the top of the cavern and look down on the class from there. He could see thousands of bubbles bursting from their regulators and rushing to the surface above.

While Joey watched the class he noticed the cave divers swimming by between him and the cement platform. They each had five scuba tanks – the sidemounts, the 80cf tanks strapped above those, and the smaller tanks hanging below. They also had really bright lights on the backs of their hands with a cable coming out of the end and connected to canisters on their lower backs. The lights were so bright he could see where they were pointed on the bottom of the basin in the middle of a bright sunny day! Joey really had to remember to ask Lindsey about those.

The first dive lasted about 30 minutes. Joey still had air in his tank but the students had breathed through most of the air in their tanks. To be fair, Joey was hanging out about 8-10 feet shallower and this wasn't his first dive. He doubted his breathing consumption was all that much better than theirs.

They spent about two hours on a surface interval. The instructor had to debrief the first dive and brief the second dive.

He also gave the students about an hour long break to bring their core body temperatures back up and to hydrate and snack a little. The water at Eddy Spring was 68F year round. And while it felt good to get into during the heat of the summer, it still cooled you off, especially when you were just planted on the platform doing skills for your instructor.

While the students were getting debriefed Lindsey saw to it that they had full tanks waiting for them to swap out and checked all their gear to make sure everything was in working order. As she was doing that, Joey got his tank filled and his gear ready for the next dive. He looked around occasionally to see if he could spot Earl but Earl wasn't anywhere to be seen. Maybe he hadn't shown up this weekend.

Once Joey finished getting his gear ready he and Lindsey had some time to themselves so they went for a walk around the basin toward Otter Creek.

"Have you seen Earl around this morning?" Lindsey asked.

"No, but there are a lot of people here today. He hasn't come up to me, anyway."

"Well, I hope he shows up. I really want to know what he wants to talk to you about."

Lindsey was more anxious about what Earl wanted than Joey was. He wondered what she was planning.

They spent the rest of the walk talking about the dive and how the students did. Lindsey had worked with this class in the pool and she said they were all solid with their skills. She expected they would get through the dives quickly and tomorrow would be a short day.

Back at the tables with the instructor and students as they

prepared for the next dive Joey noticed the deputies were standing at the edge of the basin looking toward the cave opening. Joey glanced at the time and noted it had been almost two and a half hours since the cave divers went into the cave. He hadn't seen them come out yet and judging by the way the deputies were behaving he guessed they were overdue. This wasn't good.

Joey turned to Lindsey to tell her but she was busy working with a student and he didn't want to interrupt her so he just grabbed his gear and headed to the water. As he waited for the class to join him in the water he saw a burst of bubbles pop up around the buoy over the chimney leading to the cave entrance. About half a minute later the cave divers surfaced and one of them yelled to the deputies, "Call an ambulance!"

This was not good, Joey thought. Not good for the diver that was injured. And not good for Joey. One of the search divers getting bent, or worse, while looking for a body that wasn't there was bound to make new headlines. That wouldn't go over well with Earl.

The diver that had yelled out started swimming toward the steps near Joey while dragging the other diver. Joey noticed they only had their sidemounts with them. The other tanks were missing. One of the deputies yelled, "Hey you!"

Joey looked around and the deputy yelled again, "You!" He was yelling and pointing at Joey.

When Joey looked at him the deputy yelled, "Go help him bring that diver to the steps. Joey looked at him in shock, but he quickly snapped out of it and swam toward the cave divers to help. As he approached the cave divers the one that had called out for help yelled, "Get around to his feet and push while I pull!" Joey did as he was told and pushed as hard and fast as he could.

They got to the steps in about a minute and the diver yelled, "Help me get his tanks off." Fortunately, Joey had already dealt with this with the dead diver and Earl. He saw a dive knife on the diver's BC, pulled it out of its sheath, and cut the bungees and strings holding the tank closest to him. This knife was much sharper and sliced right through them. The tanks fell to the steps and the deputies started pulling him up and out of the water with the other cave diver holding up his legs.

One of the deputies, who Joey thought was the one that had yelled for him to help, asked the other diver what happened.

"We went all the way back to the fourth restriction and turned around to exit and poke around some of the side passages on the way out. John got stuck in one of the restrictions. He got in pretty far and it looked like he A-framed. It was a really silty area and we lost all visibility."

Joey suddenly had flashbacks to his dives in the cave.

"It took us a while to get John out of there. I couldn't even tell you how long. It seemed like forever. I breathed through my stage tanks while we were trying to get John unstuck. John had taken his off because of the restriction. We finally got him out of there but the visibility was so bad we couldn't find his stage tanks and he had breathed through almost all of the air in his sidemount tanks. My stage tanks were empty so I left them behind. John breathed his tanks empty and we ended up having to share the air in my tanks the rest of the way out. This all happened back around the third restriction."

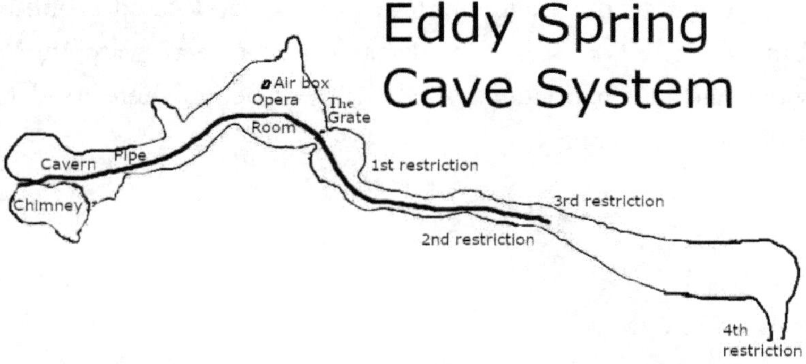

"We got back to the grate and it took us a minute to get that damn lock unlocked and the grate open. As soon as it was open John just flew through the opening and I was stuck following him because he was breathing from my tank. John didn't grab his decompression cylinder and I was so focused on staying with him I didn't think to grab mine. We left them just beyond the grate. I tried to do some kind of decompression stop even though we didn't have our oxygen but John just wanted to get to the surface. By that time we had breathed my tanks empty anyhow. John was unconscious by the time we hit the surface."

The diver talking recounted all this as the deputies pulled John up onto the grass and began administering CPR. About 10 minutes later an ambulance arrived and took over. They managed to get a heartbeat, moved him onto the gurney and into the ambulance quickly and took off to a hospital. Joey guessed they were heading to Bay Medical Center in Panama

City because that was the closest hospital with a hyperbaric chamber.

When all the excitement was over Joey looked around for Lindsey. She was standing just a few feet away watching over what had just happened. About 10 feet behind her stood Earl. And he looked angry.

33

"Les go somewhar ta talk," Joey heard Earl behind him as he was taking his BC and tank off.

Joey turned around and looked at Earl. Earl looked even angrier up close. Joey put his gear on the ground next to the table, looked for Lindsey and saw she was busy with the students. He didn't think she had noticed Earl walk up. He looked back at Earl.

"Okay."

They walked toward the dive shop away from the crowds of divers that had gathered to watch the unconscious cave diver get carried out of the water and hauled off in an ambulance. As soon as they had put some distance between them and the crowd Earl started talking in a low voice.

"We gots ta git back out ta da gulf 'n look fer dat body ag'in. I thought thins was gittin' back ta normal 'n den da dep'ties showed up dis mornin' sayin' dey wanted ta send some more divers in ta search some more. An' den one of 'um gits hurt. Dis ain't no good. They gonna keep comin' back 'n it's bad fer biz'ness."

"D-d-do you really think after all this time we have any chance of finding it?? B-by now it's probably drifted miles, or even been eaten by sharks."

"We ain't gonna know 'less we fin' 'im. Dis weekend ain't no good fer me. Too much goin' on. We'll head out Monday night. Oh…and bring y'all's lil girlfriend wit ya. We'll have better luck findin 'im wit two divers in da water."

"No way!" Joey yelled at Earl. Then he remembered they weren't standing that far from the other divers at the park. He quickly looked back toward the Grande Vista Chalet but no one had seemed to notice Joey yelling at the manager of the scuba park.

"I'm not getting Lindsey involved. It's bad enough you dragged me into this. I won't let you drag her into it." Joey sneered in a loud whisper at Earl.

"Boy! Dontcha talk ta me dat way!" Earl sneered back. "Y'all's in too deep ta think ya can git out a dis so easy. I need ta git dat body back in da cave 'n da sooner da better. If'n y'all don' git 'er ta come I'll go ta her right now an' tell 'er ever'thin 'n make 'er do it m'self."

Joey took a step back. He had surprised himself by standing up to Earl and telling him no. He didn't know where that came from. All he knew was he didn't want Lindsey involved. He had to protect her from this. But Earl had already made up his mind that she was going to be involved. If only Earl hadn't seen them together at the restaurant a few days earlier.

"No!" Joey cried back. "I-I-I'll talk to her. I-I'll make sure she's there. Just stay away from her."

"Y'all's really smitten wit 'er ain't ya boy. Ain't dat sweet."

Joey felt an almost overwhelming desire to punch Earl in the face. But there were too many people around. Too many witnesses. And Earl was bigger than Joey and would probably lay him out if he even tried.

"Both y'all's be at ma place by 'leven Monday night."

Joey nodded and walked away from Earl. He had to figure out a way to get Lindsey out of this. It would be better if he could figure out a way to get both of them out of it. But he at least had to do something about Lindsey. He considered just not saying anything and showing up at Earl's alone on Monday but he didn't know how Earl would react to that. Lindsey had been diving at Eddy Spring numerous times so Earl could probably get her address. He might make Joey bring him to her house Monday night if she wasn't with him. So he had to come up with a good excuse between now and then.

* * *

"What was that all about?" Lindsey asked, when Joey returned to the picnic tables.

Joey looked around and saw there wasn't anyone within ten feet of them. He leaned in close to Lindsey and whispered "Earl wants to head out to the gulf to look for the body again. This incident that happened here this morning didn't go over well with him. He thinks it's going to keep happening until they find the body so he wants me to put the body back in the cave."

Lindsey took a step back and looked at Joey.

"Oh no! You can't do that sweetie! You were lucky nothing happened to you the first time you went looking for that body. You can't go back out there with him."

"I-I-I don't have much of a choice. He'll come to my house

and my parents will find out. Or worse. I have to do this."

"I'm going with you then!" Lindsey exclaimed.

"Oh no! I don't want you getting involved. I didn't even want to tell you about any of it."

"Too bad mister! You don't have a choice. When are you supposed to do this?"

Joey didn't know what to do or say. He could see Lindsey wasn't going to back down but he didn't want her involved in this mess with Earl.

"Monday night," Joey sighed.

He not only had to come up with an excuse for Earl as to why Lindsey wasn't with him. He also had to figure out a way to keep her from going. And he only had two days to figure things out.

34

The week of August 29, 2011

It was Monday afternoon and it had been raining all day long. There had been a big storm in the Caribbean that the weather stations had forecast to head toward the Keys. Late Sunday night/early Monday morning the storm took a turn west and was heading straight for the gulf and the Florida panhandle. The local news stations were watching the storm closely in case it turned into a hurricane. They were reporting the current conditions in the gulf as heavy rain with 15-20 foot swells. A small craft advisory had been issued.

Even though Joey hadn't been out on his dad's boat in years he knew that meant small boats like his father's and Earl's couldn't safely be out in the gulf. What he didn't know was if Earl would heed the warnings or if he would still want to chance it. Joey decided to stop by Earl's and check in with him. He still hadn't figured out a way to keep Lindsey from coming with him or an excuse to give Earl as to why she wasn't there. Maybe Earl would decide it wasn't safe and postpone it, giving Joey more time to come up with something.

Five minutes later, relieved, Joey was back in his car and driving down the street away from Earl's house. He had rang the doorbell and waited for Earl to come to the door. Earl opened the door, looking unkempt as usual when he was home, glared down at Joey, then squinted toward the sky to the south over the gulf, then back at Joey. Joey could smell the strong odor of whisky and beer coming from Earl's breath. "We ain't goin' nowhar tonight kid. Weathers too nasty. We'll go tamorra," he grunted. He stepped back from the door and slammed it in Joey's face.

Joey couldn't believe his luck. He thought for sure Earl would be crazy enough to go even in this weather. He quickly called Lindsey and told her the good news.

"You aren't lying to me, are you? I know it's blowin' up a storm but I also know Earl is crazy enough to not care about the weather."

"No, I-I'm not lying," Joey responded and told her how Earl had answered the door smelling like booze and then slammed it closed on him.

"Alright, we'll just plan on it for tomorrow then."

But the next day was no different as far as the weather. It stormed all day long. The weather stations were reporting that this storm had the potential to organize enough to become a hurricane. People along the coast started preparing for the worst. It had been six years since Hurricane Dennis had made landfall right at Santa Rosa Island and the memory of it was still fresh in everyone's minds.

Joey drove back to Earl's around the same time as the day before and got the same response, and the same odor of alcohol coming from his breath. He had considered not even going by Earl's but he was afraid Earl would come find him if he didn't show up.

This continued for one more day. On the third evening, Wednesday, Earl told Joey there was no point in coming by every evening because the weather forecast for the next couple days was the same. They'd have to wait until next week to go out on the gulf. A huge wave of relief swept over Joey. Maybe he could come up with his excuses for Lindsey and Earl by that time. For the time being he could focus on the activities he had planned for the weekend with Lindsey.

* * *

Every year during Labor Day weekend there was a big scuba diving gathering at Eddy Spring. Divers from all over Florida and the surrounding states came to Eddy to camp and dive and have a good time. Lindsey told Joey that last year they had more than 100 divers at the event. This year was expected to have an even bigger turnout. The organizers of the event had even managed to talk Earl into lowering the entry and camping fees with the promise that more divers would show up if it didn't cost them as much. They were able to convince Earl that he would make more money by lowering the fees.

They also somehow convinced Earl to allow alcohol on the grounds during the event. When Earl took over as manager of the place he had instituted a strict no alcohol policy. Joey thought this ironic since he had smelled alcohol on Earl almost every time he encountered him. He obviously drank alcohol every day, yet he banned it from the place he managed. Not everyone was happy about the no alcohol policy, especially the campers, and many would sneak in some beer anyway. But Earl was making an exception for the big event. This meant kegs could be brought in.

Joey and Lindsey already had a campsite reserved with a group of divers that Lindsey knew. The storm everyone was concerned about was forecast to be through the panhandle by Thursday night one way or another. The weather forecasters were calling for a clear weekend. If it wasn't for the big event Earl would probably want to head out to the gulf with Joey and Lindsey. But with such a major event happening, Earl had to stick around. And it was doubtful the deputies would be bringing any more search divers during such a busy weekend. Another reprieve. Joey knew his luck wouldn't hold up much longer though.

In spite of everything that was going on with Earl, Joey was looking forward to the event at Eddy Spring. It would be his first such event since he got scuba certified and he heard they were a lot of fun. He would have preferred he didn't have the thing with Earl and the dead diver hanging over his head but he was going to do his best to put it aside and enjoy himself.

35

September 2, 2011

The big weekend finally arrived. The storm never organized enough to get named. All it did was drop rain on the panhandle all week. By Friday the clouds were gone and the weather was perfect.

Joey picked up Lindsey at her house just after four Friday afternoon and they headed to Eddy Spring. They arrived a little after five and a crowd was already forming. They paid their entry and camping fees for the weekend, got their wristbands, and headed to their campsite. According to Lindsey, within a couple of hours there would be a long line of cars all the way down the dirt road to the highway. By tonight all the campsites would be occupied and there wouldn't be anywhere left to park. Anyone who didn't show up the first day would have to park outside the entrance and carry their gear hundreds of feet, some even thousands, to the water. Joey was glad they had decided to get there early.

After setting up the campsite, Joey threw some burgers on the grill while Lindsey set up the dive gear for a night dive. This would be Joey's first official night dive, not counting the dives he was forced by Earl to do to pull out the body from the cave and then look for it in the gulf. Joey was a little spooked about going in the water at night. So far he hadn't had very good experiences in dark water. Lindsey knew this and explained that when properly planned and executed a night dive could be a really cool experience. Lindsey explained that the really cool night dives happened in salt water where there was a lot of marine life that only came out after dark. Salt water also had something called bioluminescence, creatures that were too small to see with the naked eye, but if you stirred up the water you could see them glowing. Lindsey also explained that Eddy Spring had some interesting things happen after the sun set and she thought it would be better for Joey to do his first fun night dive in Eddy so he could get a feel for it in a more controlled environment.

The dive went exceptionally well. In fact, it was probably Joey's best dive with Lindsey yet. It seemed every time they did a dive together the current did something to either make Joey look like a fool or it endangered both of their lives. There was no current on this dive, well, almost none. They did feel a little bit of flow when they dropped down the chimney but since they didn't go into the cave they didn't get to feel the full extent of it.

Even though Lindsey had downplayed this dive, especially compared to what a salt water night dive was like, Joey had the best dive ever. On previous dives in Eddy Spring Joey had seen at most two freshwater eel swimming around the entrance to the cave. On this dive there were dozens of eel swimming around. There were almost as many as at Morrison Spring. And they weren't just near the cave. They had ventured out into the basin!

Most of them were at the bottom of the chimney, which is why they had gone down there, but there were still at least a dozen in the basin as well. It was a really cool dive and Joey couldn't stop talking about it.

After the dive Lindsey and Joey placed their gear in storage tubs next to the picnic table at their campsite and headed to the bathhouses to shower. They spent the rest of the evening sitting around a campfire with friends talking about different places they had all been diving. Well, all except Joey because of his limited experience. He enjoyed hearing the stories about the different exotic places everyone had been to and hoped one day he could experience those places as well. And it would be even better experiencing them with Lindsey.

The conversation eventually turned to the cave and the missing diver. The other divers talked about the theories they had about what had happened. Some thought the diver had gone into the cave and gotten stuck in a tight spot and the body was still jammed into a passage so small none of the recovery divers had thought to look there.

"If there was a body in there the search divers would have already found it by now. Look at the map on the wall in the dive shop. The cave isn't that big," one of the divers disagreed.

"But what if he got into a part of the cave that hasn't been explored already?"

"Well, I heard he wasn't even a certified cave diver. He was an open water diver and was sneaking into the cave through the other side of the fence."

"No way!" A few of the divers in the group replied incredulously.

"I don't think he even went in the cave. Maybe he just parked his truck on the other side off the fence and disappeared. I heard he had money problems. Maybe he did this to start over," one of the divers speculated.

"Well, talk is he came from money. So why wouldn't he just call his family and get help?"

"Maybe he was disowned."

The talk went on like this for more than an hour. Joey and Lindsey sat quietly and listened. The divers engaged in the conversation were so absorbed in trying to solve the case of the missing diver that they didn't even notice Joey and Lindsey weren't participating.

Joey would have liked to tell them they were all wrong and that he found the body and was forced by Earl to pull it out of the cave and dump it in the gulf. But he didn't know these people all that well and he was sure with all the gossip they were doing around the campfire that anything Joey said would make it around the park quickly. By morning every diver at Eddy Spring would have heard the story. So he kept quiet and just listened to them theorize what could have happened to the missing diver.

The more they drank the wilder the theories got. Some of the things said were absolutely hilarious.

"Maybe a UFO came down and zapped him up into their spaceship and they're poking and prodding him as we speak."

The group burst out in laughter.

"No, no, no! I know what happened to him. He was diving in the cave at night and a giant eel came out of his lair and ate him! In fact, I think I saw that very same eel on tonight's dive!"

The laughter was even louder this time.

"Maybe he found a portal into another dimension in the cave and he's stuck over there right now trying to figure out how to get back."

Instead of laughter this time everyone got quiet. A few seconds later someone in the group started singing the notes to the theme of the *Twilight Zone*. That's when the burst of laughter came.

They sat around the campfire sipping on their beers chuckling about all the theories they had just discussed. Things seemed to be winding down. Then one of the group spoke out.

"What if someone found his body in the cave and reported it to the dive shop. And what if that creep Earl the manager decided he didn't want the bad publicity so he pulled the body out himself and dumped it somewhere?"

Joey's jaw dropped. He couldn't believe what he just heard. Was this person just theorizing or did she know something? He stole a glance at Lindsey and noticed she also had a look of shock on her face. He didn't know if she was shocked that someone came up with a theory of what really happened or if she was feigning the shock for the sake of the group.

"I don't buy that! If they got rid of the body themselves then how would anyone even know about it and why would there be search divers here almost every weekend looking for it?"

"I heard what tipped them off to anyone even being missing was the truck parked on the other side of the fence. So maybe the manager didn't tell anyone else about what he was doing and one of the employees reported the truck before he could get rid of it?"

"Well, why wouldn't he just get rid of it at the same time as the body?"

"It wasn't on the Eddy Spring property. Maybe he didn't see it."

* * *

This went on for another 45 minutes. The group had laughed at or discounted every other theory but they stayed with this one and kept coming up with more possibilities, all surrounding the manager or someone that worked at Eddy Spring finding the body and getting rid of it. Someone thought the body was buried in the woods that surround the park. Someone else suggested the body was probably dumped in Lake Seminole and eaten by the alligators that live there. Another person suggested the body was taken out to the gulf and dumped in the water.

The longer they talked about it the more distressed Joey became. Because the longer they talked about it the closer they came to describing exactly what happened. The only part they were missing was that someone who didn't work for Eddy Spring, a paying customer at the park, was the one that found the body and the one that pulled it out and the one that helped dump it in the gulf. The only part they were missing was Joey…

36

September 3, 2011

Joey and Lindsey had a pretty good day diving and hanging out with friends. Before the weekend Joey thought he might feel out of place because he didn't know very many divers. Other than Lindsey and a couple of divers from his open water class that he went diving with at Eddy Spring a couple of times, Joey hadn't made any new friends.

Joey had never had a big circle of friends to begin with. That was changing with diving. This was his first major dive event and he was noticing that divers were mostly a friendly, close knit bunch. There were a few exceptions, like the two at Morrison Spring. But they were the exception. Lindsey had introduced him to several of her friends and they all treated him like they had been friends forever.

He exchanged numbers with several of them so they could plan future dive excursions together. Joey was surprised to discover that none of them even lived in Florida. They had come to the event from Alabama, Georgia, and even as far away as Arkansas, Louisiana, and Tennessee. Most of them had done their open water checkout dives at Eddy Spring like Joey had.

Other than when the talk around the campfire the night before had turned a little too close to the truth, Joey felt at ease around Lindsey's friends and enjoyed spending time with them.

Joey was impressed with the way they all looked in the water. These weren't your typical open water divers walking along the bottom of the basin stirring up the silt. They all swam like Lindsey and with the same finning style of bending their knees and only moving their calves and feet. Joey had been trying to look more like that in the water but he still had a long way to go. None of them made fun of him over it though. Instead, they gave him pointers and helped him adjust his gear so it would be easier to achieve that look underwater.

They all did four dives that day, two in the morning followed by a lunch break, and then another two in the afternoon. They mainly swam around the basin practicing their skills. They went down the chimney a couple of times to look for eel but none of them went into the cave or even suggested it. Joey had been a little surprised by this. They all seemed to be pretty advanced divers. He saw divers heading in and out of the cave both times they went down the chimney. The group he was with stayed around the little crevices along the perimeter of the bottom of the chimney looking for an eel or two.

During the surface interval a couple of the divers mentioned the other divers heading in and out of the cave.

"Did you see that instructor coming out of the cave with his students?"

"Yeah, he always does that. I'm surprised no one has gotten hurt here yet, well, except the missing diver."

Oh no, Joey hoped the conversation wasn't going to turn to that again!

"Well, they've been doing it for years. And it's almost encouraged with the lights and the airbox in the Opera Room."

"To be fair," said the first diver, "I heard those were put in years ago because they knew they wouldn't be able to keep untrained divers out of the cave so they wanted the divers to have the light to follow out and the airbox in case something happened to give them a fighting chance."

"I guess that makes sense."

"Have you been in the cave here Joey?" one of them asked.

"U-um, I-I've been in the area to the left and peeked a little in the passage behind the grim reaper sign." Joey responded hoping no one could tell he wasn't exactly being truthful.

"That area to the left is pretty benign. You would be hard pressed to get yourself in trouble there. But you are smart to not go down the main passage without proper training."

"Yeah, I've talked to Lindsey about it. I'm saving up to take a cavern diving class as soon as I can. I might even keep going with the training if I like it."

"That's great! I think you'll like it. You have already improved a lot in the water just during the dives we've done today."

Joey beamed at the compliment. The weekend was turning out really well. He was having a fantastic time with Lindsey. He had met a great group of new friends who were all scuba fanatics. And the best part was he hadn't seen Earl around and had even forgotten about him for a while.

* * *

After the fourth dive that day Lindsey and Joey decided they were not going to do a night dive. They were pretty tired after the dive the night before followed by staying up late around the campfire drinking and laughing and then another four dives that day. They put their gear in the storage tubs, showered and changed, and sat at the top of the hill overlooking the basin in a couple of camping chairs they had brought with them. The event organizers had planned a big barbeque for Saturday night so the attendees didn't have to prepare dinner for themselves. They sat and watched all the activity while they waited for the announcement that dinner was being served.

"Well ain't dat cute? Two lovebirds sittin' tagether holdin' hands whisprin' sweet nut'ns ta each otha."

Joey's heart sank. He had been having such a good time he had completely forgotten Earl. Lindsey and Joey both turned to look up at Earl standing behind them holding a red Solo cup in one hand. They could smell the beer on his breath.

"Weatha's lookin' betta. Monday looks reeeeal good. Les git dis thin' o'er 'n done wit. Both y'all be at ma place by 10pm." Earl stretched out the p in pm for a couple of seconds so it came out peeeeeeee-em.

Before either Joey or Lindsey could respond Earl turned on his heel and stumbled away, calling over his shoulder, "Enjoy da res of y'all's weeken' lovebirds," his laughter dying out as he got farther away.

"I don't want you to go, Lindsey. This is my mess. I'll figure something out to tell him why you're not there."

"I think it will be better if I go with you, Joey. I have a lot more experience diving and maybe with the two of us we can find that body and be done with this. Besides, he is going to want the body put back in the cave, probably far beyond the grate, and you don't have the training or experience to do that. I at least need to be there to help with that."

Lindsey had a point, Joey thought. It was one thing for him to visit the Opera Room that was lit up and had a big pipe on the floor leading out to the chimney. As he had learned, open water instructors took their students there regularly. It was something completely different to pull a dead body a few hundred feet down the passage to the Opera Room, beyond the grate, and who knows how far into the cave. Joey didn't have any idea what it was like beyond the grate. Would one tank even be enough to pull that off? He didn't like the idea of Lindsey being involved but he didn't think he could do it without her.

37

Lindsey and Joey agreed to not discuss Earl the rest of the weekend. They would talk first thing Monday morning. She also got very quiet and pensive.

"What are you thinking about?"

"Oh, nothing in particular. Just people watching," Lindsey responded.

Joey wasn't accepting that response. There was definitely something on her mind. He decided not to push it further though. Instead he attributed it to her trying to process what had just happened with Earl. This was her first interaction with him since she learned about Joey's involvement in the situation.

The dinner bell sounded interrupting Joey's thoughts. Actually, the "bell" was an old scuba tank that had the bottom cut off and was hanging from a post. They used a hammer to bang it on the side. It sounded like a real bell. It looked a lot cooler than a bell though.

A crowd started forming a line near the Grande Vista Chalet where they had set up the food to be served. Lindsey and Joey got in line with their friends. The others were joking around and acting silly. Their friends had decided to skip a night dive as well and some of them were already a couple of beers into the evening. Joey and Lindsey had each drank a beer but they were taking it easy. After all the diving they had done that day they didn't want to overdo it with the alcohol.

Lindsey remained quiet and reserved throughout dinner, a complete contrast from the night before. Joey's concern for her was growing. He regretted telling her about what he had been through with Earl. Instead of telling her that night after dinner he wished he had come up with some story that didn't involve a dead diver and getting rid of the body. But he had been put on the spot and he had never been good at improvising. This situation was making him more and more angry at Earl for involving Lindsey. He needed to get Earl off her back once and for all. Off both of their backs. But he still didn't know how he was going to do that.

Joey and Lindsey remained at the table next to the Grande Vista Chalet after dinner sipping their second beer and listening to the usual conversation about different dives everyone had experienced, neither of them contributing much to the discussion. Suddenly there was a big commotion behind them under the Chalet near the fill station fireplace. Joey and Lindsey quickly turned to see what was going on.

There was a group of people standing near the tank rack looking down. A couple of them appeared to be helping someone up off the ground. Joey and Lindsey got up and moved closer to the crowd. After a few moments the crowd started to clear away, apparently no longer interested in the commotion that had just occurred. That's when Joey and Lindsey saw who had caused it – Earl. He was standing, swaying back and forth, in the middle of the few people that were left trying to help him, pushing them away.

"Ahm aight! Ahm aight! Lemme be!" He yelled at them. They backed off and Earl stumbled over to the bottom of the stairs of the Chalet and crawled up the steps to the balcony. Lindsey and Joey watched him reach the top of the stairs, pull himself up onto the balcony and almost tumble over the rail. He managed to catch himself just before that happened and stumbled to the left toward the rooms. He disappeared into the room closest to the stairs. Maybe he would just pass out in there for the rest of the night, Joey thought hopefully.

After the excitement of the moment everyone returned to what they had been doing. There were divers finishing up dives and other divers heading into the water for night dives. Joey could hear some instructors briefing their students on their first night dives. The excitement among the students was very apparent. Unlike Joey and his first night dive, they couldn't wait to dive into the black water of the Eddy Spring basin.

The small group of friends decided to relocate to the campsite and get a campfire going again. They relinquished their table, which was quickly claimed by another group that had been standing close by waiting for a table to clear. Back at the campsite a fire was quickly lit and more beer was passed around. Joey had already had two, and he hadn't planned on drinking very much but the encounter with Earl had stressed him a little so he decided another beer wouldn't hurt.

Lindsey declined another beer. She still seemed distant, preoccupied with something. She wasn't acting herself and even her friends noticed and mentioned it to her. She just blew it off with the excuse that it had been a busy week at work.

"Aww, you know how it is y'all. No one could go diving because of all the stormin' this week so we were pretty busy at the shop," she told them.

That was acceptable to everyone, except Joey.

About twenty minutes later Lindsey turned to Joey.

"I have to use the restroom. I'll be back in a bit."

"I can walk you to the bathhouse," Joey offered.

"No sweetie, I'll only be a minute. You stay here."

Lindsey quickly stood up and headed toward the bathhouse. Joey watched her disappear into the darkness beyond wondering what she had been thinking about all evening and what he could do to get her to change her mind about going with him Monday night. They had been having such a good weekend until Earl confronted them. How could he get her in a better mood again? He turned back toward the campfire and half-heartedly laughed at a joke someone had just told. But his thoughts were still on Lindsey.

* * *

Several minutes passed and Joey realized Lindsey hadn't come back from the restrooms yet. He looked at his watch and saw it had been more than ten minutes since she left the campsite. Excusing himself from the group he headed toward the bathhouse to look for her. She had probably just run into some friends on the way and stopped to talk, he thought. But with the way she'd been behaving this evening he was more than a little concerned. What if Earl had resurfaced from his room in Grande Vista Chalet and found her and confronted her while she was alone? Joey quickened his pace at that thought. If Earl did anything to Lindsey, Joey didn't think he would be able to control himself. And he didn't care who witnessed it.

Lindsey wasn't anywhere to be seen on the way to the bathhouse. When Joey got there he called her name a couple times but didn't get a response. His concern increased the more he thought about the possibility of Earl confronting her alone. He was sure Lindsey could take care of herself but he also knew how Earl could be. And Earl was much bigger and stronger than Lindsey.

He tried to calm himself by trying to convince himself she just ran into some friends and they walked off in a different direction than the one Joey had taken from the campsite to the bathhouse. Maybe she was at the campsite of this group of friends talking to them. Maybe she was already back at their campsite. Or maybe Earl had her cornered somewhere, he thought in a panic.

Joey quickened his pace even more and ran toward the Chalet to see if Lindsey might be there. As he was jogging around the restrooms next to the Chalet he heard another big commotion at the far side of the building near the stairs. Another crowd was gathering near the bottom of the steps. He sped up his pace into a run. He thought to himself, if Earl hurt Lindsey no one would be able to hold him back.

As Joey rushed through the center of the area under the Chalet he saw what looked like someone lying on the sidewalk at the base of the stairs. There was a dark pool of blood forming beneath the head. The crowd of people was growing and blocking Joey from getting any closer.

Joey pushed his way through the crowd to get a better look. As he got to the front of the crowd he immediately recognized Earl lying on the sidewalk at the bottom of the steps with the pool of blood surrounding him growing larger. Joey could see a big gash on his forehead – the apparent source of the blood – that must have been caused by his fall down the stairs.

Joey couldn't believe it. In his haze, he heard someone calling 911. Someone else was telling the others to back up and give him space and warning them not move him because they can cause further damage if he has a spinal cord injury. There was a lot of whispering in the crowd.

"Did you see how he was stumbling around earlier?"

"This doesn't surprise me too much. He almost fell off the balcony when he crawled up there."

"He must have lost his balance coming down the stairs."

"It's no wonder he doesn't usually allow alcohol here. He'd probably be stumbling around drunk every night."

Even though Joey didn't like Earl, he couldn't help but feel sorry for him and the way people were talking about him.

Joey's thoughts were interrupted as a couple of scuba instructors pushed their way through the crowd and took control of the scene. They made the spectators back up to give them space as they slowly repositioned Earl, doing their best to keep his neck straight in case he had injured it. They placed him flat on his back on the sidewalk and assessed his breathing and heartbeat.

Apparently Earl wasn't breathing and didn't have a pulse because they started doing compressions and mouth to mask breathing. As they were doing chest compressions and rescue breathing, someone ran through the crowd carrying a green case – emergency oxygen that was stored just outside the door to the dive shop. She set up the oxygen while the instructors continued CPR. Every couple of minutes the instructors would stop chest compressions and reassess Earl's pulse and breathing, neither of which seemed to have returned. About 15 minutes after they had repositioned Earl and started CPR, an ambulance came blazing in past the gate shack with lights and siren.

The paramedics quickly exited the vehicle, grabbed a medical equipment bag from one of the compartments in the back, and ran over to where the instructors were still attending to Earl. The medics took over. One of them did compressions and the other gave Earl rescue breaths using something that looked like a clear football. A minute later another emergency vehicle arrived and parked behind the ambulance. Two more emergency responders got out and grabbed equipment from the back, bringing it to the first two.

One of the new emergency responders cut off Earl's shirt and attached wires to his chest while the fourth one started an IV in the bend of his arm. All this happened while the first two continued doing CPR. They stopped chest compressions for a few seconds to look at a monitor screen on the machine they had brought from the second vehicle.

"Asystole. Continue CPR!" the one who had attached the wires to Earl said.

The two that had been doing CPR traded tasks again and continued the chest compressions and rescue breaths. A third one prepared a syringe with some medicine from a vial and injected it into the IV tubing.

"One milligram epinephrine," she said.

They continued CPR for another minute before stopping for a few seconds to check the monitor screen again.

"Still asystole. Continue CPR!"

This went on for several minutes with more doses of epinephrine being given and more checks of the monitor screen. In the meantime, the fourth responder retrieved a gurney from the back of the ambulance and rolled it next to Earl. They stopped CPR for a few seconds to move Earl onto the gurney. Two of them resumed CPR while the other two strapped him to the gurney and raised it up so Earl was at the level of their waists. They continued doing CPR as they wheeled him to the ambulance.

CPR was paused again momentarily as they loaded the gurney with Earl on it into the back of the ambulance. The last thing Joey heard from them was "Asystole. Continue CPR!" right before the ambulance doors slammed shut and the ambulance took off down the dirt road with the emergency lights on and sirens blaring as the crowd stood and watched, most wondering if Earl would survive this.

* * *

Joey couldn't believe what had happened. In a way he felt bad for Earl. Things didn't look good for him. People who knew more about this stuff than he did were already saying if Earl did survive the fall he would likely be a vegetable. They did CPR for at least 30 minutes between the instructors and the medics before they left in the ambulance. And they had another 15 to

20 minutes before they got to the closest hospital. The survival rate for someone whose heart stopped was already low. It dropped the longer he went without his heart beating on its own.

But this solved Joey's dilemma about Monday night. Even if Earl did survive it wasn't likely he would be in any condition to force them out in his boat that soon. And maybe by the time he recovered, if he recovered, things will have blown over with this dead diver thing. Joey felt bad about thinking there was a bright side to this but he had been under so much stress he couldn't help himself. He had considered doing something to Earl to end this. But the thought of something happening to Earl had never occurred to him. Seeing Earl hauled off in an ambulance had lifted a huge weight off of Joey's shoulders.

Joey suddenly remembered why he had been walking around the park in the first place. *Lindsey!* He looked around the thinning crowd to see if she was among them. As he was scanning the crowd he noticed movement above in his peripheral vision. He looked up the stairs of the Grande Vista Chalet and saw Lindsey on the balcony peeking out from around the corner of the building, her face illuminated by the light from a lamppost next to her. It looked like she was looking down at Joey. He wondered what she was doing on the balcony of the Chalet.

It was dark and she was too far away to tell for sure but the look in her eyes had changed from the far off look he had seen earlier that evening. She looked as relieved as he felt. But there was something else. She was too far away and the lighting wasn't the best, but the look on her face had a hint of satisfaction.

EPILOGUE

Three months had gone by since Earl's death following his fall down the stairs, or at least that's what Joey thought had happened. He and Lindsey never discussed what she had been doing on the balcony. Joey wanted to ask her but at the same time he wasn't sure he wanted to know.

The sheriff's office had gone to Eddy Spring with more search divers on a couple more occasions but after the same results as every other time the case grew cold and they stopped trying to find a body. The rumor was that the diver had staged his own disappearance and was probably on some Caribbean island living it up.

Joey and Lindsey grew closer to each other. They spent every weekend together and most weeknights. Joey finally introduced her to his parents. His mom actually liked Lindsey a lot, even after she learned that Lindsey was a cave diver. Somehow it was different because Lindsey was female. Joey didn't pretend to understand. But at least his mom was no longer lecturing him day in and day out about his scuba diving.

Lindsey had finally saved up enough to get the rest of the equipment she needed for her decompression diving class. She completed that class a month earlier out in the gulf on the USS Oriskany. Joey had tagged along and did a couple of recreational level dives on the tower while Lindsey was down on the flight deck with the other students and the instructor. It was his first official dive from a dive boat and he didn't even get sick. That was thanks to Lindsey and her recommendation that he take some motion sickness pills she had bought for him. He really envied her for pursuing her dreams and couldn't wait until the day he would be diving at the same level as her.

After paying his parents the last of the money he owed them Joey began saving for his cavern diver class. He would have all the money saved up in the next month and he had already scheduled the class with the same instructor Lindsey had completed her cavern diver course with. Lindsey was going to tag along and be Joey's dive buddy during the class.

He was looking forward to getting proper training to learn how to dive in caves. He wanted to be able to do it safely so he could enjoy the beauty they held. And he hoped to one day be able to actually go beyond the grate to see what was so special about it that it was worth someone's life.

ABOUT THE AUTHOR

Rob Neto is an avid cave diver who lives in the Florida panhandle just minutes away from some of his favorite caves. He is an active cave explorer and retired cave and technical diving instructor. He spent more than 10 years teaching scuba diving in Arizona and Florida. He is also the author of the book Sidemount Diving The *Almost* Comprehensive Guide, the first comprehensive book about sidemount diving. With almost 300 pages of information and photos, Sidemount Diving is on its 2nd edition and has been translated into Dutch, German and Spanish, and is currently being translated into more languages. Rob is already working on a sequel to Beyond the Grate titled Into the Darkness Beyond.

Rob is married to his wonderful, supportive wife of 20 years and has a household of furry family members. At the time of this publication his family consisted of four dogs, two inside cats, and several outside cats.

Coming Soon!

Into the Darkness Beyond

Another Joey Simmons novel!

Read about Joey's adventures and mishaps after he receives cave diver training. Joey promised himself he would be safe and not take any more risks when diving. But that soon changes and he finds himself in a situation that nearly costs him his life. He manages to save himself but someone else takes the credit and claims he rescued Joey.

Read on to see what happens to Joey and Lindsey next!

1

Joey Simmons tried to back out, but something was keeping him from being able to move. He pushed forward again but only felt his scuba cylinders squeeze him like a vise even more. The silt had gotten so thick in the passage he could no longer see the walls which were mere inches from his face.

He wiggled his hips, trying to get himself unwedged. That only seemed to make things worse. He noticed his breathing rate was getting faster. Rather than the nice, even, rhythmic respirations he had trained himself to do, the bubbles were escaping the regulator in his mouth almost continuously. He needed to regain control of his breathing.

He closed his eyes and concentrated on his breathing, something he had learned early on in his scuba diving experiences. Something he had learned during his first unofficial cave dive. Breathe in. Hold his breath for a second. Slowly release, letting the air escape his lungs steadily. Hold for another second. Resist the impulse to immediately take another breath. Then repeat. Breathe in….

Joey could feel a sense of calm enveloping him. He would figure a way out of this predicament he had gotten himself into. He had three cylinders on him, the two sidemount cylinders plus a stage cylinder he had brought along because they were diving so far back in the cave using diver propulsion vehicles, more commonly referred to as DPVs, or just plain old scooters. The additional air in the stage cylinders was necessary in case they had a DPV failure and had to swim out. Swimming out could take three times as long as scootering out. And their breathing rates were higher swimming than they were when being pulled along by the DPVs.

They… What about Mike? Was he behind Joey? Blocking Joey's exit from this narrow passage? Or did he manage to back out and wait outside the growing silt cloud for Joey to do the same? It did no good to wonder about Mike. Joey couldn't help Mike unless he got himself unstuck and out of the narrow passage he was in.

His breathing rate had slowed down and resumed its normal calm rhythm. Joey tried to back out again. He moved a fraction of an inch before something jammed him in place. He could feel the cylinder on his right side pushing up against his armpit. He must be A-framed, meaning the bottom of the cylinder that was sticking out was caught up against a protrusion from the wall. He felt around in front of him to try to feel if the passage got any bigger. He had his DPV in front of him and moved his hand around the outside of the round propellor shroud. The passage was somewhat oval-shaped, wider than it was tall. There was only enough room above and below the shroud for Joey's hand to barely fit. There was a little more room to the sides of the shroud but not enough to pass through the passage without unclipping both sidemount cylinders and pushing them ahead of him. And that wasn't going to happen at this point.

He was going to have to back out somehow. But to do that he needed to pull the bottom of the cylinder in toward his leg. The problem with that plan was his arms were in front of him. And there wasn't enough room to pull them back alongside his body so he could maneuver the cylinders and get himself free.

Eyes closed.

Breathe…

Stay calm.

Joey wiggled his hips again and tried to get the cylinder to pop up above his hip so it could get loose from its entrapment and allow himself to back out. It wasn't working, though. The stage cylinder he had brought was riding on top of his sidemount cylinder and it wasn't allowing him to move up at all. He reached down to the D-ring on his chest where the top of the stage cylinder was clipped and found the bolt snap at the end of the bungee cord connecting it to the cylinder valve. He fumbled with the bolt snap for a few seconds trying to get the gate open and the bolt snap off the D-ring. The bungee cord was stretched too tight. He could get the gate open, but the bolt snap wasn't moving at all. He had to be able to pull it at least a quarter inch to get it off the D-ring.

He tried a couple more times without success. *Well*, he thought, he was going to have to cut the bungee cord. He couldn't remember how much air he had left in the stage cylinder but cutting the bungee also meant leaving it behind. There was no way he would be able to hold onto the stage cylinder, light up the dark passageway in front of him, and control the DPV throughout the 2000-foot exit from his current location in the cave.

He reached up to his wrist and the cutting tool he had attached to the strap of his dive computer and pulled it out of its sheath. He brought his hand down to his chest and located the chest D-ring holding his stage cylinder in place. He traced his finger along the outside of the D-ring to its edge where the bolt snap was pulling on it, and then traced the bolt snap to the bungee cord. The cutting tool was a double-edged blade secured inside the holder. It had a catch on each side meant to both protect the user from getting accidentally cut by the blade and also to use to pull whatever material was being cut in and hold it against the blade. The tool was shaped somewhat like an M with the blade being the V in the middle and the catches being the legs of the M.

He positioned the cutting tool next to the bungee and slowly swiped it down, trying to catch it in the device. He felt the end of the cutting tool pop up over the bungee cord. *Let's try that again*, he thought.

Positioning the tool over the bungee again, this time he pressed down against his chest harder. He really hoped the tool wouldn't cut through his dry suit. That would make for a miserable, wet, cold exit. Never mind the decompression obligation that was building up the longer he was stuck here.

He pressed down harder and slowly pulled the cutting tool across his chest. He felt some resistance and pulled harder. A second later he could feel the tension the bungee cord had been creating on his armpit subside. He felt the stage cylinder shift slightly above him. This was it! He was going to be able to get loose from this vise.

Joey tried backing out again. He couldn't move even a quarter of an inch. The sidemount tank was still wedged up against something. He wiggled his hips again to try to get it to move out of the way. *Nothing.*

He stopped for a moment and concentrated on his breathing. Suddenly it felt harder to pull each breath in. It was too silty to see his pressure gauges, but it had been a while since he switched regulators, so he was breathing from his other sidemount cylinder. He moved his back to his neck and found the other regulator hanging from a necklace made from bungee cord. He grabbed the regulator with one hand and pushed the other regulator that was in his mouth out with his tongue, letting it drop below him. He placed the regulator he was holding into his mouth and took a big breath in.

Cough! Cough! Cough!

He had just gotten a mouthful of silt. *Dammit!* He forgot to purge the regulator. He reached up and hit the purge button, careful to block the mouthpiece with his tongue so the silt would be directed out of the exhaust ports and not into his lungs. He then cautiously took in another breath and this time got a mouthful, and lungful, of air. Now that he had air to breathe he could get back to getting unstuck.

The stage cylinder was still above him, hanging on by the bungee cord securing the body of the cylinder to his waist belt. He wiggled his shoulders to try to get it to fall off, but it barely moved. He tried to move forward again. This time he was able to move a couple of inches before meeting resistance again. At least he moved though.

He wiggled more from this new position, but it did nothing. He tried to back up again. He was able to back up the couple of inches he had moved forward before the A-framing stopped him. It felt like the stage cylinder had repositioned itself though. He wiggled his shoulders. It felt like he had more room, but it still wasn't enough to make a difference.

Moving forward again he regained that couple of inches plus maybe an additional inch. He pushed back, feeling the stage cylinder shift position again. Joey reached back with his hand to push the valve of the stage cylinder back. Maybe that would help free him. He couldn't reach the valve though. The cylinder had already shifted too far down on his back for that.

He moved forward and backward, forward and backward. Each time he could feel the stage cylinder shifting position a little more. Each time he could feel himself having a little more room than the time before.

This went on for what seemed like forever to Joey. His air supply must be getting low by this time. He thought he was about 80 feet deep. At least that's what he remembered. He couldn't the display on his dive computer through the silt to confirm this detail. Being 80 feet deep meant he was breathing 3.5 times the amount of air he would breathe on the surface due to the pressure of the water. And despite his efforts at controlling his breathing rate he still found himself breathing a little faster than usual and having to calm himself to slow down the breathing. He had to get out of here soon.

Forward.

Backward.

Forward.

Backward.

Thunk!

That was it! The stage cylinder had shifted enough that it finally rolled off his back! Joey wiggled both his hips and his shoulders, moving them more and more violently as his exasperation with his current situation grew. The more he wiggled, the more room he felt he had. He felt himself moving back a little farther in the passage than he had during previous attempts. His sidemount cylinder had finally pulled itself from the protrusion it had been wedged against. He stopped for a moment and focused on his breathing. Once back under control, he began to push himself back slowly, trying to not get A-framed again.

Wiggle. Tug. Wiggle. Tug.

Gaining a little bit of ground each time.

Wiggle. Tug.

But no movement this time. Something was tugging back at him and preventing him from moving. He could feel something pulling at his waist belt. He pushed again and felt the waist belt tighten.

The stage cylinder! It was still attached to him. The body of the cylinder was attached to a D-ring on his waist belt with a long bungee cord and bolt snap. Joey reached down and this time managed to squeeze his arm between the rocky, limestone floor of the passage and his torso. He was glad he had managed to lose that extra weight he had been carrying around otherwise he might be in a bigger predicament. Joey laughed at that thought.

He traced the shoulder strap down to the waist strap and found the D-ring. It was being held against his belly by the tension on the bungee cord coming from the stage cylinder. Joey felt around the bolt snap until he found the gate and opened it. He tried pulling the bolt snap over the D-ring. But just like with the chest D-ring, there was too much tension on the bungee. He pulled his arm back in front of him so he could retrieve the cutting tool. He was thankful he had remembered to place it back into its sheath after using it to cut the other bungee cord. He pulled the cutting tool out and squeezed his hand back between the floor and his torso to the bungee stretched across his belly.

This was going to be more difficult than cutting the other bungee cord. He had been working on losing weight, but he was still about 5 lbs heavier than he wanted to be, most of it in his gut. He pushed the cutting tool against his belly. He had to be careful because the tow cord from his DPV, the cord that pulled him behind it, was clipped onto a D-ring located on his crotch strap. If he cut that accidently he would have a really difficult time getting out of the cave.

He held the tow cord to the side with his pinky while trying to catch the bungee cord in the cutting tool. When he pushed in it pushed both his belly and the bungee cord in. He changed the angle on the cutting tool and tried to catch it again, still being careful to hold the DPV tow cord out of the way. He felt something catching onto the cutting tool. Hoping it was the bungee and not his dry suit or the tow cord, he pulled the cutter up towards his chest. *Snap!* He felt the tension of the bungee cord release from his belly. The stage cylinder was free.

He pushed the DPV forward away from him until the tow cord arrested its movement. *That was good,* he thought. At least that cord was still intact. And he didn't feel cold water seeping onto his belly so the dry suit must still be intact.

Wiggling around some more to make sure the stage cylinder was out of the way, Joey felt it shift position. He slowly started to push himself backwards out of the crevice he had managed to scooter into at full speed. He was finally moving backwards and felt the passage walls angling away from him. He also started to see the illumination from his powerful LED dive light again. The silt was clearing out. Or at least he was getting out of the thickness of the silt cloud he had created.

Joey felt around for his cut away stage cylinder as he backed out.

All he felt was hard, sharp limestone under a layer of silt about an inch thick. He kept pushing himself backwards. The light got brighter with every inch of movement. The cave line denoting the exit from the cave finally came into view below him. *Wait! That wasn't gold line. That was cave line!*

Somehow Joey had scootered off the gold line that denotes the main passage in the cave into a side passage. No wonder the passage was barely bigger than his DPV shroud! Joey wondered where that passage led to. He would have to check it out another time. Now he just needed to keep backing up and hopefully find the gold line of the main passage.

He knew it was a bad idea. For some reason he had let Mike talk him into doing this dive. Joey had been back this far in the cave only once. That was a few months earlier when the water flow in the cave had been minimal. This cave was one of 33 first magnitude springs in Florida. This not only meant a lot of water poured out of the cave, but it also meant the flow of that water was strong. The area had experienced a drought during the first half of the year and the flow had reduced to almost nothing. This allowed Joey and Lindsey, his girlfriend who was also a cave diver, to be able to swim far back into the cave using a couple of stage cylinders. It was one of the best dives he had with Lindsey so far.

The area they were in was called the Trash Room. There was an old sink hole decades earlier that people must have used as a dumping site because there was old trash scattered throughout about 200 feet of the cave passage. There was even an old traffic signal propped up on a rock in the middle of the passage where a couple of the gold lines intersected. Lindsey and Joey swam back to the Trash Room and spent about 15 minutes checking out all the old trash before having to begin their swim out to the cave opening.

Joey had told Mike, one of his regular cave diving buddies, about the Trash Room and Mike really wanted to see it. The problem was the area had gotten a bunch of rain since Joey and Lindsey did their dive and the flow was back up to normal, meaning it was significantly strong flow, and swimming against it required a lot of effort. Joey and Mike had tried to swim back to the Trash Room the weekend before, but they only got about two thirds of the way before being forced to turn back otherwise they wouldn't have enough breathing gas to safely exit the cave.

So Mike talked Joey into taking their DPVs. Joey knew it was a bad idea. They had only purchased their DPVs a couple months earlier and had just completed their cave DPV class 3 weeks before this dive. They were still learning and trying to become proficient with them. The farthest they had taken them into the cave was about 1100 feet. That wasn't even as far as they had swum the prior weekend. And only about half the distance to the Trash Room.

Mike told Joey it would be okay because Joey had already been to that area swimming with Lindsey. One of the general rules they were taught was to swim a passage before scootering it. The reason for this was to be able to become familiar with the passage at a slower swimming pace before trying to maneuver it traveling three times as fast while being pulled by a DPV. Mike was convincing though and Joey really wanted to see the Trash Room again.

Lindsey, the more experienced cave diver of the three, was working that weekend otherwise she would have been there to talk sense into Joey. But she wasn't. And they went to see the Trash Room. And on the way out, at some point, while Joey was scootering out and looking around the passage, he lost sight of the gold line and followed the wall into the tight passage he had gotten stuck in. And Mike was right behind him. He hoped anyway.

Joey looked around but the silt hanging in the water was still too thick to see much of anything. However, he was finally in passage large enough for him to turn around rather than having to back himself out. He placed his right hand on the wall next to him and slowly turned toward it until it was to his left. He didn't want to push off the wall into the silty water and get even more lost.

He followed the wall that was now to his left. The silt was beginning to clear even more, and he was starting to feel the flow of the current moving through these passages. Up ahead he saw the outline of the old traffic light propped up on the rock. He looked down at his pressure gauges. 200 psi remaining in his left cylinder. He looked at the other one, even though he knew what he would see there. *Empty…*

Nineteen hundred feet from the opening, only 200 psi left in his cylinder. And his stage cylinder was lost somewhere in the small, silted passage behind him. This wasn't good at all!

Printed in the USA
CPSIA information can be obtained
at www.ICGtesting.com
LVHW021443260823
755619LV00009B/218/J